T0323066

The Third Love

Also by Hiromi Kawakami

Strange Weather in Tokyo
The Nakano Thrift Shop
The Ten Loves of Mr Nishino
People From My Neighbourhood

The Third Love

Hiromi Kawakami

Translated from the Japanese by Ted Goossen

GRANTA

Granta Publications, 12 Addison Avenue, London W11 4QR

First published in Great Britain by Granta Books, 2024

Originally published in Japanese as
Sandome No Koi by Chuokoron-Shinsha, 2020.

A CIP catalogue record for this book is available from the British Library.

1   3   5   7   9   8   6   4   2

ISBN 978 1 78378 887 3 (hardback)
ISBN 978 1 80351 137 5 (trade paperback)
ISBN 978 1 78378 889 7 (ebook)

Typeset in Adobe Caslon by Patty Rennie

Printed and bound by CPI Group (UK) Ltd, Croydon, CR0 4YY

www.granta.com

The Third Love

A Tale of Long Ago

Long ago. Saying those words puts me in a strange mood. Long ago – what does that mean? I'm not all that young, but I'm not that old either.

Long ago. From where I stand now, that could point to a time only a few years back, or to when I was born forty-odd years ago, or to much earlier than that. Yes.

Long ago, there was a time when I fell in love. With a certain man.

I thought of him as my big brother at first, from the time we met to when the love part began. Apparently, I called him uncle at the beginning – how many times, I wonder? I hadn't yet turned two, you see.

'Stop calling me uncle,' I'm told he said as he swept me up in his arms. At that age, I didn't know enough to wipe my own mouth, so I slobbered all over his chest as I snuggled in his arms, ignoring his request and chirping 'Un-ku! Un-ku!' over and over.

'I'm only in junior high – how can I be an uncle?' he'd teased, giving me a big squeeze. Don't say uncle, my mother laughed, say big brother. Naa-chan is good too. Naa-chan. Naruya Harada. His name.

*

'You loved him all along, didn't you?' my mother remarks every so often. 'From the very beginning.' It still surprises her.

She's right, though. Even in grade school, I was sure I loved Naa-chan.

You may wonder what a child that young can know of love.

And you'd be right to wonder.

I myself had no idea why I loved him so. I only knew that for some reason I felt warm all over when he came near. A languid, enfolding warmth. I had no way to express that love, however, so I just tagged after him whenever I could, calling out 'Brother' this and 'Brother' that. I was really small then, a helpless, unformed child too young even for preschool.

I must have been four when I started kindergarten. Until then, I had spent all my time with my parents in our very happy home, so kindergarten was a huge adjustment, let me tell you. For a start, I hated my classroom. Why did other kids my age have to run around like that? Why did the organ make such a clackety-clack when the teacher played it? Why did we children have to sing all those silly songs?

The upshot was that I chose to keep my distance from the other children as much as possible, squatting in the furthest corner of the schoolyard with my eyes fixed on the ground. Ground that was teeming with plant and insect life. The green leaves radiating from the base of each dandelion. The shepherd's purse that rustled if you shook it the right way. (My mother had just taught me how.) A cluster of pointed leaves that would prick my arms if I touched them. Light-green grass with tiny buds sprouting in between the stalks. Scurrying ants, so tiny that the grass must have felt like a jungle to them. Little grasshoppers that soared to amazing heights given their size. Grass moths that darted side-ways through the air. Other insects, like the tiny grey butterflies and the pale cloudy-yellow ones who danced above my head, as well as the lethe butterflies – the ones that flattened their wings upon the soil.

Squatting there with my eyes trained on the ground, I discovered that I was able to enter into that little world, to become one with those plants and insects for extended periods of time. In that world, there were no mean kids to yank my hair or push me and the other children around. Instead, I'd found a spot where every plant and insect devoted all its energy to just trying to survive.

The time I spent with Naa-chan put me in that same frame of mind. It was warm and familiar, a bright, quiet place where I could feel calm and secure. Yet at the same time it was very lonely.

At last, the day came when I could leave that nasty kindergarten behind and move on to elementary school. I had no choice in either case, but the elementary school was certainly better than kindergarten. In school, it was only during recess that the kids could run wild and harass their classmates.

The school had a reading room, but I searched everywhere in the building to find a quieter spot. I climbed the stairs to the second floor and peeked into the classrooms, where the bigger boys and girls gawked at me, followed the corridor to take a look at the science room, where the life-size human skeleton on display glared back, climbed to the top of the staircase to find the door there shut tight, no matter how I pushed and pulled, and then back down the stairs to the basement, where the janitor's room was located.

'Well, well, what have we here?' the janitor said. 'You're a pretty small kid to come all the way down here!' He was a big man. I had to lift my chin to look at him, as if I were looking at the ceiling. He was beaming. 'Call me Takaoka,' he said. 'I've been working here for some time. A janitor's work is pretty interesting, did you know?'

I was a little surprised. None of my teachers had talked to me this way before.

'What class do you teach, Mr Takaoka?' I asked.

Mr Takaoka laughed.

'I'm not a teacher,' he said. 'I take care of the school.'

Take care of the school? Now I was even more confused.

'The teachers take care of you guys, right? Well, someone has to take care of your classrooms, and the schoolyard too.'

My gaze was fixed on Mr Takaoka. I liked him right away. He was looking me straight in the eye. For some reason, he seemed to have taken to me as well.

'Come down and visit sometimes. Not too often, though. I have to look after the school, remember.'

Happy to have found at least one place in the school to call my own, I climbed the stairs back to my classroom.

There were other quiet places too.

The science room with its resident skeleton was scary, but it didn't take long to get used to. Most of the kids who used the reading room were older, so it was daunting at first to go in there, but I soon discovered an out-of-the-way desk where I could sit without being bothered. Outside the building there was the far corner of the schoolyard's flower bed. A shady, secluded spot in the outdoor corridor that led to the gym. A hidden nook beside the school entrance.

Surprisingly, the nurse's room wasn't an option. Some children clustered there to jabber and run madly about, while others just wanted attention and knew how to get it. At any rate, that's what the nurse's room was like in my school.

Sometimes the school nurse would accost me in the halls.

'You're too pale,' she admonished me. 'And your hair's too long. Wouldn't you feel better if it were trimmed?'

My hair had never been cut. At first it was my mother who liked it long, but soon I was the one who resisted anyone touching it. By the time I was at elementary school it was down to my waist, and Naa-chan treasured it as well.

'Your hair is so soft and silky, Riko,' he would say, stroking it. I would quiver with happiness. A lid within me had somehow been opened, allowing my emotions to flow. How could I let anyone cut the hair I was growing for him to run his fingers through? It was clear to me that the school nurse hadn't a clue how deep someone's feelings could be, so deep they could make her shake inside.

'You fainted during morning assembly, didn't you?' the nurse continued, fixing me with a stern look. 'Are you eating a proper breakfast?'

Of course I was. My mother's breakfasts were delicious. Fluffy white rice. Fragrant miso soup, made with a broth of dried sardines. A sweet yellow omelette. Sliced pickles. Dried seaweed. Boiled spinach with a touch of soy sauce. All topped off with a cup of roasted green tea. By the time I finished, I was practically ready to go back to bed.

No, it was the school lunch I couldn't stand. It wasn't the taste so much as the weirdly lightweight and slightly yellowed plastic dishes the lunch was served on. One look at those dishes and my appetite vanished. Eating with a group of children bothered me too, as did being served by whoever's turn it was that day. I shuddered to see how they slopped food into my bowl – I just wanted to be left alone to serve myself, so I was more than happy when my turn came round.

My mother said that when she was a schoolgirl, students couldn't leave the room until they had finished their lunch.

'It wasn't that bad in my elementary school,' Naa-chan said. 'Come to think of it, though, the stricter teachers in the other classes would keep an eye on things until lunch period was over.'

As far as I was concerned, all mealtimes should be special. It didn't matter how good the food tasted when we were forced to eat like that – I hated it.

'Aren't you a little stuck-up?' Naa-chan said, smiling.

'It's not that. I just like things to be pretty.'

Years later, my mother laughed at this attitude of mine. My, but you were a fussy little girl, she said. But I was dead serious.

Let me talk a little more about Mr Takaoka. Why? Because our peculiar bond had such an impact on my future.

The other children didn't like Mr Takaoka very much. Perhaps they found his appearance scary. He was a big man with a massive head and a face that made one think of a demon, despite his always cheerful expression. He had a deeply furrowed brow, unusually thick eyebrows, flashing eyes and full lips. He did have a fine aquiline nose, though – indeed, had his features been better aligned, he would have looked exactly like the beautiful Indian prince in my old book of fairy tales. Sadly, that was not the case.

To me at the time, Mr Takaoka was the epitome of age and maturity, but in fact he was only in his late twenties when I started school. I found out later that his father had passed away while he was still in junior high, leaving the family impoverished. Lacking the resources to continue on to university, Mr Takaoka went out to look for work as soon as he graduated from high school, but nothing suitable was available, so for whatever reason he decided to become a Buddhist monk, moving to Mt Kōya to undertake the rigorous spiritual training the temple complex is famous for.

When he came to work as a janitor at our school, Mr Takaoka had completed the first stages of that training and had worked as an acolyte in one of the many small temples that dot the mountain. Yet the prospect of life as a monk hadn't appealed to him – he longed to breathe the air of the profane world below, so he came down from the mountain, followed up on one of his connections and secured the janitor's job. Perhaps what people saw as demonic about him was the result of the severe austerities he had undergone on Mt Kōya.

The fact that my fellow students shunned Mr Takaoka made me draw all the closer to him.

I was in the third grade when I first told Mr Takaoka about Naa-chan.

'Hmm, sounds like you're in love,' was his response. I knew that I liked Naa-chan, but that was the first time I had thought of my feelings as 'love'. Once Mr Takaoka had suggested it, though, it became clear to me. I was indeed in love with Naa-chan.

Naa-chan would often show up at our home without warning. He seldom told us in advance. When my mother opened the front door and saw him standing there, she would knit her brow and say: 'You again? You might have let us know.' Despite her frown, though, I could tell from the way she sparkled how glad she was to see him.

It was right around the time that Mr Takaoka introduced love into the equation that Naa-chan, by then in high school, began to exert a powerful attraction on all sorts of women. When he was nearby, they grew flirtatious: their attitude became more light-hearted, their speech more lilting, their movements more supple, and they unconsciously leaned in his direction.

Naa-chan was a beautiful young man, no doubt about it. Nevertheless, that alone wasn't what made him so special. There were other things. The curve of his shoulders when he looked down. The line of his jaw when he suddenly lifted up his face. His tranquil manner when talking quietly; his passion when he grew excited. Sometimes he would be flitting about, while at other times he was so still as to make you forget he was there. He was good-looking enough in his animated moods, but even more striking when he just sat there peacefully.

On top of all that, he was a great listener. You knew that you could unburden yourself to him, expose your most deeply held secrets, and he would hear you out to the end. He made all women feel that way. And not just women, either: a certain type of man, too, found him strangely seductive. My father, for example, was drawn to Naa-chan. He loved him like he might a much younger brother.

Naa-chan called my father *sempai* or senior, as one would call someone above them in school. How that made my father smile! In fact, it was to see my father that Naa-chan began visiting my home in the first place. That's right. When I was two, Naa-chan had just entered junor high, thereby becoming my father's *kohai*, or junior. Not only did they attend the same private school and, later, the university affiliated with it, they were both members of the same soccer club.

'Did you ever go see them play?' I once asked my mother. She gave me a funny look, as if the idea had never occurred to her. My mother was a real homebody. She claimed that crowds made her dizzy, and that she didn't like socializing with other wives. These were the excuses she came up with, but really she just enjoyed spending her time quietly at home, keeping her relations with our neighbours to a bare minimum. I sometimes think that her dislike of other adults was similar to the dislike I felt for the other children at school. She reserved her smiles for my father, and for Naa-chan.

'You should take up a sport, Riko, or maybe take lessons of some kind,' Naa-chan said when I entered elementary school. Thanks to his suggestion, I threw myself into studying the koto. My kindergarten classmates tended to gravitate towards calligraphy, swimming, ballet and English conversation classes, but I would rather be caught dead than do anything that involved 'learning together'.

My koto teacher, Michiko-sensei, always wore Japanese clothes. She arranged her hair in a small chignon that shone in the light, and she was very much at home in her kimono, which she put on by herself.

'For a modern girl,' she said to me after we'd had a few lessons, 'there's something about you that smacks of the old days. Your long hair really suits you. It's very beautiful. If you ever cut it off, let me have it, all right?'

That was the sort of thing only Michiko-sensei could come out with. I hated the idea of parting with my hair, but if I was ever in a fix and needed to do that, strangely, I felt that she would be the one I'd like to have it.

I loved studying the koto with her. I took practising at home seriously too. Sometimes, Naa-chan would ask me to play for him and I always leaped at the chance. He would lie back on the sofa, close his eyes and listen to me playing. I was so proud in those moments.

Let me talk a little more about Mr Takaoka.

When I was in fifth grade, the school made the decision that a full-time janitor was no longer needed, and Mr Takaoka had to go.

'This could be a propitious moment for me,' he told me not long before he left. I hadn't heard the word 'propitious' before, but it seemed fitting coming from him.

Although four years had elapsed between when I first met Mr Takaoka and when he left the school, he seemed to have grown younger. Initially I saw him as a mature man, then gradually I came to see him as a young man, and, now that he was leaving, he seemed like a much older brother.

'How come you seem to get younger and younger?' I asked him.

'It's magic,' Mr Takaoka replied. 'Someone taught me how.' I would never have associated the janitor's room with 'magic' – nothing could have seemed more unlikely – yet once he said it, I sensed that magic had indeed been squatting in the corner of the neatly kept room the whole time I had known him.

'What does magic look like?' I asked.

'I'll let you know someday,' he answered. 'But now is not the time.'

This sounded mysterious. I wanted to know more. But he had said 'someday', so I knew that he would tell me eventually, for Mr Takaoka was the most trustworthy of adults.

There weren't that many grown-ups I could trust. Just as my mother could feel comfortable only with a handful of people – my father, Naa-chan, and me – so were there only a couple of adults in whom I could place my faith.

Trusting so few meant that those I trusted, I loved deeply. I would burst into tears at the thought of my parents' death, or even their physical absence.

'Riko's a crybaby!' the boys jeered. When our class breaks were too short to find refuge elsewhere and I had to hole up in our classroom, I gave myself over to my imaginings while looking out of the window, and avoided verbal exchanges like the plague.

Most of those imaginings were of the pleasant variety, but on rare occasions my parents' mortality would pop into my head, and then the waterworks would start.

Children hate to see other children cry. The kids in my class were sure to spot me getting all weepy and the catcalls would begin.

'Riko's a crybaby! Riko's a crybaby!' they would chant. I ignored them. Armed with tissues and a handkerchief, I would cry my heart out, undaunted. I wept silently, not sobbing or even blowing my nose, so you would have thought I'd be left alone, but that's not the way children behave.

'Why does my crying bother the other kids so much?' I once asked Mr Takaoka.

'Because it scares them,' he replied.

'What's scary about it?'

'Because they can't make you stop. That means you aren't afraid of them.'

'Why should I be afraid of them?'

'Because you're the class outcast, right? And a class outcast is supposed to be afraid of the world.'

'Of the world? No way am I afraid of something I've never seen.'

Mr Takaoka laughed.

'You're right,' he said. 'People ramble on about "the world this" and "the world that"' without knowing the world at all.'

'You don't know about the world either, Mr Takaoka?'

'No, I don't. But I'm keen to try to grab hold of it one of these days.'

I wasn't sure exactly what he meant, but the idea of grabbing hold of the world excited me no end. Perhaps this is why I wasn't sadder when he left.

I felt sure that Mr Takaoka was indeed taking hold of the world out there. With the 'magic' he had acquired by his side, he was sailing the seven seas. I didn't doubt him for a second.

On the day of Mr Takaoka's departure, I picked up our family camera on my way to school. When I got there, I headed straight to the caretaker's room.

'Take our picture, OK?' I asked him.

There was no tripod, so Mr Takaoka placed the camera on the windowsill of the now empty room. I was growing like a weed at that stage, but I still felt like a first-grader standing next to him. He set the timer with his back to me. 'Hurry!' I urged him, but he merely grinned and strolled back, cool as a cucumber. He reached me a second before the shutter clicked, but by that time I was so flustered that I blinked precisely when the light flashed.

'Please, take another one,' I asked.

Mr Takaoka nodded magnanimously and went to reset the timer. This time, though, he trotted back to where I was standing.

'Think of something that makes you happy,' he said, standing straight and tall beside me.

I still have that photograph. I had snuck the camera out of the house without permission, so I used up the roll of film and had it developed that same day. I hid the photos deep in my desk drawer and, until I was in my twenties, showed them to no one except Naa-chan. There were the two shots of Mr Takaoka and me, several taken at different angles of the skeleton in the science room and a few snapped after school of the view of the town from my classroom. All the rest were of the school garden: Madagascar periwinkles in bloom, gourd vines climbing the chain-link fence and the blurs of passing bees, butterflies and other flying insects, which flew too quickly to be caught on film.

'These are all things you see every day at school,' Naa-chan said. He was right. Although I didn't try to explain, he knew me so well he understood.

'What do you think of Mr Takaoka?' I asked him.

'That he's the sort of person I'd like to be a disciple of,' was Naa-chan's answer.

I never became close to my classmates, not in junior high nor in senior high either. By then they were no longer children, yet neither were they quite adults, and they had no clue how to deal with their changing bodies. Moreover, they seemed oblivious to how much those changes were affecting them. When it came to being physically neither here nor there, though, I was in the same boat. That was why I couldn't hate them as I had as a child, an inability that carried its own kind of pain.

'I want to get married soon,' I announced to my mother one day.

'What? But you're still in high school, Riko! Who would you marry, anyway?'

'Naa-chan, of course.'

'Would Naa-chan agree?' My mother asked, incredulous.

'You don't think he would?'

'He seems to have a girlfriend, you know.'

'Yes, I've heard.'

That's right. No sooner had Naa-chan been hired than he was posted to his company's branch in Kyushu, where he had become involved with a woman.

He had shown me her photograph not long before. She was really pretty.

'You've never been in love, have you Riko?' my mother said.

Never been in love? My mother's comment floored me. It took a moment to recover. I mean, I had loved Naa-chan since elementary school.

'What you feel for him is just a childish crush,' my mother declared.

But I knew differently. She could say what she wanted, but there was no way she could shake my conviction, which was as irrefutable as the earth turning on its axis.

The New Year has always been a special moment for me. It is festive, solemn and majestic all at once, and I love it. And the New Year that marked my last year of high school was the most memorable of all.

Naa-chan was still working in Kyushu at the time, but he returned to Tokyo for the holidays, and came to visit my father on 2 January.

'Goodness!' he said the moment he laid eyes on me. 'Haven't you grown up all of a sudden!'

'It may look like that, but she's still a child in many ways,' my mother put in. Naa-chan's eyes were fixed on me, though, and he didn't respond.

I could feel the side of my body under his gaze flush. My cheeks and ears reddened, and my palms began to sweat.

'How is your girlfriend?' my mother asked him.

'All right, I guess,' he answered offhandedly. He sounded so much like a company man it made my father grin.

Naa-chan didn't hang around for very long. He nibbled at the special New Year's food and shared a *tokkuri* of sake with my father. I wanted to spend more time with him, but my mother intervened.

'Your entrance exams are coming up, so you can't dawdle with us forever,' she prodded. Grudgingly, I trudged up the stairs to my room.

I was sitting at my desk when Naa-chan took his leave, but in fact my ears had been tuned to his sonorous voice echoing from downstairs, so I hadn't been able to focus on my studies. I heard him say, 'Please say goodnight to Riko,' followed by the sound of the front door closing. I grabbed my overcoat and scarf, tiptoed down the stairs and silently slipped out of the door. Then I ran off in hot pursuit of Naa-chan.

When I rounded the corner, Naa-chan was standing there.

'Thank you,' he said. 'I didn't have to say a word.'

'Yes,' I gasped. I was completely winded.

He hailed a taxi, got in, then snatched my hand and pulled me into the back seat with him. The taxi stopped in front of a building with a small light burning out front.

'Where are we?' I asked.

'Where you've been wanting to come, Riko.'

'Really?'

'Yes,' he said with a smile. 'Back in the old days this would have been called a teahouse.'

That evening, for the first time, I was able to explore a man's body, that strange assortment of hard and soft places. Naa-chan was warm, and fragrant. I never tired of touching him.

'Did you know I was in love with you?' I asked.

We were lying side by side, waiting for our breathing to slow.

'Of course. I've known all along,' he said, toying with my hair, fanned out across the sheets. On and on he played with it, stroking it, running it through his fingers, fondling it, revelling in its silkiness.

*

I was twenty-four when Naa-chan returned from Kyushu. Through-out our separation, we had been writing letters to each other. We could have used the phone, or email, which was becoming more common – but nothing was as pleasant as writing to him, or reading the letters he sent in return. He seldom had much time to write, so most of his notes were brief:

'I miss you, Riko.'

'The plum blossoms are out.'

'I dreamed of you today.'

'The mountains here are beautiful, though I don't know their names.'

'Riko is not here. Not even my phantom Riko.'

'Things are busy at work.'

'I feel sad that you're out of reach.'

'I really admire my boss.'

'A beautiful day. I wish we could go for a stroll together.'

These brief messages were written on lined paper, in hand-writing that ran roughshod over the lines. How I cherished them!

There were few opportunities to meet in secret. His weekends were filled with golf with his business associates and other obliga-tory events, and then there was that Kyushu girl, who still seemed to be occupying his mind. All in all, he only managed to return to Tokyo about twice a year.

'She's someone I once made a commitment to,' he said to me on more than one occasion.

'A commitment? It sounds like you were married.'

'Don't you think it's important to care for those you once loved, whether you were formally married or not?'

I was not entirely won over by Naa-chan's argument, though I knew that he would never ditch a lover in a cold, unfeeling way.

The beautiful woman in Kyushu, he explained, was prone to bouts of loneliness.

'She'd wither away if I ignored her,' was how he put it.

For goodness' sake, I told him, I was about to wither away too, but Naa-chan pooh-poohed my protest.

'Come on, you're the one I'm in love with, not her. She and I are history.'

In that case, why come back to Tokyo so seldom?

But I trusted him – always had, from the very beginning – so I could never bring myself to hate Naa-chan's concern for the feelings of the woman in Kyushu. No, my sadness was of a purer sort. He simply wasn't there beside me. Without Naa-chan, wherever I went, it felt like my life was leaking away. As if a hole his size occupied the spot where he should have been and all warmth and fragrance, all air, was escaping through it.

That winter, Naa-chan and I got engaged. I didn't ask about the Kyushu woman. After all, he loved me completely, and I loved him just as much. What else could we possibly need?

My parents were beaming when Naa-chan visited us at the time of our engagement. My father especially was overjoyed.

'Just think, you've been close since childhood, so you understand each other's feelings,' he said. 'You can really trust each other.'

My mother was happy too, but she didn't forget to give me a dose of reality when Naa-chan had left.

'Naruya is a charming man, no doubt about that,' she said. 'I fully understand how you feel. But he will cause you hardship too, Riko.'

Hardship. What kind of hardship? With Naa-chan beside me, I could endure any sadness. How could hardship enter into it?

But I had no desire to argue with my mother.

'That may be true,' I said slowly.

*

I wonder, did my mother take satisfaction in having been proved right when she looked at how my marriage was turning out, or did she grieve for what had befallen the daughter she loved? My guess is she didn't understand her own feelings.

As my mother had predicted, my marriage to Naa-chan was plagued with problems from the start. The first problem was that he had not made a clean break with the woman from Kyushu. I never attempted to pry into his activities. Never even tried to listen in on his phone calls. Nevertheless, I knew what was going on. Why? Because he never tried to hide anything. I could always tell what was going on between him and his women.

The woman in Kyushu visited Tokyo to see him once every six months. Naa-chan never tried to conceal their meetings with excuses about playing golf with his colleagues, or having to work on his days off.

'I'm stepping out for a bit,' is all he would say, then, as if pulled by a string, he would make a beeline to wherever the woman was.

'Don't go,' I might plead, but it did no good. He was never cold to me on those occasions, of course.

'You're right – I love you most, Riko,' he would say, 'so I have no reason to see anyone else.'

Then he would take me in his arms. I could tell how much he was itching to leave, though – I could feel it in his fingers, his shoulders, his chest.

'Do you want to go that much?' I would ask.

'Have a heart. You know how much she wants to see me,' he would reply with complete honesty.

Aah, how I loved that honesty. Yet I loathed it just as intensely. Why wouldn't he lie to protect the woman he loved most? Make an effort to understand her feelings? However warm his embrace, in the end he would hurry off to see the other woman, wherever she might be waiting.

'It's always to you that I return, Riko,' he would say. That was true – he always came back home. But so what?

The man who left and then returned. That was Naa-chan. As a result, my married life never enjoyed true peace.

One thing I would never do was open up to my mother about the state of my marriage. Still, I bet she had a pretty good idea what was going on. After all, Naa-chan was living in our house.

This living arrangement had nothing to do with the old practice of adopting a son-in-law. Rather, my father didn't want to part with his only child, and Naa-chan willingly agreed to his entreaties that we live together. In truth, however, I wanted to create an intensely private space for just the two of us. A small apartment, perhaps, where we could live quietly, away from the world. Yet I doubted I could preserve such a sanctuary by myself. Perhaps I lacked confidence. Looking back, I think I had an inkling that I couldn't contain Naa-chan within such a space, and that what I hoped to be deep and intense would turn out to be shallow and cold. As long as we were all living together, my mother and father were able to fill in the gap when Naa-chan was off visiting some other woman. Yes, that is clear to me now. I was leaning on my parents, like a child.

'Why don't you two find your own place?' My koto teacher, Michiko-sensei, was the only one to ask this question. My parents certainly didn't. Both of them wanted to have Naa-chan close by – my mother was clearly as infatuated as I was, and my father doted on him.

'You're really old-fashioned for someone so young!' Michiko-sensei said, laughing.

'What was your marriage like?' I asked.

'Normal. My three sons are pretty normal too.'

'Your husband is . . .'

'He died a long time ago. He was a good man, but it was an arranged marriage, so romantic love wasn't part of it. That's why I want to experience it for myself one of these days.'

I couldn't help but smile at that.

'Why are you smiling? Does the idea of an older woman like me falling in love amuse you?' she said, looking into my eyes.

That wasn't why I had smiled, but I couldn't find the right words to explain.

I had no way of knowing that, before long, Michiko-sensei would fall in love, and with a most unexpected person. There were so many things I didn't know. It hits me now, when I talk about the old days like this. It's scary, to be honest. Yet, as things turned out, I was fortunate to have been kept in the dark.

The woman from Kyushu wasn't the only one. There was someone else.

I think we'd barely been married two years when I first sensed it. The atmosphere surrounding Naa-chan had begun to change. Do you find it strange that I would intuit the presence of other women in such a vague way? That wouldn't surprise me. I would be the first to admit that anything so indefinite, so uncertain, is hardly likely to lead anywhere.

Sadly, though, unsubstantiated though it may have been, it turned out my hunch was right. Who could it possibly be?

I spent days turning that question over in my mind. He wasn't coming home early. Instead, despite his junior status, he was being asked to work overtime virtually every evening, with frequent dinners with clients, so that he seldom got home before ten.

Even after his return there would be constant calls from his office, often late at night. Very occasionally, I could hear a woman's voice on the other end. I could tell right away, though, that she was a co-worker of his, rather than someone trying to lure him away from me. I knew this wasn't the woman with whom he was involved. Such a person wouldn't pester him in the middle of the night. Discretion might be part of it, but I felt the main reason was that, since Naa-chan always satisfied his women, she would have nothing to gain by tracking him home to where his wife was waiting.

I knew this because Naa-chan fully satisfied *me* when we were together. Sure, he might see other women, I reasoned, but why complain about that when he loved me so much? Perhaps it was just a way to console myself, but I was too content to pester him. Probably the other women felt the same.

It was around this time that we began receiving nightly phone calls from a man.

At first, I thought it was someone from work, but it wasn't that. He sounded older than Naa-chan, and spoke in a soft baritone.

'My husband isn't back from work yet,' I told him the first time he called.

'Thank you so much,' he replied. 'I will try again later. Might I ask, until what time may I phone?'

I answered that any time was all right, and he thanked me so politely I could feel him bowing at the other end of the line. The man did not call again that evening. The next time he called was a few days later, on a Sunday. I said I would get Naa-chan. Once again, I sensed the man bow in return.

Their conversation lasted a few minutes. Strangely, though, I could feel the presence of a woman at the other end. This despite the fact that I had felt nothing of the sort when the man and I were talking directly to each other.

Was there a woman sitting beside the man, who took the phone when Naa-chan came on the line? I thought so at first, but it seemed I was mistaken, for I continued to hear that gentle yet resonant baritone, however faintly.

'Who was that?' I asked when the call ended.

'An old acquaintance,' he answered.

An old acquaintance? I was about to ask for more details, but just then Naa-chan gently covered my lips with his and, though it was midday, took me to the sofa, where we began making love. He and I were occupying two rooms on the second floor of my family home: one served as our bedroom, while the second had been converted into a sizeable living room with a wooden floor and a small kitchen in the corner. How many times we embraced in those two rooms!

My body had recoiled from daytime sex at first – my parents were living downstairs, after all – but Naa-chan trained me well. We made love everywhere, in the bedroom, on the sofa, with my back or front pressed against the wall, on the cold floor. I always opened to his touch, however unbecoming our position.

Making love with Naa-chan was wonderful. There was the deep, physical pleasure, sure, but more than that, I always felt spiritually and emotionally completed, if that makes sense.

The man's occasional late-night phone calls continued. Gradually, I began looking forward to those brief conversations in a mild sort of way.

'I'm terribly sorry, but my husband hasn't come back yet.'

'Sorry to have disturbed you.'

'Not at all.'

'Thank you, as always.'

'Thank you too, and good night.'

Our conversations were limited to standard greetings of this sort; yet, over time, I began to feel close to the man. At times, I even felt like asking about the nature of the relationship he and Naa-chan had enjoyed back in the old days, but I hesitated to broach the subject. It was less out of concern for his feelings, and more that I didn't want to destroy whatever slight intimacy we might have developed.

His voice bore a slight resemblance to that of my father.

I didn't have to wait long, though, to discover the man's identity.

I have mentioned that I continued practising the koto after my marriage. Now I had lessons with Michiko-sensei every other week, rather than weekly as I had when I was single.

One day – the same day that Naa-chan was dispatched on an overnight business trip by his company – Michiko-sensei asked that we change the time of our lesson from the early afternoon to the evening. Had Naa-chan been returning that night, I don't think I would have consented to the change, but he wouldn't be back, no matter how late I stayed up, so I agreed.

I remember once confiding to Sugawara, an old college friend, how happy I felt waiting for Naa-chan to come home at night. I'll never forget how shocked she looked.

'What an exemplary wife!' she said. It may have sounded like a compliment, but I could tell there was an underlying criticism: what a boring life you lead!

I knew she was unlikely to understand, so I didn't try to explain. To some people, the work I did for Naa-chan with such joy – keeping house, looking after his needs – was considered pure drudgery. I didn't care, though. What they thought was irrelevant to me.

I loved thinking about Naa-chan in those hours I spent waiting for him to come home at night, it was that simple. I was completely immersed in my love for my husband and no one could interfere with that joy, with the sweet anticipation I took in waiting to welcome the man in the flesh. Where else in the world could I find such happiness?

That evening, at five o'clock I began my lesson with Michiko-sensei. By the time we finished, over two hours later, it was already dark outside.

'Shall we have dinner together?' Michiko-sensei asked me. 'There's a small Western-style restaurant not far from here that's pretty good.'

I had worried that I'd be causing her extra work if I stayed for dinner, but the fact that we would be going out removed that concern, so I nodded my assent.

The phone call came when Michiko-sensei was changing clothes in one of her back rooms.

'Sorry, but could you get it, Riko?' she called to me.

Nervously, I picked up the receiver. I had never worked in an office, so I had no experience dealing with phone calls from strangers. Answering someone else's phone put me on edge.

'Hello,' I said timidly. There was a momentary pause at the other end of the line.

'You're my mother's student, aren't you? Could you please call her for me?'

The man was apparently Michiko-sensei's son. I, too, had to pause in surprise, though, when I heard his voice. Why?

It was the first time I had talked to a member of my sensei's family for one thing. More to the point, however, the voice on the phone sounded exactly like the man who had been calling our home so frequently. There could be no mistaking that gentle manner which sounded slightly like my father.

At any rate, that evening the three of us – Michiko-sensei, her son and I – shared a meal at that small restaurant. Her son was in his mid-forties, halfway in age between Naa-chan and my father, although he looked much younger than he sounded on the phone.

'He's my third son,' Michiko-sensei explained. 'He's married, but he worries about me, so he stops by for dinner quite often.'

Her son scratched his head in embarrassment. 'Well, I don't know,' he said with a shrug. 'I think my wife likes it if I eat out sometimes.'

There was something about that shrug that Michiko-sensei and I found terribly funny, and we burst out laughing. Her son reminded me of my father on many fronts: his way of speaking, his demeanour, the mild-mannered air that – I sensed – women found so relaxing.

I was sure now that it was the son's voice on those late-night phone calls, yet that evening I never asked him about it. If I was wrong, it would be terribly awkward; moreover, those calls were to Naa-chan, not to me.

The son bowed when we parted at the station that evening. It was a deep bow, the same as I had imagined the man on the phone making.

'It was a great pleasure,' he said as he hopped on the train heading in the opposite direction from mine.

My second encounter with Michiko-sensei's son took place half a year later.

By that time, the dark shadow the Kyushu woman had cast over my marriage had lightened considerably, but I had no idea who was behind the 'different atmosphere' that seemed to be affecting Naa-chan.

Discussing Naa-chan purely in terms of his relationships with other women may not be entirely fair, but there's not much I can do about it. He wasn't the type who jumped into bed with whomever happened to be around, that's for sure. Yet, as I said before, his nature made it impossible for him to reject a woman with whom he had shared a heartfelt conversation.

I was vastly relieved that the shadow of the woman in Kyushu had faded, but puzzling over who the new woman might be constantly occupied my mind as I whiled away the hours I spent waiting for Naa-chan's return.

What was so curious about this new woman was that, whereas I had felt the woman in Kyushu attempting to toss a net over Naa-chan, to bind him to her, nothing of the sort seemed to emanate from this one. To the contrary – and I know this may sound strange – I sensed neither envy nor malice directed towards me, though I was his wife. Instead, and this may also strike you as strange, my impression was that she valued, even embraced, my presence.

I think I have mentioned how women, including my own mother, could see me as a rival when it came to Naa-chan. Yet this still-nameless woman seemed to hold no animosity at all. Rather, she seemed to pay me the deepest respect – that feeling radiated through Naa-chan so strongly that I didn't question it.

What could it possibly mean?

It didn't take long to discover the truth of the matter.

The trigger was yet another phone call.

It had been quite some time since I had heard that low, mellifluous voice on the other end of the line. Night had already fallen.

'May I speak to your husband, please,' the man said.

His usual opening, but this time there was a new urgency in his voice. I handed the phone to Naa-chan and settled back on the sofa. Normally, I couldn't have overheard their conversation, but on this night the man's deep voice had risen a few decibels.

'What? You mean right now?' Naa-chan was saying.

'Yes, please, if at all possible,' the man pleaded. He sounded desperate – his voice was now so loud I could make out what he was saying.

'But it's so late,' Naa-chan said, bewildered.

'She's already on her way.'

'My wife is here.'

'That's why I'm calling.'

They seemed to be arguing about something. Who was heading this way? Why was my presence a problem?

Their call wrapped up quickly.

'I'm stepping out for a bit,' Naa-chan said the moment the call ended. Fine, I replied. But I had no intention of leaving things as they stood.

I set off on Naa-chan's heels. I felt no self-disgust in doing so, for I was propelled by sheer curiosity. In all likelihood, the person heading our way was the nameless woman he had been seeing. Had I thought she hated me, I never could have pursued Naa-chan like that. Yet I was convinced that she felt something akin to affection for me.

I really mean that. I was just so curious. I wanted to meet her. Even become her friend, if possible. Was that weird? You may well think so. For sure. To me, though, it's not weird at all. I have never had many friends, so if I were to have a true friend wouldn't it have to be someone who loved Naa-chan as I did? That had always been my belief.

We assume that two women who love the same man are fated to become sworn enemies. But however rare, couldn't there be cases when, instead of hatred, a true intimacy might develop? At least, that's how I felt at the time.

Naa-chan plunged into the night in pursuit of the woman. I followed, keeping a careful distance between us.

The woman was wearing a formal kimono. I could only make out her shadowy outline, but I was sure I had seen her before.

'What made you come here?' Naa-chan asked her.

'What, I'm not allowed to?'

'Riko's home. Do you want to alarm her?'

The woman's voice was familiar too. I was taken aback. My first reaction was: no way! Yet deep in my heart it made a kind of sense. In fact, I felt I had known all along, from the moment I overheard Michiko-sensei's son on the phone that evening. (I had assumed it was him, though I couldn't be absolutely sure.)

'Riko knows what love is,' the woman's voice said.

'What if she does?' Naa-chan snapped. I was tempted to call out, to tell him not to be so cold, but I held back. I wanted to hear what she had to say.

'Women are a lot stronger than you men seem to think. And I have no intention of stealing you away from Riko. None at all. In fact, I like her a lot.'

Aha! There in the dark, I broke into a smile. She had said that she liked me. Besides, she seemed to feel, as I did, that we who loved Naa-chan were friends, not enemies.

A minute later I heard the approach of another set of footsteps. By now, the shadows of Naa-chan and the woman had become one. No, that might give the wrong impression. There was no passionate embrace – rather their shadows overlapped in a way that seemed even more intimate.

The footsteps came to a halt in front of those blended shadows.

'Stop that! You promised one meeting would be enough, didn't you?' It was the voice on the phone. The self-possessed, resonant tone of Michiko-sensei's third son.

'My goodness, did you follow me all this way?' the woman replied, sounding amused. 'But why do I have to stop?' Now she was practically laughing.

'Riko is such a fine young lady, Mother,' he replied. 'How can you be so mean?'

So, there it was. The woman whose shadowy form had joined with Naa-chan's there in the dark was my koto teacher, without a doubt.

'I'm not doing anything to harm Riko,' Michiko-sensei told her son.

'Don't you think meeting Naruya alone like this hurts her?' the son reproached her. 'Just think, they were enjoying a quiet night together at home until you showed up.'

'Ohhh,' Michiko-sensei exhaled. Her breath was like a bubble worming its way to the surface.

'Let's go home,' her son said, tugging her arm.

'Do I really have to go?' Michiko-sensei said, turning to Naa-chan. But it was her son who answered her.

'Yes,' he said.

Faced with Naa-chan's silence, Michiko-sensei finally let her son lead her away. She was a picture of defeat, totally different from how she had looked when she was waiting for Naa-chan.

Naa-chan stood there silently until the two disappeared from sight. I considered running home before him, putting on an innocent face to make it look as though I had never left, but I couldn't bring myself to rush off, so I stood there in the dark and watched Michiko-sensei depart.

Her faltering steps made her look much older. While I was glad she was leaving, I felt guilty seeing her chased away like that.

At my next lesson, I made up my mind and confronted Michiko-sensei about Naa-chan.

'You mean you know?' she replied guilelessly, clearly surprised.

'You came near my home the other night, didn't you?'

'Yes. I really wanted to see Naruya again,' she said, flashing a smile.

'Are you and Naa-chan in love?'

The innocent way she was acting, I felt, gave me leeway to be equally frank.

'No, you're the woman he loves, Riko. I'm happy just being with him. Remember, I told you that I'd never been in love. Well, when I'm with him it feels like being in love.'

Like being in love. I rolled the words around on my tongue.

'So, you say you're not in love? But that your feelings resemble love?'

Michiko-sensei thought for a moment.

'I'm not sure,' she finally answered in a quiet voice. 'I think I like Naruya, but I've never thought of sleeping with him, or marrying him, or anything like that. I like him, that's all. Being together makes me happy.'

I was about to say, 'Come on now, isn't that love?' But then I checked myself. I was talking about my feelings, not hers.

'How did you and Naruya first meet?' I asked instead. I wanted to know how all this had started.

It was like this, she said, and launched into her story.

Their first meeting had not been, as I had assumed, at Naa-chan's and my wedding. No, Michiko-sensei had known Naa-chan long before, while he was still in junior high.

It had been a chance meeting. Michiko-sensei was on her way to a session with her koto master – the woman had died a few years back, and though I had never taken a class with her, I had met her briefly at one of our class recitals – when she suddenly felt faint and had to sit down.

She was squatting there by the side of the street when a student called over to see if she was all right. He took her to a park nearby and sat her down on a bench to rest. That student was Naa-chan.

She wanted to give him a token of her gratitude, but when she asked for his address he waved her off and bounded away.

Yet she did not give up the idea. From then on, once a day for a week, she visited the small coffee shop situated near where they had met. She supposed, correctly, that he might take the same path again. At the beginning, her sole intention was to give him a small gift as thanks for his help. However, once she had seen him pass by on his way home from school, Michiko-sensei's feelings became harder to pin down.

She realized she didn't want to give him a thank-you gift.

Etiquette, propriety, the repayment of a debt – such worldly things would not come between them. That's what she resolved as she sat there in the coffee shop, watching the boy through the window.

For Naa-chan looked that free and easy. His face, his movements, the way he talked and joked with his friends – everything about him was pure and natural. He was like the passing breeze, or the shining sun.

Who among us has the gall to bestow gifts of thanks on nature? All we can do is join our hands in gratitude for what we've been given.

Michiko-sensei had no way to track down Naa-chan's name,

let alone how to contact him, so she simply filed his memory away in her heart and ended her visits to the coffee shop.

Nevertheless, coincidence was to bring the two of them together again.

One night, Michiko-sensei had a dream. In the dream, she and Naa-chan were holding hands. She could feel his vital energy flowing in an unbroken stream from his hand into hers.

When her three sons and their families gathered together at New Year's, Michiko-sensei entertained them with her account of that dream.

Her eldest son shrugged. Her second son frowned. Their wives tittered. Only her third son and his wife listened attentively until she finished.

'Children of nature do exist in this world,' her third son said.

'Junior high school students aren't exactly children,' Michiko-sensei replied.

The wife thought for a moment. 'Actually, I know another boy like that,' she said.

Not long afterwards, they discovered that the two schoolboys were in fact one and the same, for the next time the third son and his wife visited Michiko-sensei, the wife brought with her a photograph of the boy she had been talking about.

'This is what he looks like,' she said, pointing him out.

Michiko-sensei gulped. 'This is him?'

'Yes, he's a student in the junior high school where I work,' her son's wife cheerfully replied. 'The girls all love him. This picture was taken by someone in the photography club, and it's being passed around the entire school as if he was a movie star or something.'

The boy in the photograph was the one who had helped her that day, no question about it.

All three were excited by the sheer coincidence of this, but it did not lead to any personal connection between Michiko-sensei and Naa-chan. The wife worked in the school office, and while she was close enough to the action to get her hands on the boy's photo, she couldn't put one of her relatives in touch with a student.

Time passed, and Michiko-sensei's memories of Naa-chan grew less frequent, so seeing him at our wedding sent her over the moon.

As soon as she calmed herself, she resolved not to let this stroke of luck pass. Unbeknownst to me, she never took her eyes off Naa-chan during the wedding, and thereafter began using every trick in the book to get close to him.

'Of course,' she told me, 'I had no desire to take him away from you, none whatsoever. But you know Naruya's natural beauty is even more striking now that he's an adult. To me, it's as if you took every woman's image of the "male ideal", squeezed them to the last drop, and then poured that essence into a man.'

I couldn't help laughing. 'Sure, Naa-chan is charming,' I said, 'but is it a good idea to praise him to the skies like that?'

'Why not?' Michiko-sensei replied. 'We can heap praises on him until we run out. What else do we have to dream about if we can't dream of men?'

I wasn't at all sure about that. Weren't there other things women could dream of?

Looking back, I'm sure I was correct. It's risky when a woman places all her dreams on a man, no question. At the same time, though, a woman has the right to choose to take that risk.

That night, I questioned Naa-chan about their relationship.

'What are your feelings for Michiko-sensei?' I asked.

'I'm very fond of her,' he answered immediately.

'You're fond of her? What does that mean?'

'It means what it says. That's all there is to it.'

Naa-chan floors me like this from time to time. I may be naive about how the world works, but I still have a pretty good idea of how men and women relate to each other. Enough to know the pain a man can cause when he says he's 'fond of' another woman.

In retrospect, I see I may have reached a crossroads in that moment. There were two paths I could take – either follow my many sisters who have striven to lay claim to the men they loved, or resign myself to the futility of holding a man to his promises.

In the end, I chose the latter path, acknowledging that justice and reason don't govern what takes place between a man and a woman. Was I stupid?

'Not at all,' said Mr Takaoka much later. 'After all, justice and reason are merely ideas people make up along the way.' Was he trying to console me or was he joking? (Either way, my decision was a response to the pain I was feeling, nothing more.)

After that, Michiko-sensei no longer intruded on our relationship. I continued my lessons as before, and never grew to hate her. Yet there's no question that the affair opened a small but very deep wound, one that still hasn't healed.

I'm not saying that there was *always* some woman whose shadow loomed over our domestic life. In fact, the days that followed those events were a happy time for me.

The house we shared with my parents had a big front yard, and I asked my mother to mark off an area for our use, a small square in the south-east corner. The first thing I did was to lay out an old-style flower garden. I started with a circle of red bricks and planted a variety of white flowers inside it: white kerria, Easter lilies, white violets, jasmine, white bellflowers and Christmas roses. I searched for them everywhere, going through catalogues, visiting shops and carefully planting what I could find. Some flowers liked direct sunlight and others didn't, but I jumbled them all together: as a result, some thrived, others died, while still others appeared and disappeared in what gradually became a riot of plants. The whole thing was weird and chaotic, but it was a chaos I enjoyed. I also tracked down the name of the wild white flowers – called *hakidamegiku*, or 'garbage chrysanthemums' – that lined the road, flowers that I had loved in my childhood. I'm sure there were people who thought they didn't belong in a flower bed, but I was furious that such an unfortunate name had been attached to such a pretty flower. I found a patch growing nearby, dug them up and stuck them in my garden.

'Our flower bed looks a lot like you,' Naa-chan laughed. Shy but wild. Those were the adjectives he used.

We had two rooms in our part of the house, which I loved decorating. There wasn't space for large furniture, so I focused my attention on pieces that could fit in my hand. I am no seam-stress, but I loved embroidering small, unobtrusive designs in the corners of the fabrics that I bought. I arranged white flowers in small glass jars, which I placed on windowsills, and positioned a number of baskets around the two rooms, which I filled with different objects on a rotating basis.

I liked dressing up too. My wardrobe wasn't extensive by any means, but I took deep satisfaction in putting on one of my favourite outfits each day and then arranging my waist-length hair to suit them; depending on the clothes, I might braid it, put it up, or let it hang freely down my back. I never felt ashamed in front of Naa-chan. Being confident in how I looked made my days brighter, since I could take pleasure in glancing in the mirror whenever I liked. You may laugh at how self-satisfied I was then. That doesn't bother me. If you can't be satisfied with yourself, then how can you ever be satisfied with anything else?

'You're free like a cat,' Naa-chan would say sometimes. Were that the case, then I was a house cat, not a stray. I was free only within the confines of our home, with Naa-chan and my parents close at hand. I was not entirely unaware of that fact. Looking back, I may have been mildly depressed, but I never complained to Naa-chan.

'I guess you're right,' was all I would say in response.

Time passed. Our marriage was already seven years old. The few years since the incident with Michiko-sensei had been a period of relative tranquillity for me. There were still women buzzing around Naa-chan, but no sign that he was attached to any of them. Instead, it was the factional strife at his job that was wearing him down, little by little.

I had seen TV dramas about conflicts between managing directors, vice-presidents and other corporate officials, but now it seemed that Naa-chan was being sucked into one such complicated mess in real life.

'How bad is it?' I asked him once.

'Underlings like me can't tell if fights are actually going on at the top or not,' he said, 'but we do get hints of what's happening behind the scenes, and we don't know how to react. I just want to work hard, but . . .'

I just want to work hard? That was so typical of Naa-chan, I couldn't help but laugh. If one chooses to believe that what seems complicated is actually very simple, then the shadows cast by what has been overlooked are bound to accumulate. This, in a nutshell, was Naa-chan.

Our lives were still all right when we could laugh together like that, but as time passed, Naa-chan became more and more exhausted.

'I like the work, but the rest weighs me down,' he took to saying.

'You shouldn't complain to Riko like this!' he laughed bitterly to himself as he plied his shoehorn in the entranceway on his way to work. I saw him off, but watching his retreating back I couldn't help but notice how much older he looked. It worried me that the bad work environment was making it harder and harder for him to do his job.

How I wished I could drive away all that was causing him pain. I wanted to protect him, to hold him close to me. I didn't have that power, of course. Naa-chan didn't want me to, for one thing. For another, in so many ways, he wasn't a man I could ever hope to keep to myself.

Eventually, though, I did come to know of Naa-chan's new love interest.

I believe I've told you that there were no apparent signs of another woman at that time.

Certainly, I had no wind of any such thing. Yet that didn't mean she didn't exist.

For the first time, Naa-chan had hidden something from me.

He had not attempted to conceal his involvement with Michiko-sensei, or the woman from Kyushu. True, he hadn't told me exactly what was going on, but the fact that he wasn't trying to hide anything meant I could sense their presence, for the details would naturally leak out. Once I knew something was taking place, I would question him, and he would answer me truthfully – that was the protocol we followed.

This time, though, Naa-chan was as secretive as could be, at least as long as the affair was going on.

I didn't find out about Naa-chan's new love until it came to an abrupt end, and he was falling to pieces. Even then it took a while to hear the whole story from his lips.

Naa-chan had fallen in love with the fiancée of his company's vice-president, who was himself the son of the company's president. The girl was the youngest daughter from a family that had helped to found the family business. They had been nobility until the close of the Second World War. Distant relatives, the vice-president and his fiancée had been betrothed to each other at an early age, after which she was pampered and watched over like a hothouse flower, far from any polluting breezes.

That was the girl that Naa-chan had fallen hopelessly in love with. He would slip away to see her whenever there was a break at work, meetings which had increased even as he was being tossed about by the factional infighting in his office. Is it any wonder he was so exhausted? After all, he was seeing the treasured daughter of an elite family, so protected she wasn't permitted to stay out late, which meant their secret affair took a terrible toll on their nerves.

Despite the risk, they continued to meet. In the end, though, her family discovered what was going on.

She had two older brothers, and one night they broke into one of their clandestine trysts and stole her away. They had taken her in that brief moment when Naa-chan was in the bathroom, so that when he returned to the private room of the restaurant she was no longer there.

Where had she vanished to? Utterly beside himself, Naa-chan searched and searched until, finally, he came to the realization that her brothers had grabbed her and carried her back home.

The restaurant staff must have taken pity on Naa-chan. Although they had witnessed the whole abduction, they said nothing to him. To me, that silence bespoke their compassion.

Naa-chan and the girl never met again. The two brothers made sure of that, keeping a strict watch on their sister and never letting her out of their sight.

As I mentioned before, Naa-chan himself recounted all these details once the dust had settled, but long before that it had become clear that he had lost the love of his life.

It took some time for him to get back on his feet. For me as well, for the pain was excruciating. Naa-chan may have lost his lady love, but I had lost not only love but much else besides. I had loved Naa-chan and Naa-chan alone since childhood. After our marriage my love had grown even richer, yet more complicated. Now I stood, shattered, amid the ruins of that love.

Naa-chan lay in bed at night lost in thought, looking at the moon, while I lay beside him, weeping as I gazed at his face. Yet he was unaware of my tears, for they flowed not on the surface but within my heart. On the outside, I was always smiling. That rigid smile froze the muscles of my face, froze my heart, froze my feelings for Naa-chan.

I was a bloodless statue. A heartless, cold thing, incapable of change.

The few years that followed were a blur – I can remember hardly anything.

Naa-chan was stymied at work, moved to a meaningless job and then ignored. I didn't know if the cause was the factional strife in the office or his affair with the vice-president's fiancée. Nor did I care.

Although I said those years were a blur, that doesn't mean my mind was swept clean. A bit of amnesia would have helped, but that wasn't on the cards. No, the feeling that I recall from those days, one that still returns at times, is that of overwhelming sadness. Sadness that Naa-chan no longer cared for me, first of all. Beyond that, though, an even deeper sadness that I had lost all desire to look after him, even though I had once been happy to place my heart at his feet, had found such pleasure in guessing what might please him and then doing my best to provide it.

Now, as I look back on those days gone by, I realize that it isn't being loved that makes love fulfilling. No, that's merely a necessary precondition. Loving, being loved, that's only the first step, isn't it?

As love progresses, I think the real issue becomes what one can give to the other. That, I feel, is the rarest, sweetest part of a loving relationship.

Sexual love, for example, can be given. So can many other things that are part of daily life. One can calm one's beloved when they are in turmoil. Or, if they're stuck in the doldrums, one can shake them, sending ripples across stagnant waters that may eventually develop into rolling waves.

I can be of help to this person, is the feeling. This more than anything else provides the greatest happiness true love can attain. I feel that in my bones.

Yet now there was nothing that I could give to Naa-chan. Nor did I desire to do so. Not the tiniest ripple disturbed the still, dark surface of my heart.

It was painful to be with Naa-chan when things were so cold between us, so I began spending more time outside the house.

My flower garden had grown wild, and our rooms were a mess. My mother was worried about how things looked, I could tell, but I never opened up about our problems to her, nor did I ever complain.

I took long walks every day. In the past, after Naa-chan left for the office, I had done the laundry and the cleaning and cheerfully planned our dinner menu, but now the idea of housework left me cold. Almost by way of apology, I turned on the washing machine every few days and vacuumed once a week. I had no patience with washing dishes, however, so the kitchen sink was a disaster area.

Around this time, I cut off the hair I had so cherished. As I coldly watched it pile up on the floor of the salon, I recalled that Michiko-sensei had once said: 'If you ever cut it off, let me have it, all right?' It felt like the distant past.

I left the chaos of our home each day with my now-short hair uncombed, clothed in whatever happened to be lying around. Aimlessly, I wandered the streets in the pale morning sunlight. A surprising number of people were out there as well. In my frame of mind, it seemed that they were all a little lost. Since I felt at sea too, I took to following them around wherever they went. The idea of this somehow soothed me.

I was walking along on one such day when, in the distance, I saw something heading in my direction.

Something that flashed in the sun.

It was a cloudy day, yet it shone beautifully.

As it came closer, I saw it was a man pedalling a bicycle.

'Oh,' I exclaimed in surprise.

For the man on the bicycle was none other than Mr Takaoka, the janitor at my old elementary school.

Mr Takaoka recognized me immediately.

'It's you!' he said, pulling up directly in front of me. 'You're the kid who liked hanging out in the science room.'

'Yes, that's me,' I said with a laugh. I hadn't laughed in a really long time. I'd even forgotten I knew how.

'Where are you coming from?' Just like the old times, I spoke informally, as if there was no age difference between us.

'From far away,' he said. From far away. I tried saying the words to myself. Yes, Mr Takaoka had travelled a great distance, I could feel as much. Not from the next town, not from the next province, but from a place that was truly far, far away.

Time flew by as we talked. In mere moments, we were back where we had been – so many years had passed, yet it felt like we'd been seeing each other every day.

'When did we last meet?' he asked.

We were sitting on a bench beside a small river.

'I was in the fifth grade, so I must have been ten.'

'And how old are you now?'

'Thirty-four.'

'So then it's been about a quarter-century.'

'Oh, my.'

The word quarter-century gave me a start. Could it have been so long?

'I thought our paths might cross today – I could feel the magic working,' Mr Takaoka said with a smile.

'Really?'

'Really.'

How weird could things get?

I recalled Naa-chan's reaction on seeing Mr Takaoka's photograph: 'He's the sort of person I'd like to be a disciple of.' I hadn't given much thought to Naa-chan's comment at the time, but now, seeing Takaoka after so long, I could see what he meant.

I want to be his disciple too, I thought keenly. Now, right away.

For Mr Takaoka did indeed seem free from all worldly desire, like a Buddhist sage. He appeared to have been dwelling in a distant realm, free of the dark and oppressive ties that bind men and women, the cravings of the mundane world, the need to compete.

Perhaps he had been that liberated when he was a janitor. But I had been too young to fully appreciate how much his laid-back attitude had soothed me.

'Hey, Mr Takaoka,' I asked him. 'Where are you heading on your bike?'

'Nowhere in particular,' he answered quietly, looking into my eyes. 'In fact, now that you're here, I think I'll stop for a while.'

'What kind of work are you doing these days?' I asked.

'No job right now. I worked for a temp agency, but I quit once I had saved the money for this road trip.'

A road trip. The expression entranced me.

'Across the hills and mountains, always pedalling forward,' Mr Takaoka explained.

'All day long?'

'No, I'm in no rush, so I rest when I'm tired, find a handy spot to lie down when I'm sleepy, cook something when I'm hungry. The day passes before I know it.'

He seldom bunked down under a roof, he said, choosing to sleep in the open air. I wondered if it was really possible to sleep outside with what appeared to be so few possessions. He laughed.

'Hey don't forget, I'm the guy who underwent training on Mt Kōya back in the day!'

Yes, I had heard him mention that once.

'Did you do the thousand-day austerities?' I asked with some trepidation.

'They don't practise those on Mt Kōya, but I did get used to living outside for days at a time,' he said.

Mr Takaoka had seemed to be growing younger year by year when I was a student, and now he looked younger still. Riding his bike every day had left him tanned and hardened – the outdoor life suited him physically, that much was clear. Indeed, he left a

much younger impression than did Naa-chan, whose perpetual
suffering was taking a toll.

'Mr Takaoka. Please, teach me magic,' I finally spoke aloud
what I had been thinking. I was willing to do anything to sweep
away the clouds darkening my life.

Where could Mr Takaoka's campsite possibly be? After not
meeting for so long, now he was bound to show up within an
hour whenever I went on my walk.

I walked at various times of the day. Sometimes I returned to
bed after Naa-chan left for work and went out around noon; sometimes I woke in the middle of the night, couldn't go back to sleep,
and headed off at the crack of dawn; and sometimes I waited until
the afternoon to leave the house. Whatever time it was, before long
I was sure to see him in the distance, making his way towards me.

'Where are you coming from?' I would ask when he reached
me.

'From far away,' he would reply, as he had the first time.

His bicycle was always well polished, the handlebars and
spokes glowing.

'How do you cook your food when you're camping?'

'Over a fire is best,' he answered. 'But I can't do that in a city,
so I use a camping stove. Building a fire up in the hills can't be
topped, though – it makes me feel like a million dollars.'

Like a million dollars. That cracked me up.

'Are there any wild animals up there?'

'You bet. A whole bunch. You get deer, wild boar, sometimes
even a bear, but they stay away if there's a fire. Would you like to
join me one of these days?'

'I'll take a pass,' I replied immediately. I had no interest whatsoever in experiencing life in the wild. It was all very well for Mr

Takaoka to live that way, but nothing could convince me to sleep under the stars. Was that necessary, I asked, if I wanted to master the magic he possessed?

'No, don't worry about that,' he replied, clearly amused. 'Magic isn't something that requires camping out.'

'If you want me to teach you magic, you have to tell me more about your life first,' Mr Takaoka said.

The air was warm. Summer was gone, autumn had arrived, but winter was not yet round the corner. That kind of day.

We were sitting at our usual spot, on the bench beside the river. The grass that had been so thick at the height of summer was shorter and sparser now: it bowed gently in the breeze as if petitioning something.

This was the setting when I opened up to Mr Takaoka about my relationship with Naa-chan, a topic I had never broached before with anyone. How Naa-chan and I had first met. How falling in love had felt. My pain when I found out about the other women. Our strange relationship with Michiko-sensei. The sadness I felt now, at this moment.

I had expected my story would take a very long time to relate, but once I started talking it took less than an hour. Mr Takaoka listened quietly until the end.

I let out a deep sigh when I finished, but Mr Takaoka's silence continued a while longer.

'When I talk it out like this, it sounds like someone else's story,' I said at last.

'Someone else's story,' he said. 'I like that. That's how I always think about my own life.'

'If it's someone else's story, I must be a complete idiot to let it torment me like this.'

'Maybe you get so deeply involved precisely because it's someone else's story.'

'What?'

I looked into Mr Takaoka's eyes. He was close enough to touch, his face slightly above mine. It was deeply tanned, with lines that suggested his maturity, and yet he looked far younger than the Mr Takaoka I had known before.

'I mean, the tale you just told me is your tale, isn't it?'

'My tale?' I repeated.

'Yes, your tale. The real world consists of separate fragments, so many it's almost impossible to get an overall view, yet we are able to create our stories by stringing a few of those fragments together in some kind of order, right?'

'But still,' I demurred. 'The love I feel for Naa-chan is real love, the pain his women cause me real pain.'

'I'm not saying any of that isn't real.'

'Then what?'

I could feel my cheeks flush as my frustration mounted, a reaction Mr Takaoka seemed to enjoy. It made me angry that he continued to look so relaxed.

'Legions of psychologists and novelists agree that tales are essential to our lives,' Mr Takaoka went on.

I found his way of speaking smug, even disdainful, which made me all the angrier; nevertheless, something in his manner seemed to be loosening me up, for it did strike me that I was involved in some sort of tale. My yearning for Naa-chan, the emotional carnage left by his betrayal, the fact that I had made him the centre of my universe – all were reminiscent of a tale told long ago.

When I turned to look, Mr Takaoka was smiling.

*

'There are so many kinds of stories,' Mr Takaoka says quietly.

The dusk is deepening – I had not realized it until that moment. How long had I been sitting there next to Mr Takaoka, lost in thought?

There are so many things to ponder. Naa-chan. My mother. My father. My surprisingly few friends – only Sugawara and Michiko-sensei, really. (I wasn't sure the latter could be placed in that category, but I decide to include her for now.) The things I love. The things I hate. Finally, me myself.

When I look back on my life this way, my existence begins to seem uncertain, fleeting. Sitting there beside Mr Takaoka, sunk in my reverie, I realize again that it is just as he has said: my life is composed of nothing but fragments, fragments that I myself have stitched together.

In my life to date there is no settled path, nor any real foundation.

'My story isn't worth much to this point,' I spit out. 'It's just boring.'

'You're wrong,' Mr Takaoka replies calmly. 'People's stories tend to be simple. A man and woman meet, fall in love, then separate.'

'Then I have to leave Naa-chan – is that what you're saying?'

'You're the one who decides the direction your story will take, not me.'

'Leave Naa-chan? You can't mean that!' I cry out. My voice is strange, unfamiliar to my ears. It sounds as if I am screaming within a deep cave, where no one can hear. Yet my scream resounds throughout the cave, fills it, spills into the air outside, drops from the sky to reach the people below, spreads endlessly on its way towards some distant destination.

'Do you really love him that much?' Mr Takaoka asks quietly.

'Yes' is my simple answer.

'Then you, too, can learn magic,' he says as we sit on the bench by the river in the fading rays of the sun. You, too. Those words pierce my heart. You, too. Is it possible that he has also been driven mad by love? Was he drawn kicking and screaming into the world of magic as a result? It certainly seems that way.

And so, at night, I began to dream.

I dreamed I was a little girl. Big Bro number one told me that I was seven, I recall, yet I was terribly small for that age. I was not alone – my whole family was in wretched shape. Ma was skin and bones, Pa was a runt, and my three brothers were small and weak.

The hovel where our family lived froze us in winter and roasted us in summer. But I enjoyed the spring and fall, when I could scamper along the ridges between the rice fields, catching *tombo* dragonflies and chasing *amabira* butterflies.

Big Bro, Pa, Ma, *tombo*, *amabira*: these words were unfamiliar at first, but I knew what they meant. Dreams are like this, my dream self thought. In fact, it was a pleasure to be in a dream while at the same time knowing it was a dream. However painful a given moment might be, in the end I was sure to wake up.

My family – my big brothers, Pa, Ma – all cared for me a lot. I had a Big Sis too, and another Big Sis who was even older, but neither lived with us. I was vaguely aware that the Big Sis closer to me in age had been sold to an establishment in Edo two years earlier. Many of our neighbours sold their daughters at the age of ten to reduce the number of mouths that had to be fed. Most of those daughters went to work in inns within walking distance, but the prettiest were packed off to distant Edo to be trained as entertainers in the pleasure quarters.

The Big Sis just above me in age was a sweet girl. 'Hush, hush,' she would croon when I started to cry. 'You're the cutest girl in the world,' using the word *tsuboi* for cute. I was heartbroken, though, when her own cuteness resulted in her being sent away to Edo.

The pity I felt when she was sent away was not the emotion of a child but that of an adult. Yes, there can be no doubt that, emotionally, I was responding as a woman in her mid-thirties, born and raised in modern Tokyo and married to Naa-chan, and not as a seven-year-old girl from a dirt-poor village in old Japan. In my dream, though, I could be both ages at the same time. Experience the feelings of both.

Time in my dreams could easily expand or shrink. One whole night might be spent dreaming of a single day; the next night could encompass an entire year.

I grew steadily in that way. I was seven, then eight, then nine, until I had reached that age when my two big sisters had been sold. Ten years old.

My dream life was jumping ahead in fits and starts, yet my daytime world remained more or less the same. Naa-chan's depression continued, but I could only look after him in a desultory, mechanical way.

Mr Takaoka seemed to have gone off on another of his road trips, for I hadn't seen him in some months. That was hard on me, but my new dream life made it less hard than it otherwise would have been.

My absorption in Naa-chan had left me quite ignorant of my surroundings. I had few friends, couldn't unburden myself to my father and mother, and although I applied myself to the koto, that only made me feel better when I was actually playing. As a result, all I did every day was wander about my immediate neighbourhood.

*

By contrast, my dream world was filled with unfamiliar land-scapes. Our work in the fields began as soon as the snow in the mountains melted enough to leave patches that, from a distance, looked like human forms. Until then we worked shoulder to shoulder before the hearth, weaving straw to make sandals and the like. I had never seen sunsets so red, nor had I noticed how the sky's colour changed from moment to moment with the com-ing of the dawn. Neither had I experienced anything like the frightening quarrels of my big brothers, the wordless night-time sex between Pa and Ma, the incomparable sweetness of the water we drank during our breaks in the fields, or the delicious white rice we ate only once or twice a year. The world of my dreams was harsh yet filled with a brilliant vitality, a vitality stretched so tight that it could snap and cut me if I touched it.

When I woke and considered my life in the modern world – the stagnant repetition that made me feel as though I was sleep-walking through each day – it struck me that the real world was the dream, not the other way round.

Time in my dream world moved forward step by step until I reached the age when I was ready to be sold. The arrangements were made by a man named Zōroku, a broker in the sale of young girls. He was ready to provide the money for my purchase, more than enough to get my family – Pa, Ma and my three big brothers – through the coming winter. It appeared that I had been chosen to make the trip to Edo, like my sister before me.

On our way to Edo, Zōroku stopped at two villages and picked up two more girls, both about my age. It was clearly more efficient to purchase three commodities on a single trip instead of just one.

Yes, commodities. We usually think of commodities as life-less, soulless objects, or perhaps horses or cows raised for market, but the two other girls and I were nothing more than things to be bought and sold.

Being sold was one thing; what hit me hard was the fact that those doing the selling – Ma, Pa and my big brothers – didn't look all that sad to see me go. How could the family that loved me remain so calm and composed when the time came to sell me off? My conscious self – the part of me that belongs to the modern world – just couldn't fathom it.

Why aren't you sadder? I asked my mother. It's fate, was her reply.

So that was it. The awful poverty of our family was fate; the hunger we felt each day, fate; the daughters sold off at the age of ten, fate; the sons too poor to marry, fate. It was fate that crops drowned when there was too much rain, or were fried to a crisp when the sun was too hot, or were driven into the mud when typhoons hit – anything and everything was attributed to fate.

One could never stand against fate. One could only quietly accept it. Our village lived by that principle. There were some who rejected working the fields – who gave up farming and ran off to Edo, or even turned to thievery – but no one knew where they were or what they were doing.

The night I dream of being sold, I am woken by the sound of my own sobs.

'What's wrong?' asks Naa-chan, beside me in bed. My sobs must have woken him too.

'Ma,' I say, without thinking.

'Who is Ma?' he asks, baffled.

Of course, he has no way to decipher the name I had called out in my sleep. I half-blame the silent mother who had sent me away without a tear the day I was sold, but who is sadder – the modern me, or the girl sold off to Edo?

My image of Ma bears no relationship to my real mother, so I guess it must be the sadness of that ten-year-old girl that I'm feeling.

I may be awake, but in my heart I am still my dream self.

Naa-chan is clearly bewildered.

'You don't look the way you usually do, Riko,' he says, peering into my eyes. I have been avoiding his gaze for a long time, but now I look back.

His eyes are brown, their pupils bright.

This is the man I loved. The man I still love. Yet now I measure my feelings for him from a distance, as I might regard someone who bears no relation to me.

I miss Ma and Pa, and my big brothers, and that cramped, windowless shack.

All three of us girls had been told that Edo was a big, colourful place. That it was a stroke of good fortune to be sent there from the village.

'You'll all get to dress up in pretty kimonos,' Zōroku told us. We walked on and on until, finally, we came to the Naitō post station, one of the checkpoints through which travellers had to pass to gain entry to the great city. We thought our journey was about to end at last, but another full day of walking lay ahead, for our path took us to the far-eastern end of the city. Zōroku was intent on reaching our destination while it was still light, so we left the post station before sun-up.

That destination turned out to be a desolate spot on a narrow canal. The wind was strong and the water rough. I could see rice paddies in the distance. Night was about to fall, so we were hustled into a 'boar tusk' boat, a narrow craft with a pointed prow. The boatman was a taciturn sort; he stood and plied the waters with a long pole. We continued along the canal for a while, then turned into a broad river.

'This is Ōkawa, the big river,' Zōroku said. Pine trees lined the shore, their branches jutting out over the water. We could see groves of trees on both sides of the river as we moved along until, once more, we turned off on to a smaller canal. The wind picked up again, and we were tossed about. The three of us huddled together whenever a big wave struck.

At last, we pulled into a spot where many pleasure boats were moored. The boatman laid down his pole.

'We get off here,' said Zōroku. He rose from his seat and we staggered from the rolling deck on to dry land. Men were parading back and forth, and sounds of revelry rose from the moored boats.

We could do little but trudge along behind Zōroku as the path twisted and turned. Soon we reached a road lined with small shops next to a great willow tree. It was here that visitors to the pleasure quarters could rent the wide-brimmed hats that many wore to shield their identities. The road came to a dead end at a black gate, with a moat that apparently served as a drainage ditch stretching out on both sides. Being new to the Yoshiwara, I had yet to learn that this moat was called Ohagurodobu, Tooth-Black Ditch, named for the black dye that courtesans used on their teeth, and that it surrounded the entire Quarter.

'This is the Ōmon, the Great Gate,' Zōroku said, pointing at the looming black structure. The Great Gate of Yoshiwara. Ah, how ignorant I was then. The modern, dreaming me has heard the name somewhere, but knows little more than that. The girl I was back then saw just a big gate.

We were all hustled through the gate. It would be ten years before I would pass through that gate again, on my way out. I would not leave the Quarter once in all that time.

*

Yoshiwara was like a big village.

The two girls I travelled with had been sold to different houses from the one I was headed for. I say 'houses', but they were not the kind of house I was used to, no Ma or Pa living there, for sure. No, these were so-called teahouses, or *mise*. Nevertheless, over time my house did become my home. There may not have been parents, but there was a community of men, women and young girls.

The house to which I had been sold was a mid-sized establishment that fronted on Yoshiwara's main avenue. I learned later that my travel companions had been purchased by smaller houses a stone's throw from Tooth-Black Ditch.

When I arrived they stripped me of the clothes I was wearing, caked with dust from my long trip, and led me to the bath. As a ten-year-old girl I was dimly aware of the awful things girls in the Quarter could be forced to perform, so I trembled at the thought that some beastly man might have his way with me when I had finished bathing.

The person who helped me bathe, though, was a sharp-looking girl who appeared slightly younger than me. She was dressed in a pretty kimono, with her hair cut short at the shoulders.

'Were you sold here too?' I asked.

'No,' she replied with a laugh. She said she had been born in the Quarter. Her mother currently managed the girls and women who worked in the teahouse, but before that she had been an *oiran* herself.

'You'll become a *kamuro* like me,' the girl said.

'*Kamuro*,' I mumbled the unfamiliar word.

'We're the assistants to the *oiran* – we do whatever they tell us to do.'

'Do we have to let men have their way with us?' I asked in surprise.

'Have their way?' she repeated instead of answering my question. The words seemed to amuse her. 'Oh, I see, do you mean the ways of the bedchamber?' she replied. 'It sounds so crude when you say it like that.' She giggled, taking in my bewildered expression. As a modern woman sojourning in a dream of the past, I am offended that my words struck her as crude, yet the girl didn't seem contemptuous of me at all. Rather, she seemed to enjoy my confusion.

'B-but,' I stammered.

'Travellers have such interesting ways of talking,' she said with a laugh, even more amused. The modern me is a little put off by the effrontery of this girl, who was probably younger than I was at the time, but my Edo self was already beginning to look up to her. Indeed, the girl's gestures and speech were strangely enticing for her age.

Born and raised in Yoshiwara, she had naturally absorbed the ways of the Quarter – it had not been necessary for her to study them. She lived in an elegant, mysterious world that took as its sole purpose the gratification of male desire, a world whose mores transcended any moral judgement about the rights or wrongs of selling women's bodies. That world fascinated me.

'We *kamuro* sleep in the room beside the kitchen,' she explained. All houses in the Quarter had two storeys, with a lattice of thick red bars that faced the street. Courtesans entertained their customers in rooms upstairs, while the ground floor consisted of a large reception hall, the kitchen and bath, and the *andon beya*, a windowless storage room where customers who failed to pay their debts might be locked up.

The following day my hair was cut to my shoulders, the same

length as that of my fellow *kamuro*. And so it was that my life in Yoshiwara truly began.

Six months have passed since my dreams started. Winter has come and gone, and spring is well under way when who should pop up with the budding green leaves but Mr Takaoka, back from his travels!

I was housebound all winter, but with the first signs of spring I have begun pottering around the garden, straightening up the house and exploring the neighbourhood on foot.

My long months spent in dreams of the past have drastically changed my feelings about the present. The more I dream, the more my feelings about Naa-chan are altered – the pain I feel seeing his face, saying his name, even listening to him breathe, is no longer there. I love Naa-chan as I always have. Whatever else happens, it's likely that will never change. It's part of me, like my body, my voice.

But where my love for Naa-chan once filled me to overflowing, that love is now joined by a host of new things. It's as if a space in my heart has opened, allowing a rainbow of colours to flow in.

Now I can love the evening sky in the same way I love him. I can also love the mother and daughter I met on my strolls – the latter reminds me so much of my youthful dream self. I can love the falling cherry blossoms as never before. I can even love the tulips blooming in almost nauseating profusion in my neighbour's front garden.

It is right at this point that Mr Takaoka returns. I'm sitting on our bench by the river looking at the water birds when I sense someone come up behind me. I feel a surge of joy and immediately spin round. Even without looking, I can tell it's him.

*

I have missed his smell. It is the scent of grass. Of wind. Of green leaves. Of flowers.

'Where have you been?' I ask him.

'Here and there,' he says. I laugh, for I had expected his answer to be just like that, without a single place name.

'What's so funny?' Mr Takaoka says, staring at me, puzzled.

'You really haven't changed a bit!'

'I guess not,' he says, unsure what I am talking about.

But I have no doubt. Compared to other things in my life – the changes taking place in my dream self and my altered feelings towards Naa-chan, to name just two – the Mr Takaoka standing before me is the same as always. Seeing him instantly puts me at ease.

'The magic is still working,' I say.

'Is that so? That's good.'

'I'm not so sure.'

'Believe me, it's good. Magic is exciting, isn't it?'

'Exciting? Is that what you call it?'

'Sure. Most things in this world are,' he replies laconically. Really? Could most things be seen as exciting? Given all that has transpired between Naa-chan and me over the years, I couldn't disagree more strongly.

'Are things dragging you down?' he goes on.

'Of course, lots of things.'

'Really?'

He opens his eyes wide. That innocent look annoys me.

'Did you feel like that when you were very young?' he asks, studying my pouting face.

When I was very young? The phrase sends me straight back to my grade school days. I recall the janitor's room where Mr Takaoka hung out. The quiet places I loved. The classmates

I hated. As for all those things I neither loved nor hated, he was right – almost everything was exciting in one way or another when I was a child. Things I liked, even things that left me cold. Although my idea of 'exciting' might be quite different from other people's.

Mr Takaoka sits beside me there on the bench, entirely relaxed, looking out over the river.

Night after night, my dreams of Edo continued.

Life in Yoshiwara was a constant challenge. Living in the shack with my family had been difficult too, but the problems presented by the Quarter were of a wholly different nature.

We *kamuro* attended to the *oiran* in every detail, serving them and running errands. We didn't rise early as farmers did, but we worked late, until midnight or even dawn. I was always short of sleep. I had heard stories about the fabled opulence of Yoshiwara, and it was true that the clothes we wore were top-quality, and we ate white rice every day, albeit mixed with other grains like millet, barley or wheat. At first I felt guilty towards Ma, Pa and my brothers at mealtimes.

It turned out that the cost of all the pretty clothes and fine food was added to the money we owed, so we had to be frugal. All the debts an *oiran* ran up over the years had to be paid off before she could leave her house. Thus, while a *kamuro* would often go on to become an *oiran*, she would still be held accountable for what she owed from that early period of training. This is why it took so long for a woman to free herself from the Quarter.

Ah, but a person can get used to anything, can't she! I quickly grew accustomed to a standard of living – my clothes, the food I ate – that, however constrained, far surpassed life in my old village. Indeed, Yoshiwara was a place that encouraged, even demanded luxury, so that it seemed only natural for women to pile debt upon debt.

In this way, little by little, within a single year, I acquired the airs of a denizen of Yoshiwara.

It was the custom that patrons ordered dishes prepared by *daiya* – what we call caterers today – which we *kamuro* carried on trays up to their rooms. To my Edo self, the menu was mind-boggling, almost unbelievably sumptuous. My heart pounded imagining what it would be like to be an *oiran* who feasted on such delicious food every day. They must be truly happy!

Or so I thought at first. Later, I was surprised to discover that *oiran* were not permitted to eat the same catered food their customers did. At least, that was the policy at my house. However, an *oiran* who attracted numerous patrons did have her own special food prepared in the house kitchen, which was very different from what was eaten by the *kamuro* and the other men and women who served. That special meal was prepared in the afternoon before things got busy and was carried upstairs for her to eat at leisure. And after their customers had left, several *oiran* might also gather together to polish off what remained, washed down with cups of leftover sake in what could turn into a lively party.

Oiran who lacked customers, however, were a sad lot. They were served the same humble fare we *kamuro* received. Consequently, anything left from what the *daiya* had delivered was not thrown away but secretly warmed up and eaten the following day by those patron-less *oiran* and we *kamuro*.

My favourite dish was day-old sashimi lightly grilled over a brazier and eaten with miso or chilli peppers. I was shown how to make this by my fellow *kamuro* Omino, the younger girl who had helped me in the bath on my first night. She also taught me that a dash of vinegar added to a simmering pot of vegetables could deepen its flavour, making an otherwise bland dish very tasty.

Omino was my sensei when it came to Yoshiwara. Although her mother was a former *oiran* who now helped manage the house, I saw little evidence of any emotional connection between them, despite that blood tie.

Omino slept in a big room next to the kitchen, the same place the other *kamuro* and female servants bunked down, all packed together on the floor like sardines, and her meals were equally wretched, a far cry from those her mother enjoyed. In fact, virtually no distinction was drawn between someone like me, who had been sold to the house, and Omino, who had grown up in it: we were both being raised for the sole purpose of someday becoming a popular, and therefore profitable, Yoshiwara *oiran*.

My happiest times in Yoshiwara were the hours I spent in training.

All the Yoshiwara *oiran* – at least those working in the bigger houses facing the main avenue – could read and write. This surprised me. I had assumed that girls sold so young and raised for the explicit purpose of having their bodies purchased by men would be illiterate.

But I was completely wrong.

Of course, the education of *kamuro* varied from house to house. An *oiran* from one of the big houses, which entertained high-ranking samurai and daimyo officials, had to be highly educated to hold her own in the verbal repartee expected in those encounters. If, on the other hand, her house was a small one, little education was provided.

Since my house was medium-size, we rarely had to entertain samurai from daimyo households. Yet I came to realize that even an average samurai possessed a more thorough education than I had received.

To be honest, my modern self had done very poorly in classical Japanese at school. For the life of me, I couldn't get my head around all those unfamiliar verb endings: *keri*, for example, or *haberi* and *eumajiu*. It was all gibberish to me. Perhaps that was why I was overly impressed with quite run-of-the-mill samurai who had no trouble reading the old texts, and who dashed off all sorts of messages on the packets of paper they carried with them.

During the daytime hours the *oiran* would rest in their rooms, reading novels, perhaps, or plucking their three-string shamisens. Many of the novels they read reminded me of the mysteries and romances that are bestsellers in Japan today. One *oiran* in my house loved the Heian romances, works written a thousand years earlier, like *The Tale of Genji* and *The Tale of Utsuho*, as well as collections of popular Buddhist stories.

Her name was Komurasaki and I called her Big Sister, as I did all the *oiran*. Although not the most popular in our house, she was much sought after by our more elite patrons, the best-read and most knowledgeable, for not only could she exchange missives with them but she could also write witty thirty-one-syllable *waka* and seventeen-syllable haiku poems – no mean feat.

'Is that book actually interesting?' I asked her one day. Of the many books stacked on Komurasaki's shelf, one in particular seemed to have captured her attention. The books were printed using woodblocks, and all were illustrated. The page she was gazing at had a picture of a man and woman holding hands and running across a meadow.

'Aha! So, this *kamuro* likes books, does she?' Komurasaki said, acting surprised. When I nodded, she invited me to her side and recounted the story behind the illustration.

The man was an aristocrat named Ariwara no Narihira, the woman the future Princess Kisaki of Nijo. They were pictured in the act of eloping together. The man's kimono had an unusual diamond pattern.

The book was the ninth-century *The Tales of Ise*!

My modern self picked up on this fact in the course of my dream. I smiled to remember how passionately our classical Japanese teacher in high school had described Narihira's great charm, and yet how many of us dozed off during the lecture. But now I found myself entranced by Komurasaki's delicate fingers moving across the picture.

'I'll lend it to you sometime,' she said. Then, as if she had completely lost interest in me, she rolled over and returned to her book.

It always takes time to adjust to the present after dreaming of life in the Quarter.

In the morning, as Naa-chan sleeps beside me, I find myself going over the world of Yoshiwara in my mind.

The Quarter was laid out like an eel bed, with a single main avenue that ran in a long, straight line from the entrance deep into the interior. Since the houses opened only on to that avenue and there were no windows, virtually everything was in darkness.

The *oiran* entertained their guests in shared rooms. That's right – only a select few had rooms of their own, which meant that up to four *oiran* would cavort with their guests in a single chamber. Screens and curtains made it impossible to see one another, but there was no way of concealing the sounds or any other signs of what might be going on.

In my house, only three *oiran* had their own rooms. Two were designated 'room-holders', while the third, an *oiran* named Ibuki, had the highest rank of all, that of *chū-san*. She even had a separate

parlour in which to entertain her guests, which she kept exqui-
sitely decorated and fragrant with incense. There, Ibuki would
spend her nights with a single customer on a bed of multiple
futons stacked one upon the other, befitting her privileged status.

Lighting in the Quarter was provided by lamps suspended from
the ceiling and *andon* – much like the paper-covered lamps still
in use today – placed on the floor. One of our responsibilities as
kamuro was keeping all those lamps filled with oil.

I loved the dimness of the Quarter.

It is strange indeed to wake from my dream world to the
disconcerting brightness of the modern world. Both electric light
bulbs and oil lamps produce illumination, but what a difference!
Electric light renders the outlines of objects clearly. Lamplight
obscures those outlines, yet somehow suggests the depth of things.

There seemed to be no relationship between *The Tales of Ise*
that Komurasaki was reading next to the *andon* and *The Tales of
Ise* that I read in my high school textbook. As a student I found
the book quite tedious, written in a preposterous language riddled
with what I saw as faults. Yet the longer I looked at *The Tales of
Ise* that Komurasaki was reading in the dim light of the Quarter,
the more colourful and appealing it became. (You might expect
it would be brighter, since Komurasaki read during the day, but
fewer lamps were lit then, making it even dimmer than at night.)

The modern me might have been a poor student of classical
Japanese in high school, but thanks to the training I was receiving
in my dream, I could somehow work my way through the old
cursive text, though it wasn't easy going. As a *kamuro*, the pas-
sage that took my breath away was the 'Akutagawa' chapter, the
so-called sixth episode, where Ariwara no Narihira abducts the
future Princess Nijo.

Narihira is carrying her on his back as they hurry along a dark path. When they are about to cross a river, the princess speaks. 'What is that?' she asks, pointing at the dew on the grasses.

Narihira cannot stop to answer, for thunder is crashing about them. Rain is falling in sheets when he finally finds shelter for her in a nearby storehouse. Then he stands guard at the door, sword at the ready.

Narihira remains on guard until the sun comes up. Unbeknownst to him, however, a demon has entered the storehouse and swallowed the princess in a single gulp. She emits a small cry and then vanishes. Narihira is devastated to discover her gone. Yet he is able to compose a poem through his tears:

> 'What is that?
> Might it be a string of pearls?'
> 'No, my love, it is the dew.'
> Would that I too had vanished
> With the dew.

Narihira's grief in that moment always brought me to tears. On the very night that, after so much effort, he could finally be alone with the young woman, a demon devours her.

I shed only a few tears in the dream, yet back in the modern world I find myself sobbing over Narihira's calamity as I did when I dreamed of being sold by Ma and Pa, perhaps even harder. When I wake in the night to wipe the tears from my eyes, I always check on Naa-chan sleeping beside me. This time he is crying too, his brow knitted in pain, as if in response to my weeping. Tears are seeping from behind his closed eyelids, now one trickle, now two. Might the two of us be sharing the same dream?

*

'You know the girl in the sixth episode? Well, she wasn't really eaten by a demon,' Mr Takaoka remarks one day.

'What?' I exclaim. 'If that's the case, then why was she missing when morning came?'

'Her brothers took her back home.'

'Really?'

'Well, that's what the commentary says.'

'But isn't the commentary unreliable? I mean, *The Tales of Ise* isn't a true story anyway, right?'

'Mm, I'm not so sure about that. Parts of it are true – and that applies to the character of Narihira as well.'

I smile. Mr Takaoka makes it sound as if he knew Narihira, and they had talked face to face. I consider Mr Takaoka's version, where the girl's brothers whisk her away from Narihira. Which would have been more difficult for Narihira to accept, I wonder: that she had been swallowed by some sort of demon, or that her family had forcibly taken her home? If the girl's brothers had swept him aside like a piece of trash to reclaim their sister, wouldn't that have inflicted the deeper wound? If a demon had swallowed her, perhaps Narihira could have accepted his defeat at the hands of monstrous Nature. Resistance would have been futile in that case, no matter how hard he fought. Had her brothers taken her, he would have had to live knowing that she was still somewhere out there in the world. She would be alive, yet forever beyond his reach, her marriage to someone else a foregone conclusion. Wouldn't it have been even harder to reach some sort of closure if Narihira had known she was still around? Might he then have been fated to carry his love for her into the future, an unending source of pain?

But what I am really thinking of is my own stubborn love for Naa-chan. I recognize my own pain in Narihira's.

*

I had been living in Yoshiwara for four years, and the date of my investiture as a newly minted *oiran*, or *shinzō*, was fast approaching. It was an important step, and thus highly formalized. An *oiran* had to sleep with her customers. A *shinzō*, however, didn't do that straight away. There were a number of rituals we were to undergo first.

Two *kamuro* from our house would become *shinzō* that fall, Omino and me. Our first ceremony would be the *shinzō-dashi*, the public presentation of all the *shinzō* in the Quarter. The *shinzō-dashi* was a once-in-a-lifetime event for the women of Yoshiwara. *Oiran* blackened their teeth while *kamuro* did not. Ten days before the *shinzō-dashi*, therefore, the patrons of our big sisters – that is, the *oiran* in our house – subsidized a teeth-blackening ceremony for us. That symbolized our impending promotion to *oiran* status.

At last the day of the ceremony arrived. That day, our house sent gifts of soba noodles to the many teahouses and agents who helped direct customers our way. We also prepared celebratory red rice for the occasion.

The event itself was carried out on a massive scale, and again was paid for by our older sisters' patrons. Needless to say, houses whose *oiran* had attracted wealthy patrons could mount the most strikingly elaborate ceremonies.

Large bamboo steamers, shallow baskets normally used for the steaming of dumplings and the like, were stacked in front of the house, and a plank of fresh wood was laid on top to make a platform. It resembled one of those long tables you find in a corporate boardroom. Arranged on top of this platform was a many-hued array of fabrics – satin, silk crepe, brocade, and so on – as if a hundred flowers were blooming there in profusion. Nor was this the only display. The rooms of our *oiran* big sisters were also decorated with colourful cloth, as well as things that might be shared: tobacco pouches, folding fans, hand towels, steamed sweets and so forth.

For the next seven days, Omino and I were paraded around Yoshiwara by one or another of our big sisters, sporting a new and different kimono on each occasion. Our big sisters' patrons had shelled out for these kimonos, which had been set aside for this very event. Had there been no patrons ready and willing to contribute the necessary support, then our sisters themselves would have had to borrow funds from the house to pay for the kimonos. In the Yoshiwara system, it was always the women who ended up being squeezed for money. Therefore, while Omino seemed utterly thrilled by the extravagance of it all, my feelings were more complicated.

'Isn't it beautiful,' Omino murmured rapturously, running her fingers across the cool surface of one of the kimonos she had received.

'It's beautiful, but it's scary too,' I said, sunk in my gloomy thoughts. But, hold on a minute – hadn't a tiny smirk just flitted across Omino's lips? It passed quickly, but I was sure that's what it was.

Aha, I thought. Omino was no fool, that was clear. The truth was that she understood the depths of Yoshiwara far better than I did. A gaudy world subsidized by ever-mounting debt, an underlying darkness that threatened to snatch the *oiran* and pull them down.

She and I were grappling with the same problem. We each had a dream of how we could escape our poverty. A dream of meeting a man we could share our lives with. A man who, just possibly, might care for us with all his heart.

Still, as *oiran* there was nothing we could do to change how things stood. We had no choice but to accept what fate might bring. In which case, our best option was to enjoy the present as fully as we could.

Omino's smirk encompassed all of that.

Finally, the time came when Omino and I were to begin sleeping with our customers. But that did not mean that as new *oiran* we were made available to just anyone. A fledgling *oiran* might develop a deep-seated fear of sex if, at the very beginning, she was treated roughly by some unknown man unable to control his passions. To avoid that outcome, the first man an *oiran* slept with after her initiation, as part of what was called the *mizuage* or 'water-raising' ritual, had to be someone fully experienced in the arts of love.

My partner was a man a bit past forty. What I remember most about him was that, while his face was tanned and firm, his naked torso was pale and pudgy. But he was a masterful lover, that much I could tell as his fingers gently caressed my body, patiently manipulating it, opening it for the first time.

When our lovemaking began there was a cool, even icy separation between my two selves – one a modern, mature woman who presumably knew what there is to know about sex, and my other young self from centuries earlier, who had never before been touched by a man. As our lovemaking progressed, however, the two sides began to merge in a manner I found very strange. The two mes – the woman in her thirties and the virginal girl – were astonished by the man's sexual technique.

Is this what it was all about, sleeping with a man? The woman me felt this most strongly. Sex with Naa-chan, the man I love, is filled with warmth and happiness, but there is little in it that is surprising. Rather, it makes me feel peaceful and secure. A tender affection governs the way his body and mine join together – it feels as if I have returned to my true home.

What took my mature, experienced self wholly by surprise was the variety of techniques the man used to awaken the sexuality of the young *oiran*. Could sex be like this? My amazement knew no bounds. I discovered that there was a place within my body that was pulsating with life, with muscles that I could learn to control. By tightening and releasing those muscles in time with a man's movements, I could heighten his pleasure as well as my own.

Until then, I had believed that sexual pleasure couldn't be fully experienced unless the emotions were engaged. Yes, that's what I had assumed. I don't mean that Naa-chan is lacking in technique. On the contrary, somewhere along the line I had grasped the fact that he is a better lover than most. It wasn't necessary for me to experience other men to figure that out.

And, yes. I have always been satisfied in Naa-chan's arms. Undoubtedly, my physical response is a big part of that. And yet a question stuck in my mind: if an absolute stranger made love to me exactly as Naa-chan does, would I enjoy it as much? No, that couldn't happen, I decided. Instead of feeling pleasure, I assumed, my body would stiffen, and sadness would close my heart.

Yet – how can I put this in words – by opening me the way he did, the man from Yoshiwara had set my body free, allowing it to experience pleasure that was entirely physical. It was like the rush of blood to the head the first time you execute a flip on the bar in gymnastics, or do a perfect spin on the dance floor. That sort of feeling.

The man had been a complete stranger, someone I neither liked nor disliked, someone I had never even talked to. But the way he handled my body provoked virtually no disgust, no anger. Perhaps that was because he did not regard me as a woman.

Instead, he treated me as he would a valuable piece of crafts-manship. A beautiful object, lovingly created by a highly skilled artisan, who had put everything into it even while knowing it was destined to be sold.

The man had used all his skill and care to polish this object, thereby completing the process of making me a perfect commodity. That had been his sole goal.

And so it was that I learned what sex freed from emotion really felt like.

So now I was a *shinzō*, a new *oiran*. That's right. Now I would start sleeping with my customers.

My first was the eldest son and heir of an armour merchant in Shitaya. He looked to be in his early thirties. His father ran the business and showed no sign of retiring, so little responsibility rested on the son's shoulders, allowing him to lavish great sums of money enjoying himself in the Quarter.

'Merchants from the bigger shops are better than samurai,' Oshina, our manager and Omino's mother, was fond of telling us. 'They can spend money more freely. I'll be charging a pretty penny for you two, you can be sure of that.'

As we would now be entertaining customers, Omino and I were given new names. She would be known as Izumi. My *oiran* name would be Shungetsu.

Izumi was critical of the name chosen for me, which meant 'Spring Moon'.

'I mean, what about the other times of the year?' she fretted. 'Don't you think it might be bad luck?'

She argued that, since we had to maintain our popularity all year round, it was better to have a name that wasn't limited to a specific season. But her mother laughed that off. 'The spring moon is veiled in mist, you see, so it feels within reach, yet isn't. Like an *oiran*.'

In fact, I was quite fond of my new name. Spring Moon struck me as both gentle and sincere. With such a name, I thought, I might be able to penetrate more deeply into the heart of Naa-chan, who had been so beaten down, and give him hope. That's how I felt, anyway.

My dream life in Yoshiwara was making my waking, modern self very curious about what the world of the Quarter had been like. That makes sense, don't you think? I mean, almost a third of our life is spent sleeping. I was spending all that time not in modern Japan but in the Edo period. So it wasn't mere curiosity that spurred my research – rather, I felt compelled to find out. Yes, it was compulsion that drove me to discover all I could about that place called Yoshiwara.

The books I read said that a man had to make at least three visits to be accepted as a regular by an *oiran* in Yoshiwara. One of my sources put it this way:

On his first visit – visits to a house being referred to as 'climbing the tower' – the guest would be shown to one of the rooms on the second floor, where he would describe to one of the young men who received guests which of the several *oiran* who had welcomed him at the door he wished to see. Then a *kamuro* would bring him tea and a tray with smoking implements, while the young man would fetch the *oiran* in question. Following custom, the guest and the *oiran* would sit separately, and neither would drink the sake that the young man had readied. Even when food was brought, the *oiran* would refrain from eating. Once the revelry had started and things had grown lively, the young man would guide the guest to the *oiran*'s room and they would sleep together.

The next time the guest 'climbed the tower' – that is, his second visit – was called 'the reversal.' The *oiran* had been largely silent on the first visit, but now she would converse with the guest, though she would be reserved. Sake and food would be laid out, as on the first visit, but this time the guest was obliged to tip the young man. Then, the guest and the *oiran* would go to bed.

The third visit was referred to as becoming 'intimates' or regulars. It carried with it the recognition that the guest was pleased with the *oiran*, and that his visits would continue. On this occasion, the guest was obliged to tip not only the young man but the woman who managed the house as well. This would be the last visit where he was required to give separate tips to everyone. The status of a regular meant that the *oiran* would remove her *obi* before she and the guest went to bed. Until then, she had kept her kimono fastened until they were under the covers.

My goodness, what a strict set of rules! My eyes widened in surprise as I pored over my paperback copy of *An Illustrated History of Yoshiwara*. I found the book endlessly rewarding: when my experience in the Quarter confirmed what I had read in the book, I felt as satisfied as knowing my home was swept and clean; when my experience differed, I was excited to feel that I was privy to secrets no one else knew.

Yes, that paperback was my bible as I shuttled back and forth between dream and reality. I read it during my breaks from housework, took it as a companion on my walks, immersed myself

in it while curled up on the sofa on evenings when Naa-chan
was late.

'You've turned into a real bookworm, haven't you?' Naa-chan said
to me one day. 'What are you reading?'

'Nothing special,' I said lazily. Naa-chan came over and looked
down at the title.

'Yoshiwara?' His voice was a bit too loud, making him sound
rather stupid.

I had reached the point in my dreams where my first customer,
the young master from the armour shop, was showering me with
gifts. Nor was he the only one – almost every day, other men of
Edo sought to excite me with all sorts of erotic stimuli. So is it any
wonder that I allowed some of my feelings as the *oiran* Shungetsu
to spill over into my life as a modern woman?

I lay there sprawled on the sofa absorbed in my reading,
feeling as I did in the Quarter reading popular novels during
those long afternoons when there weren't any guests. I had no
inclination to jump up and hide the title of my book, for in that
moment Naa-chan had come across as such an uncultured boor I
had practically written him off.

The young man from the armour shop had other interests
above and beyond the ladies of Yoshiwara. His clothes were always
fashionable, he had mastered the tea ceremony, and he followed
the theatre closely. On every visit, he was sure to entertain me
with lively reports of what was going on in our great city. Other
men also came to my house to ply me with gifts and regale me
with fascinating stories.

'Yoshiwara still exists, right?' I asked Naa-chan, hoping to head
off further discussion of why I had chosen that book in particular.

'Yeah, I guess so. I've never been, though.'

'Have you ever paid for sex with a woman?' I asked bluntly. Shungetsu was lingering in my heart, egging me on.

'What?' Naa-chan exclaimed, looking at me. 'What's wrong with you, Riko?'

'Nothing,' I replied.

The men of Edo weren't nearly as good-looking as Naa-chan. People were a lot shorter back then, and standards of personal hygiene were lower. Naa-chan took the gold medal, too, when it came to his glowing, blemish-free skin and his well-groomed exterior. The biggest difference, however, was dental. Naa-chan's teeth had been straightened when he was a child, and he still visited the dentist regularly, whereas Edo men tended to have uneven, yellowed teeth, the complete opposite of the immaculate whiteness of men like Naa-chan.

Nevertheless, I was no longer attracted by the fierce gleam of his teeth. Edo men definitely weren't as well turned out from head to toe, but they really knew how to have a good time, and I felt close to them.

'Why would you ask me something like that?' Naa-chan said, his voice dripping with pride and indignation. 'I would never think of paying to sleep with a woman.'

So, you'd jump into bed with women other than me but never crack your wallet to buy one? You fickle hypocrite. You make yourself out to be so high and mighty, but I bet you never gave a thought to the feelings of the women who make their living that way. Cheapskate!

When I cursed Naa-chan, I sounded like Shungetsu of Yoshiwara. Unspoken though those curses were.

'I'm hungry,' he added, all innocent. 'What's for dinner?'

I lazily watched Naa-chan from the couch as he went to the next room to change his clothes.

*

Mr Takaoka laughed out loud when I described my dream life to him.

'Your magic world sounds like a lot of fun!' he said.

I'm not so sure about that, I thought, sceptically. Life in Yoshiwara is hard – a vast, indescribable darkness lies at the very bottom of everything. So I'm not sure 'fun' sums it up. One thing's for sure, though – thanks to Yoshiwara, my blind faith in Naa-chan has been worn away, so I'm not nearly as upset by every little thing he does.

'It might not be completely enjoyable, but I bet you can have *some* fun,' Mr Takaoka said. 'Maybe I'll pay a visit to your dream world.'

'Are you able to do that?' I was flabbergasted.

'I'm not sure. Perhaps I can, and perhaps I can't. If you give me a little tug, I just might manage to squeeze in.'

According to Mr Takaoka, there had been rare cases where he was able to rope a particular person into his dreams.

'Who did you rope in?' I asked.

'That's a secret. Let's just say that someone I have admired since long, long ago has visited me more than once.'

'Long, long ago.' I tried repeating the words to myself, rolling them around on my tongue.

They struck me as far more profound than they once did.

At this moment, I am here. Sitting with Mr Takaoka on a bench beside a river. Yet at the same time I exist in a world long ago. As a Yoshiwara *oiran*.

How much time separates our present and the world of Yoshiwara?

For me, now, that old world is both past and present. True, looked at historically, the Edo period is long past. Yet I *am* living in Yoshiwara, no doubt about it. I'm not remembering what happened back then – no, I am *present* in Edo at this very moment, body and soul.

'When you say long, long ago, just how long do you mean?' I asked.

'Mm, let me see. Well, writing had already been invented. People weren't all that different from now. They walked upright on two legs; their eyes were no more deep-set; they wore clothes; they waged one war after another. So it wasn't really that long ago.'

I laughed when Mr Takaoka said, 'upright on two legs'. Who knows, perhaps he could travel even further back in time, to before humans walked on land.

I imagined Mr Takaoka there at the beginning, when our earliest ancestors hadn't yet evolved, and those life forms that came before were struggling to survive. I could feel the wind blowing across the river. Did this river even exist back then? Or was this spot not even solid earth, but sitting at the bottom of the ocean, invisible, in a world where space was vague and indistinct?

'I still can't grasp what long ago means,' I said, rising from the bench. Mr Takaoka got up too. Then he nimbly hopped on to his bicycle and was off in a flash.

Who does he remind me of? thought the me that is Shungetsu. I know his face well. Too well, in fact, to recall who he makes me think of.

That was my reaction when I first met Takada. He was a person of few words. He kept his eyes fixed on me, only nibbling at his food. He had been brought to our house by Mr Yamashita, a regular of my friend and fellow *oiran* Omino, now Izumi. Mr Yamashita was a well-off salt merchant from Shinagawa, and one of our most valued customers.

'Mr Takada is a samurai, you know,' drawled Mr Yamashita, introducing his companion while Izumi poured the sake. Mr Takada nodded stiffly, visibly out of place in his surroundings. It appeared he seldom visited the Quarter.

'Mr Takada chose Shungetsu, so he is clearly a man of discernment,' Mr Yamashita said. 'Still,' he pontificated, 'she has a way to go to catch up with Izumi.'

In school, I had learned about the four-class system – samurai, peasant, artisan and merchant – that shaped traditional Japan, so I had thought when I first arrived in Yoshiwara that samurai naturally ruled the roost. Once I had started working as an *oiran*, though, I came to understand that merchants were not nearly as lowly as their official status suggested.

Although the role of the samurai swordsman had been crucial in the early years of the Edo period, when battles were still being fought, samurai had less and less to do once the long peace was under way. While high-ranking samurai retained their wealth and power, their poorer cousins, the lower-ranking samurai, struggled. They might have to take on side jobs to survive, and were sometimes forced to relinquish their status and marry into merchant households, where they adopted the surname of their bride's family.

I studied the interaction between Yamashita and Takada carefully, trying to figure out their relationship. It appeared that Yamashita was selling salt wholesale to the Edo estate where Takada's feudal lord resided with his family the six months of the year when he was required to be in the city. Takada was the person responsible for his clan's finances – in today's language, he was their chief accountant – which meant he and Yamashita were business associates. Yamashita, I surmised, had brought Takada to the Quarter to entertain him, and thus deepen their tie.

Even spending the night together didn't seem to make Takada more relaxed. When I saw him off the next morning, I wasn't at all sure whether or not he was satisfied with me.

Although I had written him off, Takada defied my expectations and showed up three days later, this time by himself.

'How happy I am that you have chosen to visit me again,' I said.

'Sure,' Takada mumbled, looking down at the ground. There was something cute about this that touched my heart, even though our relationship was still only at the second, 'reversal' stage. I was supposed to be strictly business with all my customers – that was the nature of my profession – so it was unacceptable to warm to a man, even slightly, and yet . . .

Caught off guard, I was staring at Takada without being aware of it. He stared back.

That's when I realized who he reminded me of.

Mr Takaoka. Not so much Mr Takaoka today as the way he was when he was young.

'Thanks for coming all this distance to see me,' I whispered under my breath.

Takada began visiting me frequently. He became my regular the week following the reversal, after which he climbed the tower to visit me twice a month.

Samurai received a stipend from their fief by way of salary, but it appeared that Takada's was not all that generous. I never asked what the exact numbers were, but as the *oiran* Shungetsu I had an eagle eye, so I could tell from his behaviour that his life was straitened compared to our better-off customers.

Takada may not have been loaded with money, but, strangely, he looked like a man who could afford anything. He enjoyed the city of Edo to the fullest.

He told me all kinds of things about the place. The spiels of the street vendors. The lively shops that lined Nihonbashi. The story of the man from Ikenohata who was fishing late one night when a *kappa* sprite popped up from the water. The love affairs featured in so many of the plays being performed in the theatres.

Takada would lull me to sleep at night with these stories, adding so much detail it felt as if he were unrolling before me an illustrated scroll of life and love in Edo. There was an irrepressible energy in the men and women who populated them, a life force that propelled every aspect of their existence – their expressions, their gestures, even their kimono patterns. An *oiran*'s kimono and accessories were designed to attract men, so they had to be dazzling. But Takada didn't focus on the parts of Edo that dazzled: rather, he showed me the city in its raw state, glowing with a wild abandon.

By this time, I had been entertaining customers for long enough that I was growing more than a little tired of the superficial, ostentatious performance of life in Yoshiwara, which may help explain why Takada's unembellished stories drew me in the way they did.

It didn't take very long for me to fall in love with Takada – in Yoshiwara lingo, he had become my 'special someone'.

Meeting only twice a month was hard to bear, but Takada's slender purse made it impossible for us to see each other more often. As each day passed, my desire to see him only mounted.

I needed to see Mr Takaoka. I spent several empty days on the bench by the river waiting for his return, and reflecting on my dream life in Yoshiwara.

It seemed only yesterday that I was sold off and taken to Edo, yet several years had passed since I had become the *oiran*

Shungetsu, and a year since Takada had become my special someone. In waking time, only twelve months had passed since my
life in Edo had begun. Nevertheless, my emotions in that dream
world had undergone a dizzying transformation. What could that
possibly signify?

I was beginning to grow a little worried. It was as though my
heart, Shungetsu's heart, was a small boat on a wide river being
steadily pulled towards Takada as towards a great waterfall, with
no chance of turning back. I felt helpless.

The deeper our tie grew and the more I discovered about him,
the more mysterious he became to me. He belonged to the lower
ranks of the samurai, yet it appeared that he had been born into an
elite family. However, some sort of incident had occurred that had
resulted in their destruction. His father had committed *seppuku*,
his brothers had been scattered, and he himself had been taken in
by a less illustrious samurai family as their adopted son. Thanks
to his innate intelligence he had gone on to distinguish himself,
but there were strict limits as to how high a samurai of humble
background could rise, and so he was more or less stuck in his
present job – this, at least, was the story I was told by Izumi, who
had heard it from Yamashita, the man who first brought Takada
to our house.

Takada had a nobility about him. He naturally exuded dignity
and calm, and had a wonderful sense of humour. Weren't those
the same characteristics that Mr Takaoka possessed? Yet I was
reluctant to draw any conclusions about the two men. Could they
really be one and the same person? Or was the similarity pure
coincidence?

I needed to see Mr Takaoka as soon as possible. I was eager to
understand how he and Takada were connected before my dreams
carried me any further. I sat there on the bench by the river for

days and waited. Yet Mr Takaoka never showed up. Perhaps he had hit the road again on his bicycle. Or was wandering about some foreign land, whistling a carefree tune.

Shungetsu was now head over heels in love with Takada. Something bad was bound to happen. I found myself growing more and more ill at ease. Yesterday, Shungetsu had felt a strong but controllable affection for Takada; today, she was being driven wild by her need for him; tomorrow, I felt certain that she would begin to dream of absconding with him, of escaping Yoshiwara altogether.

I had to do something before it reached that point. Desperately, I tried to stop her heart from sliding down that slippery slope. Yoshiwara could be surprisingly lenient, even magnanimous, to those who accepted its rules and conventions. Yet it was unforgiving to anyone who defied them.

An *oiran* was not permitted to lose her heart to a customer. Instead, she was to feign love in order to provoke love in men. Once a man was hooked, she ramped up that pretence to squeeze as much money out of him as she could. That was the essence of Yoshiwara. An *oiran* drew men to her like moths to a flame or, better perhaps, small birds to a stick of birdlime – on the surface, she and her customers played the game of love, but what lay beneath was an entirely different story. It stood to reason, therefore, that any *oiran* who refused to entrap a customer, who simply let him depart without extracting as much money as she could, would be disciplined. Woe to the *oiran* who helped her customer save money!

The penalties varied from house to house. The simplest forms involved physical punishment of one kind or another. Beatings were probably the least severe. *Kamuro* were regularly disciplined by the men who owned the houses or by the women who managed them. At that early stage of our training, it was not at all uncommon for us to be knocked around or locked in a closet. Nor did our misdeeds have to be major ones – they could be very minor, like sleeping in an unseemly position or being less than attentive to our duties. Nevertheless, great care was taken to avoid leaving any permanent marks. Our bodies, after all, were valuable assets, future sources of income for the house.

In my years working, I never witnessed an *oiran* from my own house eloping with a customer, or running away to escape the profession. I think that may have been because, while our managers and the owner were certainly strict, the only thing required of us was that we carry out our duties to our customers, whether we be *oiran* or *kamuro*, male or female attendants. It probably helped too that we *oiran* always managed to get along well together.

Not long after Takada and I became regulars, however, an *oiran* from three houses down the street did attempt to elope. Her name was Yukiyanagi. She was was their highest-ranking *oiran* and she had fallen deeply in love with her special someone. Adopting male disguise, she had attempted to slip out of Yoshiwara's Great Gate, the Ōmon.

It was pouring buckets that particular day, so far fewer people were out than usual. When the weather was good, night-time would find the avenue swarming with people come to gawk at the women on display, but on this evening the teahouses quickly swallowed up their regular customers, leaving the main thorough-fare sparsely populated and the side streets deserted. This was the evening that Yukiyanagi chose to make her escape in an attempt to unite with Sadakichi, the man she loved.

She had been with a customer that night. She gave the man a sleeping potion and waited until he was dead to the world. Then she put on his clothing. As Yukiyanagi had a slightly bigger frame than most women, it seems to have actually suited her.

The person who saw through her disguise was a *kamuro* named Otoki, who glimpsed Yukiyanagi at the very moment she was about to pass through the Great Gate. Otoki belonged to the same teahouse as Izumi and myself; she was not much younger than us, and we had served as *kamuro* together. The three of us got along well, especially after we had sneaked off to an alley not far from Tooth-Black Ditch to share some leftover delicacies we had stolen from our house.

The teahouse Yukiyanagi belonged to was even more prosperous than ours. Yet the *oiran* who worked there were always pale and tired-looking, and rumour had it that they were being driven hard, forced to accept far more customers than the norm.

'Their *oiran* won't last long at this rate,' commented our manager Oshina. 'I heard another two of them had to make the trip to Chujo the other day.'

A 'trip to Chujo' meant being taken to see a doctor who did abortions. That was the preferable option; otherwise, the manager of the *oiran*'s teahouse would perform the procedure herself.

Izumi and I trembled in fear when we heard stories like this. At that time, knowledge about how to prevent pregnancy was extremely vague and unreliable. All the methods recommended to protect the bodies of *oiran* like us – potions to drink, ways to cleanse ourselves after sex, and so on – would be dismissed today as utterly unscientific, and yet there were no alternatives. Needless to say, the same thing applied to any diseases we might contract.

When Otoki spotted Yukiyanagi it was around midnight, the 'hour of assured return', when *oiran* were supposed to withdraw from the front of the teahouse, where they had been stationed to attract clients. Otoki had been hiding in the shadows near the Great Gate, waiting to 'ambush' (that was what the denizens of

Yoshiwara called it) any of our regular customers who failed to visit our teahouse before leaving the Quarter. The rules prohibited such behaviour – on the surface, at least, a customer could not leave without frequenting the place where he was a regular, and *kamuro* like Otoki were dispatched to accost them and drag them back to where they belonged.

Yukiyanagi wasn't rushing to escape, we were told: rather, she was wobbling along unsteadily, mimicking the movements of a man on his way home after a night out, when Otoki caught sight of her. In all likelihood, she was the only person who would have seen through her disguise. Yukiyanagi was already passing through the Gate, and Otoki told us later that, for a split-second, she considered letting her go.

'It was such a gloomy night, you know,' Otoki told Izumi and me later. 'And I admired her so much. No one looked more beautiful parading down the Avenue.'

Izumi and I just nodded.

'So then, why did I stop her? Is this what they mean when they say the devil made me do it? I wanted Yukiyanagi to escape, to start a new life with the man she loved, but instead I snatched her hand and called to our man to grab her. If the night hadn't been so dank and depressing, perhaps I would have kept my mouth shut,' Otoki whispered, looking down at her lap.

Izumi and I understood the situation very well. When she saw Yukiyanagi about to make her escape, Otoki had been seized with a terrible jealousy: in that moment, she hated Yukiyanagi, hated the fact that she might be able to escape the Quarter and set up house with her beloved. No, she could never let that happen. Nor could we blame her, for we were all forbidden from even thinking about leaving Yoshiwara.

*

Yukiyanagi paid the ultimate price for her misdeed. She was tied to a tree in the courtyard of her teahouse where, for several days, she was given neither food nor water.

The first couple of days we could hear her sobbing. After that, nothing. When she was on the verge of death, her breathing no more audible than that of an insect, they finally untied her. Izumi, Otaki and I were too distraught to speak about any of this, so we went about our daily business as if nothing was out of the ordinary.

For the next few months, we were told, Yukiyanagi lay on a mat no thicker than a rice cracker in a crude, windowless storeroom and was fed nothing but the thinnest of gruels.

It was there that she died.

Yukiyanagi's cruel fate left the me that inhabited today's world shaking with fury. When I woke from this part of my dream, I couldn't get her out of my mind. I wept, just thinking about her life and the way she met her end. I opened *An Illustrated History of Yoshiwara* and vented my fury at the book, especially the pages that described the punishments meted out to *kamuro* and *oiran*. It was outrageous, I thought, one of the many injustices women had suffered throughout history.

Strangely, however, the part of me that lived in Yoshiwara as the *oiran* Shungetsu could not see the outrage for what it was.

'That's just the way things are' – those were the only words that came to Shungetsu's mind, an echo of what Pa and Ma said so often back home.

It's fate.

It's fate if a drought ruins the harvest, or a typhoon flattens your crops, or the authorities strip you of your rice for taxes despite your terrible poverty.

The oppressed of the Edo period were treated no better than animals. This thought kept running through my mind as my shared life with Shungetsu continued. Animals never complain about their environments. They adapt to whatever circumstances they are placed in to survive. In much the same way, Shungetsu was doing her best to adapt to the environment of Yoshiwara. She never gave a thought to changing the system – instead, all of her energies were directed at finding the easiest and most comfortable way to accommodate herself to things as they were.

Couldn't there be another path, though? A way in which she and Izumi could team up to somehow change the policies of their house? Couldn't the whole Yoshiwara system be transformed into something healthier for those who worked there, not to mention more efficient for the house?

I ground my teeth as I pondered these questions.

I began reading all I could get my hands on that dealt with the plight of contemporary women working in a similar field. I went to the library and borrowed everything they had on the sex industry, pored over the accounts of sex workers and read more broadly about the world of the 'water trades', studying day and night to try to come up with a way for Shungestu to help eliminate the exploitation of the women of Yoshiwara.

In the process, my own looks began to suffer and I lost weight. I stopped leaving the house, combing my hair, or even bathing regularly, let alone wearing make-up. In the grip of this obsession, I was helpless to stop the constant cycle of thoughts swirling around in my head.

In contrast, for the me that lived as the *oiran* Shungetsu, making sure that my face, hair and skin were beautiful was part of my job. My make-up had to be perfect, my hair glossy, my skin fresh-looking, my outfits gorgeous. As if in inverse proportion to

Shungetsu's beauty, my modern self was now growing progressively more bedraggled and pitiful.

'What's wrong with you?' asked Naa-chan one day, when my appearance had pushed him past breaking point. 'Are you physically ill?'

No, I mumbled in response. Naa-chan was a sweet man, I thought distractedly, as if it had nothing to do with me.

Clearly, Naa-chan's career was going nowhere. He was returning home much earlier than before, and even when he and a few of his contemporaries – whose careers were going as badly as his – went out drinking together, that never lasted until the small hours of the morning as it once had.

'What do you say – shall we take a trip sometime soon?' he asked one day.

'A trip?' I said vaguely.

'You look tired, Riko. Maybe a hot springs would pick you up.'

'Hot springs?' My first thought was, what a nice idea – I could take Shungetsu and Izumi with me.

'I just heard of a nice place on the Izu Peninsula. Here, take a look,' he said, pulling a glossy pamphlet from his briefcase and handing it to me. Wouldn't my friends in Yoshiwara be surprised to see colour printing like this, I thought as I fiddled with its edges distractedly. Going with Naa-chan hadn't entered my mind.

The inn Naa-chan had chosen was located at a hot springs deep in the mountains of Izu. We rented a car and left first thing in the morning, but it still took us all day to reach our destination.

I wasn't expecting much, but the lakes and mountains were beautiful, as was the sunlight on the trees, and as we pulled over yet again to take in the landscape, in spite of myself, I found myself enjoying the view. When we stopped at a roadside restaurant for lunch, Naa-chan ordered a big *okonomiyaki* omelette and a plate of fried noodles the colour of brown sauce. I had a single order of cold soba noodles.

'Why not choose something a little more decadent?' Naa-chan said. 'After all, we're on a trip.'

Decadent? The word struck me as so funny that I laughed out loud.

'I haven't heard you laugh like that for ages,' Naa-chan murmured, his eyes cast down. I stole a glance at him. The face I love. Yes, I thought. I do love that face. I love his voice. The way he talks. The realization moved me deeply.

It had been ages since I had felt that way. What he said was true. For a long time I hadn't been able to smile at Naa-chan, not once. I had been sunk in my thoughts of life in Yoshiwara, but I had also been secretly nursing my resentment of him, and the way he had betrayed me. Only after setting out on this trip with him, I felt, had I realized just how long that betrayal had been eating away at me.

I had chosen to avert my eyes from his cruelty: instead, sunk in sadness, I had found refuge in a dream world, pretending that what I found there could somehow distance me from my pent-up resentment. I wasn't blind to the grudge I held. And yet by pushing it from my mind, I was ruining my life – that much was now clear.

'I have to ask,' I said as lightly as I could to Naa-chan, who was still staring at the ground. 'How are things with that woman? Is it really over?'

Naa-chan had clammed up, and I was at a loss what to do as I sat beside him in the car. The scenery from the restaurant to the inn was beautiful: even the grass verge that ran along the guardrail of the twisting road was filled with the glories of the season. Yet Naa-chan drove straight to the inn without stopping once.

Though he normally had no trouble parking – he could parallel park, row park, back into a space, the whole skill set – this time, strangely, Naa-chan struggled, turning the wheel this way and that until, finally, he had the car lined up correctly. He was still sulking when he unloaded our bags. We carried them across the pebbled ground to the main entrance without exchanging a word. When we walked in the door of the inn, the staff were lined up shoulder to shoulder in the old-fashioned way. 'It is our pleasure to welcome you,' they called out in unison. Startled, we took a step back, but Naa-chan returned to his old self and rescued the situation.

'Thank you so much for your kind attention,' he replied, his voice warm. 'We are the Haradas.'

Exchanging our shoes for the inn's slippers, we padded down the long, winding corridor to our room, guided by one of the maids. She and the rest of the staff were clad in close-fitting kimonos, very different from how we wore them in Edo. Our kimonos were loose to allow air to circulate, while theirs were so tight the layers of cloth squeaked rubbing against each other. Wouldn't they move a lot more freely, I thought, if they cinched their kimonos harder round the waist but loosened the fabric round the neck and the chest? That's what was running through my mind as I walked.

'It sure is a long way,' Naa-chan whispered, as if to himself. I didn't answer.

We faced each other across the low table as the maid poured us a cup of tea. Our long silence dragged on.

What would Shungetsu do in this situation? I thought.

For one thing, she wouldn't face Naa-chan; rather, she would go and sit next to but slightly behind him, perhaps, plying her fan and tilting her head in his direction. An *oiran* might not say very much, but she had many ways to coax a man to talk by using her body.

In this moment, though, I was Riko, not Shungetsu, so I certainly wasn't going to act that way.

'I've known what was going on for a very long time,' I said, feeling him out. 'The woman in Kyushu, Michiko-sensei, the most recent one too.'

Naa-chan's eyes slowly widened, growing bigger and bigger, like a flower spreading before the sun.

'You knew about her as well?'

'You bet I did,' I said curtly. I could hear a bit of Shungetsu in my voice.

'That's all over,' Naa-chan said quietly. 'I guess it bothered you when you found out, huh?'

Those words cut me. He had never considered my feelings, that was clear, no matter which other woman was casting a shadow over our marriage. He felt no shred of guilt as he flaunted each before me, treating the time they spent together as perfectly natural. And now he had the gall to ask if his latest affair 'bothered' me.

This could only mean that he had assumed that I was *not* all right with this woman, unlike the others, so he had hidden her presence.

'Did you love her that much?' I asked. My voice had also become quiet.

'Did I love her? It's all in the past now. It feels like a very long time ago.'

'A very long time ago? How long – three hundred years, perhaps?' I asked seriously. Long ago? Did he think my grief could be chased away with those simple words? Not a chance. Besides, to me, three hundred years wasn't that far away, not at all.

Naa-chan didn't respond. Maybe he thought I was trying to make a joke.

'Is it really over?'

'It's over.'

'Do you love me now?'

'I've always loved you. Very much.'

'But how deep does that love go? Is it the same love you've felt for other women?'

'No, I don't think you could call that love. In fact, I don't think I've ever fallen in love.'

His answer caught me by surprise. I had expected him to draw a line between falling in love – what was called *koi* – and *ai*, or 'true love'. But I may have been giving him too little credit. After all, the assumption that married love was *ai* while love between lovers was merely *koi* reeked of all the old stereotypes.

'I'm fed up with all this talk about love,' Naa-chan said, clearly but quietly.

And yet, how long did I listen to Naa-chan that evening? I had set the ball rolling soon after our arrival in the late afternoon, but after that it was all him. His words flowed non-stop while we soaked in our private outdoor bath and during dinner, which started at six. He was still going strong when the maid came to lay out the futon for the night. He talked about a wide range of things: his feelings for me, for the other women in his life, for the latest one who had caused me such pain. That was when I found out that her brothers had taken her back.

The more the words came tumbling out, the more he had to

say – about his changing heart, emotions he had never revealed to anyone before, his feelings for me.

He talked about *koi* and *ai*. Did all that romantic stuff really exist, or were these abstract terms just an elevated form of word-play?

He extolled the simpler forms of love. He said he loved women *and* men, just as he loved the snow, the moon, flowers – there was no end to it.

He said that he loved me in that way, that he always had and always would. It was that simple. That I had no idea how important that love was, how much it comforted him.

That he still couldn't understand what had happened between him and the woman. It was both frightening and strange, as if a bolt of lightning had struck a stony crag, giving birth to a host of unfamiliar gods.

Naa-chan's words may not have been what I had been hoping for, but they did hit home. For the first time in our marriage, the tangle of words trapped inside him had begun to unravel and emerge, bit by bit. I had become a vessel, as it were, into which he was stuffing all those pieces. That's what it felt like, anyway.

Oddly, this time it was not Riko alone who listened to Naa-chan unburden himself, it was also Shungestu. Until that point, I as Riko had united soul and body with Shungetsu in my dreams of Edo, but this was the first time she had fully joined me in my waking world. Thus it was as Shungetsu *and* Riko that I listened to what Naa-chan had to say. The mingling of our spirits was transforming me into a new person, someone I had never encountered before.

Perhaps this was because Naa-chan's story about the woman was too painful to confront alone. Then again, I might have unconsciously determined that in this situation, faced with a man baring his soul, my best strategy was to team up with the experienced Shungetsu.

Thanks to Shungetsu's presence, Naa-chan's revelations were less crippling than they otherwise would have been. No, check that – given my nature, it's entirely possible that I had chosen to avoid the physical and emotional pain of those revelations by beating a blind retreat into Shungetsu's heart. Either way makes no real difference, for in the end I was able to wring out from Naa-chan a tear-choked vow of love for me.

Shungetsu wasn't convinced. Mere words, she scoffed.

Mere words, perhaps, Riko parried, but how lovable he looked when he was struggling to get them out.

Words are unreliable, as you well know, Shungetsu persisted. What counts is the heat of his body and the strength of his embrace.

No, Riko stood her ground. I want to believe him.

Naa-chan did indeed hold me tight that night, tighter than ever before, and his body was on fire. This is good, Riko, I whispered to myself over and over again as we made love for the first time in ages. This is good, for now at least.

When we returned from our trip, I threw myself into gardening.

The perennials were just getting started, but this time they were joined by a bumper crop of nameless weeds. Before my Yoshiwara nights began I had taken pains to pull all the weeds out, but now I actually enjoyed seeing them mixed in. I learned their names, too. Snake strawberry. Oxalis. Nazuna. Plantain. Ōbako. In summer, the ones called 'paper strings' outstripped all the others; while in the fall, true to their name, they sent out long, whip-like tendrils resembling the cords used to wrap presents.

Yes, the ties that bind the Yoshiwara of Edo and present-day Tokyo are long and slender too, I thought, as I regarded their pale-red flowers.

Women who sell their bodies work in dimly lit places. In that respect, the Edo period and the modern day are probably identical. The dimness of Yoshiwara as portrayed in literature, film and photography was not due solely to weak lighting. When I see women in the sex industry today – how they look, where they work – I am always reminded of the shadowy teahouses of the Yoshiwara.

Sure, it's only natural, you may say. After all, they sell sex just as the women in Yoshiwara did. All those media images have been created with that connection in mind. But I suspect that's not the whole story. What men and women do, they do in secret. It is a hidden part of life. It might even be considered a sort of game. A secret game played in the shadows.

There had been no shadows, however, in my love for Naa-chan. Rather, light had flooded our relationship – it was as if my love for him was light itself.

Yet as I spent more time in Yoshiwara, I came to realize that a certain darkness characterized relations between the sexes, though I couldn't put my finger on it. Might it be that Naa-chan was a man singularly ill-equipped to deal with those shadows? I was beginning to think so. Nevertheless, he had fallen for that woman. Someone who was forbidden fruit. Someone he might love but could never find true happiness with. What had Naa-chan felt when forced to confront that darkness for the first time? It certainly baffled him – that much was evident as he rambled on and on about their relationship that evening in the hot-springs inn. He had been left with nowhere to turn, and it was clearly eating away at him.

Naa-chan and I were a couple who lived in the light. He and that woman dwelled in the shadows.

Why, oh why, are people drawn so irresistibly to the dark?

Shungetsu's love for Takada was deepening. She was taking ever more risks to meet him.

She enlisted the help of not just her *kamuro* but of a man-servant in her house, plying him with money to arrange a tryst in the windowless storeroom on the first floor, where she and Takada could embrace each other. For another secret meeting, she left a customer fast asleep in her bed after two in the morning to sneak out to the dark area beside Tooth-Black Ditch.

One time she was almost caught by Oshina-san, the manager of her teahouse, who surprised her as she was giving instructions to her *kamuro* on where to find Takada.

Shungetsu had just given the *kamuro* a bowl of leftover seafood, a kind of tip to accompany the instructions.

'Well, well, what have we here?' Oshina said, grabbing the luckless *kamuro*, who was clasping the bowl to her breast, by the scruff of her kimono.

'Please!' squealed the *kamuro*.

'Where did you get that bowl?' Oshina demanded to know.

'It's not mine,' protested the startled *kamuro*, thrusting the bowl back at Shungetsu.

Oshina turned to Shungetsu, who was reclining on her side, arm propped on an elbow-rest, and looked her slowly up and down.

'All right,' Oshina said. 'What game are you playing?'

'Playing? Who, me?' Shungetsu cocked her head coquettishly. It was a trademark gesture of hers, one she often employed with men. 'We were just having a little fun,' she went on.

Oshina started to say something, then stopped.

'All right then,' she said at last, glaring daggers at Shungetsu. 'I'll let it drop. You know the rules, right?' And with that, Oshina walked out of the room.

Takada's origins were more illustrious than Shungetsu had first thought, the introduction by the salt dealer Yamashita having told but part of the story. The rest emerged in dribs and drabs from comments Takada dropped along the way.

If you traced his line back, you ended up at the clan of one of the pre-Tokugawa shoguns. That much Shungetsu could deduce from the language Takada used. Yet he hardly looked like some-one from a noble family when he came to see her holding a bowl of sweet red bean soup from the street, or when he drew from the folds of his kimono a little wind-up *oiran* doll he'd found on a vendor's straw pallet in front of Asakusa's Thunder Gate, making Shungetsu laugh.

'If you go back far enough,' Takada said nonchalantly, 'all those shogunal families were no better than country samurai.'

'All this girl has to hear is "samurai birth" and she gets jealous,' Shungetsu said.

'Yes, tilling the soil is gruelling work for sure,' Takada said with a laugh.

It's not so bad for those who farm their own land, Shungetsu thought. But there are so many peasants, like the tenant farmers I was born to, who slave their whole lives just to get through each day. For the first time in a long while, Shungetsu thought back to her own family that had been forced to sell their daughter to Yoshiwara. The faces of Pa, Ma and her big brothers flashed through her mind. But only for a brief moment. Now, her only desire was for the man Takada, to love and be loved, to hold and be held by him, until they melted into one another.

'Do you love me that much?' asked Takada, gazing into her eyes.

'I do,' she answered without hesitation.

'Poor you,' he murmured, pulling her to him. 'Poor you. That you love me, and poor me that I love you. It's terrible for both of us.'

It felt strange, Riko thought, for a couple so much in love to speak of that love in such doleful terms. Yet, once again, the way Takada was talking – at once droll and distanced – reminded her of Mr Takaoka.

'I want to run away,' Riko heard Shungetsu whisper into Takada's ear. Clearly. Finally, the words had been spoken. Riko was surprised that she felt no fear when Shungetsu said them; instead, she felt calm. I want to run away. Riko felt she knew exactly what Shungetsu was feeling.

For Riko wanted to escape as well. From Naa-chan. No, not from Naa-chan per se, but from the time she spent with him now, with that woman's vague presence still squatting in a corner of his mind. To escape back to the days when she could love him with all her heart.

'I want to run away.' Once Shungetsu had spoken those words, step by step she began to turn from the conventional path. Her behaviour became erratic.

When will you take me away? she asked Takada whenever they met.

Do you really love me that much? Takada would whisper in her ear, trying to placate her, but to no avail – instead, she only grew more insistent. Take me away, please, she'd repeat over and over.

What was it about Takada that made her love him so? I asked

myself this question many times. Well, he was a samurai for one thing, and handsome too. He was fun to talk to. He paid his debts. True, he wasn't wealthy, but no one rivalled him when it came to the depths of his affection for Shungetsu.

Even so, I wondered.

If their escape was successful, what did they have to look forward to? A life spent in poverty, beset by constant worries of discovery. To make matters worse, Shungetsu's Ma and Pa back home would be crushed under the weight of the debts to the tea-house that she had left behind and that they would be saddled with.

If their escape failed and they were caught, the consequences would be even more catastrophic. The cruel fate that had met Yukiyanagi not that long ago was clear evidence of that. Escaping Yoshiwara was nothing but a fool's dream.

I had access to Shungetsu's innermost feelings, so I decided to take a look deep inside her. What I found were very simple, basic emotions:

Fear.

Excitement.

Joy.

Sadness.

Most of all, a fierce commitment to the path she had chosen. A sense of accomplishment that came from her determination never to look back. That feeling had convinced Shungetsu that she could achieve something worthwhile – it outweighed all the fears engendered by the idea of escape from Yoshiwara.

Shungetsu's passion, her willingness to press forward at what-ever cost, was like a fire that filled her body, her heart, and I could only shrink before its intensity. Where could such heat come from? Well, Shungetsu was entirely unafraid of death. Even if she and Takada were to rot away in some wild and unforsaken field, she would have no regrets.

But what about Takada? Where did he stand? Faced with Shungetsu's passion, he might well end up like a lover in a puppet play, driven to walk the road to his inevitable death. What, then, were his true feelings about this relationship, one that could end in their double suicide?

I decided to speak through Shungetsu to find out.

'Takada-sama,' I asked. 'Don't you have a family, parents perhaps, or brothers and sisters?'

Takada thought for a moment.

'No. Not any more,' he said slowly.

'Not any more?'

'I did, once upon a time. But they took off.'

'Took off?'

'Yes, they left, went far away.'

An image of Mr Takaoka on his bicycle, travelling the world so free of family ties, came to mind. Once again, it struck me that he somehow existed there in front of me, within Takada.

'Is it really all right if I drag you away like this?' I asked as Riko, not Shungetsu.

'Sure, that's fine.' In a voice that sounded like Mr Takaoka, not Takada.

'We might die, you know.'

'Yes, you're right. I have no problem at all with dying. It's forgetting that I fear.'

'But doesn't death put an end to everything?'

'If it does, then it might be a lot easier.'

Takada – no, that's not right, Mr Takaoka – had me stumped. Death would be easier? It sounded like whistling past the grave-yard.

My eyes settled on the back of Takada's hand. It looked strong. Beautiful, in fact. Shungetsu placed her palm on it as though making a serious pledge. In that moment, the fire burning within her reached its zenith.

At long last the fated night arrived. The night when Shungetsu would make her escape from Yoshiwara.

She had laid no intricate plans. Even if plans were made and arrangements secured in advance, you could always be discovered and brought back, as had happened to Yukiyanagi. Wasn't it better, therefore, to let yourselves be guided by passion as you ran forward, hand in hand, through the night? This was what Shungetsu had resolved.

Takada too seemed absolutely resolute. When he came to the Quarter this time he was not the aloof Takada he usually was – now he exuded readiness to act on their plan, making him look uncharacteristically serious, even imposing. Oshina the manager had not taken him seriously until then, but now she deferred to him for reasons she herself did not understand.

Takada had been coming twice monthly to see Shungetsu, but now he stayed with her for a third night at the end of the month. Oshina greeted him in the politest terms on his arrival, and he was quickly escorted to Shungetsu's room. Finally, they were alone.

The moon was riding high in the sky. Drums and flutes echoed from the bustling streets.

'It sounds like a festival,' Shungetsu said.

Takada was resting his head on her lap. 'Was there a festival where you grew up?' he asked.

'We called ours "sending the god home".'

'What was it like?'

We held it when the rice harvest was coming to a close, to show our gratitude to the mountain god, who came down to the village every spring and stayed with us until the harvest was done. If, for whatever reason, he left before the harvest, it was said that terrible things would happen: a horde of locusts would descend on us, the rice would become diseased, the harvest would fail and ogres would invade the town, circling the houses and devouring anyone who might stray outside.

The festival was meant to bid farewell to the god who was returning home. As thanks for the god's willingness to remain through the season, thereby ensuring the harvest, the villagers danced and sang the sacred *kagura* tunes while colourfully clothed children paraded through the fields, trailed by horses and cows, also draped in bright cloth. All danced to please the god.

'Did you dance?' Takada asked.

'Me dance? Not on your life!' Shungetsu laughed. Her brothers, though, were terrific dancers and singers. They paraded in orange and yellow outfits borrowed from the village headman, the oldest singing in his clear, strong voice, the younger two dancing and whirling about.

'Was that thunder?' Shungetsu asked, cocking her head. Lightning flashed across the desolate stretch of reeds beyond Tooth-Black Ditch. A good deal of time elapsed before the thunder rumbled. It was still dry, but rain was surely on the way.

When the storm began, Takada and Shungetsu were already in bed. The rain was coming down in full force long before the midnight clappers sounded, and the streets, packed with people only a few hours before, were deserted – not even a kitten was out and about.

'I wonder if it will end by four o'clock?' Shungetsu – no, actually Riko – muttered. Four in the morning was the deadline for special guests to be delivered to the Great Gate. I spoke up because I knew that Shungetsu had set her mind on escaping with Takada that very night, and I hoped bringing up the downpour would temper her enthusiasm for the escape. But my words seemed to have the opposite effect.

'Takada-sama,' Shungetsu said, looking down at him. She was sitting on the tatami, her legs curled to one side. She spoke softly, but the import of her words was unmistakable.

'Please take me away now,' she said.

Takada gave a slow nod. A brilliant flash of lightning filled the sky. At almost the same moment a great crash filled the room, as if a thunderbolt had struck next door.

'Now there's just the two of us,' Shungetsu murmured, enraptured.

The darkness of the city of Edo surprised me.

Hand in hand, Shungetsu and Takada crossed the wall surrounding Yoshiwara, waded across Tooth-Black Ditch, and fled.

Shungetsu had been leading an indolent life, but she was still a fit young woman. Perhaps it was due to the long years she had spent working in the fields. Or maybe she had just been blessed at birth with a strong constitution. She was never winded, no matter how far they ran. She was dressed entirely in men's clothing: before they left, she had deftly donned a man's kimono, added shabby leggings borrowed from a young manservant in her house, and put on a pair of Takazaki split-toed socks. She was Takada's guide as they slipped through the barriers and made their escape.

How did Shungetsu find the best route to leave? Perhaps I could claim some credit there, for as Riko I had collected a number of books, and even drawn a decent map of Yoshiwara. The surrounding landscape. The location of the bridges leading out. The route one should follow if heading east.

And now Shungetsu is leading Takada. How nimbly she runs through the reeds, how full of life!

Presently, the rain began to let up. Shungetsu and Takada quickened their steps along the unfamiliar path. From time to time, lightning flickered on the horizon. They could no longer hear any thunder. All around was dark: the moon a mere sliver, the sole lights those at the foot of the larger bridges, or in the nightwatchman's quarters at the bigger estates.

Only the distant flashes of lightning gave them a dim sense of where they were. The next second, the inky black returned. The night and the weeds underfoot made for hard going, but they wanted to put as much distance as possible between themselves and the Quarter before dawn.

'Let's make for Chiba.' Who came out with that? Chiba wasn't yet a place name, so it must have been me, not Shungetsu. The situation had discombobulated me, blurring the dividing line between the two of us. I was Shungetsu, she was me, and the power of her love was entering me as never before.

Shungetsu's love for Takada was so pure it was frightening. Until that moment, I had considered my early love for Naa-chan to be the purest and most beautiful in all the world. Yet it couldn't hold a candle to what Shungetsu was feeling now. I was stunned.

I don't care about dying.

I had given voice to those words any number of times, as if to test whether I really meant them, but they never carried the weight of truth. In that moment, however, Shungetsu was unequivocally prepared to die, no ifs, ands or buts about it.

Driven by that powerful emotion, we set off in the dark

towards Shimōsa. When I mistakenly called it Chiba, as it is known today, Takada had registered my meaning. That simple fact indicated that Mr Takaoka was there, inside Takada. I was growing more and more certain of it.

Shungetsu led the way until we reached the bridge at Arakawa, after which the positions were reversed and Takada became the guide. He seemed to be using the stars to fix our direction.

'Can you read the stars?' Shungetsu said admiringly. Her adoration of Takada could be kindled by the slightest thing, I thought. The pathos of it brought me close to tears. Shungetsu appeared about to cry as well, as her passion for him mounted.

Takada gave her hand a firm squeeze in reply. Shungetsu trembled at his touch. She was happy in body and spirit, happier even than when they lay together.

They ran all night, as fast as the wind. Shimōsa was now within sight. The sun was coming up.

'What on earth is that?' Shungetsu asked. No, judging from her choice of words, it may well have been me doing the asking. The words were those of a modern woman, not a Yoshiwara *oiran*.

It is said that an *oiran*'s distinctive speech originally stemmed from the desire to conceal her impoverished origins: her unfamiliarity with formal language, her provincial dialect, her lack of education, and so forth. That unusual rhythm also whetted the male desire to frolic in an alternative world, enhancing Yoshiwara's unique attraction.

Outside Yoshiwara, however, Shungetsu was not an *oiran* but a normal young woman. Her manner of speaking had become mine, just as my heart had merged with hers.

'They look like white jewels!' we exclaimed as one. White

jewels. Pearls, in other words. Dew blanketed the grass, and the drops shimmered in the pale morning light.

Takada didn't respond. Instead, he seemed lost in thought. Shungetsu regarded him quizzically. Now, for the first time in their journey, they were able to stop and rest.

'I feel as if I've been here before,' Takada said.

'It does seem identical to that scene in Komurasaki's book. But what do you mean, "you've been here before?"' Shungetsu or I asked. 'Have you eloped with someone like this?'

Takada shook his head.

'No, the woman departed this fleeting world very long ago.'

The woman? Shungetsu and I widened our eyes. Might Takada have fallen in love like this in the past? We felt no pang of jealousy about who she may have been, though, nor any resentment towards Takada. How could there be, when we were alone like this here, just the two of us. Why allow jealousy to ruin such a blissful moment?

'Who was she?' Shungetsu and I asked. No blame was involved – we merely wanted to learn more about Takada.

'Someone from long ago. Her name was Kusuko.' He seemed to have understood our desire to know, for now he spoke without hesitation.

This is the story he told.

Long, long ago in a certain place lived a young prince named Takaoka Shinnō. This prince was very talented: he wrote beautiful poems while still a child, was well versed in the great books of distant Cathay, and knew the Five Classics of Confucianism inside out.

When the prince's father eventually rose to become emperor, he took into his palace a woman named Kusuko. She was already wed to another, so officially it was said that the emperor needed to rely on her knowledge of Chinese medicine. In fact, however, the two of them were deeply involved.

The boy prince was strongly drawn to Kusuko, his father's beloved. A fragrance followed her wherever she went, a thin mist that induced a strange rapture in him. At the same time he was infatuated by her physical being, which was seductive but at the same time utterly pure.

Nevertheless, Kusuko was his father's beloved. A somewhat later tale told the story of a Shining Prince Genji who slept with the young wife of his emperor father, but little Prince Takaoka Shinnō was incapable of such duplicity. His feelings were simple and straightforward – he adored Kusuko without a thought of making her his.

For her part, Kusuko seems to have enjoyed the adulation of the young prince, so innocent and free of guile. For obvious reasons, the prince couldn't visit Kusuko in the inner sanctum of the palace, where she and the emperor's other women were quartered, but she did have her own villa, where the young prince was always welcome.

These visits lasted only until he reached the age of nine. Then, when he was eleven, his father abdicated the throne and everything changed.

It was about this time that the stench of raw ambition began to rise around him. The court was even more rife with secrets and schemes than usual, and many accused Kusuko of manipulating the retired emperor like a puppet on a string.

Spurred on by Kusuko, so the rumour went, the prince's father was planning to retake the throne. This rumour engulfed the entire court.

'What a terrible thing,' Shungetsu and I said. 'But did this woman you call Kusuko,' we asked, 'really try to foment an uprising?'

'No one knows what actually happened,' Takada calmly replied.

Conspiracy followed upon conspiracy, until in the end Kusuko was driven to kill herself by drinking poison, and the young prince forced to renounce his title and enter a Buddhist monastery.

'What does this story have to do with you?' Shungetsu and I ask.

Takada's voice is quiet. 'Because I am that prince,' he replies.

Shungetsu and I look at him in disbelief. 'I thought this all happened long, long ago,' we say as one. 'Even further back than when court ladies vied with each other to read the Tale of the Shining Prince.'

'Yes,' Takada says. 'My story took place a long, long time ago. But I was there. Just as surely as I am here with you now, eloping hand in hand like this, even though it seems to defy belief. Can't you see the connection now?'

It seems to defy belief. Shungetsu and I ruminate on this for a moment.

As Shungetsu, I had escaped Yoshiwara's confines exactly ten years after my arrival. Now, fresh memories from Shungetsu are flooding in: my family selling me to Zōroku the broker, our trip to Edo, my surprise at seeing the Great Gate of Yoshiwara for the first time, the years I was confined within its walls. Now here I am, standing in an open field, having escaped the inescapable.

Truly, none of this is believable.

'Yes,' I reply. 'It's all incredible to me, not just our escape, but the fact that I am here at all. It's so very strange.'

My voice is now quiet too. I still can't believe that I have really escaped Yoshiwara. Beyond that, just being present, in this spot, at this moment, strikes me, and Shungetsu too, as highly peculiar. Why were we born into this world to begin with?

But that is just a fleeting thought. After all, I am here now with Takada. What more could I ask?

'What on earth is that?' I say a second time, pointing at the dewdrops on the grass.

The storm picked up again, pushing Shungetsu and Takada on. A heavy rain like this would wash away their footprints, hopefully foiling any pursuers. Perhaps this new optimism made them less vigilant.

They were growing tired and footsore, now that the initial excitement of their escape had worn off.

'The thunder is coming back,' Takada said. 'Let's stop and rest for a moment or two.'

Just then they saw a dilapidated storehouse not far away.

'Let's take shelter there,' Shungetsu said.

Takada told her to enter – he would stand guard for at least a while.

'Please come inside if the rain gets worse,' Shungetsu said.

Takada would always remember how forlorn she looked at that moment. For he would never see her face again.

The storm was indeed growing worse, the claps of thunder more deafening, the flashes of lightning even more blinding than when they left Yoshiwara the night before. Could this be one of those places where storms originate? There were several such spots, he knew, on the plains of Musashino.

Takada stood there, legs apart, in front of the storehouse. He was listening intently for the footfalls of their pursuers beyond the rain and thunder. But he could hear nothing. He flinched as rain and thunder pummelled the spot. Anxiety was mounting in his chest, a strange premonition he found he couldn't brush away. Had Shungetsu's anxiety been passed on to him? A chill ran up his spine and sweat sprang from his brow, though the air was cool.

Suddenly, lightning flashed and there was a deafening thunderclap. The camphor tree beside him had been struck. Startled, Takada looked up to see the great tree aglow in the gloom. Much like the glowing stalk of bamboo where the old man found the moon maiden asleep in the ancient Tale of the Bamboo Cutter. Would something emerge from the camphor tree as well? Takada prepared himself for the worst.

He stared at the tree, but nothing emerged. Takada then turned and fixed his eyes on the storehouse behind him.

Was Shungetsu safe in there?

Anxiety tightened its hold.

He could sense nothing moving in the dark interior. Hurriedly, he threw open the doors he had closed but a short while earlier.

Light entered the storehouse.

But there was no sign of movement. Shungetsu was nowhere to be seen. It was as if she had vanished into thin air.

'Where are you, my love?' he cried.

There was no answer. Only the sound of the rain, and an occasional muffled clap of distant thunder.

'Where have you gone?' Takada's grief-stricken voice resounded once more in the empty space.

Again, there was no answer. The place was deserted – not a trace of Shungetsu anywhere.

'Come back, Shungetsu!' Takada called a third time. His voice echoed through the storehouse, but not a soul was there to hear it.

*

The season has changed once again.

In the old days, a garden in winter had struck me as somehow desolate. Now, however, I'm surprised by how much life it contains. Bulbs and seeds are sound asleep awaiting their time to sprout, while just below the hard surface of the ground grubs and earthworms fatten and a host of fungi and protozoa decompose, radiating heat and giving birth to organic matter.

I sometimes think of my present self as being like my winter garden.

Months have passed since my dreams of Edo ended. Whatever happened to Takada? And how did he figure in the story that he told me of the young prince and Lady Kusuko?

I visit the bench beside the river where I spent so much time in late autumn, hoping to discuss all this with Mr Takaoka. I sit there patiently in the faint sunlight, feeling the cold creep up my legs. It has been so long since I saw him.

'Will he ever come?' I murmur under my breath. And then I hear the sound of approaching footsteps behind me.

'I made it,' he says, as if we had been meeting every day.

'It's been a long time.'

'Yeah. Then again, it hasn't really been all that long.'

I look up at his face from the bench. He looks down at me.

'Shall we take a stroll?' he asks.

'Sure.'

So off we walk, shoulder to shoulder.

I cut right to the chase. 'You were Takada, right?'

Mr Takaoka pauses. 'Well,' he says reluctantly, 'maybe not entirely.'

'What happened to Takada after that?' I ask.

'It's really Shungetsu we should be concerned about, isn't it?'

'I guess you're right.'

A chilly breeze is hitting the spot where my blouse meets the nape of my neck.

'I'm cold,' I say. Mr Takaoka puts his arm round my shoulder.

'Now we look like lovers,' I say.

'We were lovers there, weren't we?'

'But here we're not.'

'You don't have to be lovers to warm someone when they're cold,' Mr Takaoka says smiling. 'That's just compassion.'

We walk on until we reach a small shopping street, where we come upon an old-fashioned coffee shop.

'Look, it's named Pearl,' I say with a smile. He laughs.

'What's so funny?' I ask Mr Takaoka, giving him a poke in the ribs.

His expression turns serious.

'Those two, didn't it strike you as strange how they threw themselves into their affair so completely?' he says.

'Yes, I must say I was rather jealous – I'd like to live that way myself.'

There's a cowbell hanging in the entrance of the coffee shop that clangs as we open the door.

'Yoshiwara looked magnificent, but there was something cold about it, too,' Mr Takaoka mutters as he scans the handwritten menu. I think back on my days there. How lively the evenings were. The repartee with the male patrons. The *oiran* parading in their splendid kimonos.

'Yes, cold and rather depressing,' I reply, 'but I can see why it's called the floating world. It's strange, when you're there you feel like you're actually floating.'

The elderly proprietor totters over to take our orders. Mr

Takaoka chooses black tea, I opt for hot chocolate. Tiny rain-drops are dotting the windowpane. The rain looks cold, I say. Mr Takaoka gives an almost imperceptible nod.

It turns out that Shungetsu and Takada had been followed.

It was the *oiran* Izumi who had sounded the alarm. Unlike the *kamuro* who identified Yukiyanagi, however, Izumi felt no com-punction about what she was doing – neither self-recrimination nor jealousy figured in her act. She simply didn't question the rules that governed her life. The rules of Yoshiwara.

As the daughter of the teahouse manager, Oshina, Izumi had lived her entire life in the Quarter, so perhaps it was only natural that she upheld the system that governed it. That was all she knew.

The posse who tracked Shungetsu and Takada down were the manservants of the house.

'The lightning was gorgeous,' I murmur. Mr Takaoka stares at me.

'You had time to notice something like that?' he says, some-what critically.

'Of course not. That's why its beauty hit me with such force.'

Mr Takaoka doesn't respond. The tea and hot chocolate arrive. With shaking hands, the old man places the cups in front of us, then shuffles back to the counter.

'As I recall, one of the manservants was a bit older than the others.'

'Yes, the guy who always guided me to your room had a wicked look, like a villain on the Kabuki stage.'

'Yes, that's him. He was sleeping with Oshina.'

Mr Takaoka looks up in surprise, as if he's spotted something floating in the air. 'So that was it,' he says.

But he knows the whole story already: Izumi had alerted her

mother Oshina to our departure, and she had set the brawniest of the manservants on our heels.

'When did you realize that I had been abducted?' I ask.

'I had no idea what had happened when I looked in the storehouse and found you gone. What an idiot I was!'

'So how did you figure it out?'

'I found the sash of someone from your house lying on the ground near the storehouse. That's when I knew.'

That made sense: one of the men who had grabbed me must have dropped it. Shungetsu never found out, though. For the rest of her days, it pained her to imagine Takada's distress at finding her gone without knowing why.

'So what did Takada do after that?'

'He didn't want to believe Shungetsu had been dragged back to her house, so he told himself that an ogre had swallowed her whole.'

'An ogre?'

'Yes. Right before they ran away that evening Shungetsu had been talking about the festival in the village where she was born.'

That's right. Takada had asked her about the festival. She had told him about the god who, in good years, stayed until they harvested the rice. The ogres who would devour the villagers should the god leave any earlier. That story.

How pitiful that Takada couldn't face the fact that their elopement had failed. Knowing that makes me sad.

'But what could he have done? There was no point remaining there, so Takada went back to the official residence where he worked. No word had come from Shungetsu's house. He was a samurai who paid his debts promptly, so he owed them nothing. It was a clean break. But he was heartbroken. He spent the next year mourning his loss.'

Mr Takaoka is looking down at his cup of tea on the table as he speaks. This is good, he says, taking a sip.

'What happened to Shungetsu?' he asks.

I hesitate for a moment. Should I tell him or not? But then I go ahead with Shungetsu's story.

A month before the elopement, a wealthy man had offered to redeem Shungetsu. A rice wholesaler, one of the two biggest in town, had fallen for her at first sight, and through an intermediary had proposed to make her his third mistress.

Shungetsu had sensed that they were physically incompatible. As someone who entertained men by touching and being touched, she instinctively understood that. Of course, compatibility was hardly the first priority in her line of work, but once she had discovered the joy of sleeping in the arms of a man like Takada, the prospect of spending the rest of her life as the plaything of someone like the rice merchant aroused nothing but disgust.

The rice dealer was a good-looking, burly man in his early forties. He was well versed in the ways of love, and more than capable of paying off a woman's debts, so from an *oiran*'s perspective his credentials were flawless – he was the perfect candidate to become Shungetsu's sole patron, her *danna*.

'But Shungetsu couldn't stand the idea,' I tell Mr Takaoka. 'And having realized this, the prospect became more and more unbearable.'

'Takada would have been eager to take in Shungetsu,' Mr Takaoka says. 'He was as committed as she was to their escape. His life to that point hadn't been smooth sailing either: although born a high-ranking samurai, he had been forced to toil in obscurity. I guess it was only natural for him to find solace in a woman's arms.'

Mr Takaoka and I sit there tracing the history of Takada and Shungetsu's love affair frankly and dispassionately, as though we were talking about a scandal involving two complete strangers. Yet for me at least, a world of sadness lay beneath our casual tone. Poor, poor Shungetsu. If only she hadn't fallen in love. Had kept her passions at arm's length.

Shungetsu was forcibly returned to her teahouse, to be locked away in a small room and rarely fed, just like Yukiyanagi. In the end, though, her house needed her to look her best for the rice merchant, so she was garbed in beautiful kimonos and reacquainted with the arts of seduction before being sent off to be his mistress.

Her failed elopement was kept an absolute secret – no one in her house was allowed to even mention it – and so the sad story of Shungetsu and Takada never saw the light of day.

'When did your dreams stop?' Mr Takaoka asks.

'After Shungetsu passed away.'

'When did that happen?'

'She died of tuberculosis, less than two years after being redeemed.'

Mr Takaoka picks up his cup and tilts it to his mouth. It's cold now, he says, returning it to the saucer.

'Takada lived into his sixties,' he says. 'At the end of his life, he journeyed to the Asian continent, which is where he met his end.'

The continent? I hadn't expected that. It takes me a moment to recover my thoughts. Takada had lived such a lively and adventurous life, had even travelled abroad, while Shungetsu's time on earth had been so brief.

'Why did Takada journey to the continent?'

'My guess is that when his heart and mine overlapped, our

memories did as well, so that he was tracking down things that had happened to me long, long ago.'

'The night we eloped,' I press him, 'Takada told me the story of the prince and Lady Kusuko. Is that what you're talking about?'

'Yes, that may well be.'

'Will you be able to give me more details someday?'

'Of that story from long, long ago?'

'Yes, of that story from long, long ago.'

'Now you've put me on the spot,' Mr Takaoka says with a quiet smile.

Long, long ago. The simple repetition of the words calls back memories of Shungetsu's love for Takada and the pain it unleashed. It is an affair long ended, with both lovers long dead, yet I have to stifle a sob.

Why such a rush of feeling? To answer that question, I must look within. Sitting there, I turn things over in my mind until, finally, I arrive at an answer.

Yes, that's it. There can be no doubt.

Shungetsu is not dead. Her body perished, but she was a figure of dream in the first place, so it's hard to say she ever truly existed. Nevertheless, the power of her love has taken root in me, and it's not going anywhere anytime soon.

I, Riko, am still in love with Naa-chan. That love is a distant echo now, an ancient memory, and it has changed markedly from what it once was, yet it is still there. It hasn't disappeared.

When I unleash the passion that Shungetsu had for Takada, however, free it from its box, so to speak, it is reborn in my heart in all its immediacy and power. I have tried to push Shungetsu from my mind since my dreams of her stopped, and though I did still glimpse her feelings occasionally, I assumed that they had largely disappeared.

But I was wrong.

For I am still in love with Takada.

I wish I had spent my life with him. Fled with him to the ends of the earth. If that was impossible, I wish I had died with him there that night.

It was true, an unfulfilled love could live on, its thin flame flickering in one's heart.

The bulbs have sprouted, pushing up a number of pale-green leaves. Soon there will be buds, and after that flowers.

I love each and every one of my flowers: narcissus, crocus, snowdrops. It warms me to imagine how soon they will display their immaculate blossoms. Loving flowers is different from loving people. It is quieter, and brighter. I can look into my own heart as I water and weed.

Last Sunday, Naa-chan and I visited a mall. We window-shopped the spring sales, ate pasta at the food court, shopped for dinner and, when we had finished all that, we sat at a table in the big atrium while Naa-chan drank coffee from a plastic cup.

'Is it good?' I asked him.

'Same as always,' he answered brightly.

These days, Naa-chan always puts on a cheerful face. Yet at the same time he looks a little haggard, a little melancholy. I can tell his last break-up lies behind that expression. How do I know? Because I look the same way. Cheerful, but a bit melancholy.

Mr Takaoka had said as much earlier, at the Pearl cafe. We could have had a similar conversation on the bench next to the river, but I doubt we would have been as calm and collected were food and drink not set before us.

It is not as if I am in love with Mr Takaoka. Yet I am deeply attached to him.

Mr Takaoka probably feels the same. He is not in love with me, in other words, not in love with Riko. Yet he is still hopelessly drawn to that part within me that is Shungetsu. Our conversations are not as lively as they once were. A weariness has crept into them. Yet it is a weariness that both of us cherish.

'Look at all the kids,' Naa-chan said. Toddlers were frolicking on the playground equipment – their happy voices occasionally resounded in the vaulted atrium.

'Would you like children?' Naa-chan said, casting a sidelong glance in my direction.

'I think I'd be happy if we were blessed with a child,' I replied brightly.

'Me too,' he chimed in, even more cheerfully.

Back in my garden, I see tiny insects crawling on the leaves of the buttercups. I pluck them off with my gloved hand and deposit them in a plastic bag we picked up at the food store. Yes, I do still love Naa-chan. Even now. My love might be fragments of what it once was, but it still exists.

The air was dry inside the mall. How cautiously we had talked to one another. Perhaps Naa-chan, too, was searching for what fragments remained of his love for me.

I spot more insects on the buttercups. One by one, I carefully pinch them between my fingers and toss them in the bag.

A Tale of Long, Long Ago

Long, long ago.

For some reason, Takada's words came back to me as I lay on the birthing table.

Yes, that's how he had described his relationship with Lady Kusuko to Shungetsu on the night of their elopement.

I had assumed that was the first I had heard of Lady Kusuko, which fixed it in my mind. Now I realized I had misremembered. It hit me in that instant my baby was being born.

Remembering is a strange thing. Memories bubble to the surface unbidden – we cannot pick and choose. Never could I have imagined that Takada's first mention of his love for Lady Kusuko would pop into my head on this of all days.

Long, long ago. Takada had spoken of Lady Kusuko using those words well before Shungetsu first thought of escaping Yoshiwara – in fact, it may have been shortly after he and Shungetsu were first introduced. His story of falling in love for the first time, over a thousand years ago. Of how the woman was loved by his father and thus forbidden fruit. And how, forced to suppress his passion, Takada had taken to admiring her from a distance.

Takada had told this to Shungetsu as a bedtime story, without mentioning Lady Kusuko by name. His voice was so soft and gentle then, dream-like really, that I could remember it even now, with childbirth pressing upon me.

Wouldn't such a confession be bound to make a new lover like Shungetsu jealous? And she *was* jealous.

To be remembered by such a man, to be spoken of in such a dreamy voice – for that she would willingly rot away to nothing.

Perhaps it was then that Shungetsu fell in love with Takada. With a man who could worship a woman like that. How wonderful to be thought of that way, if only for a moment. And to honour him to the same degree. Yet the chances of an *oiran* entering into such a beautiful relationship, where one was free to worship and be worshipped, were virtually nil – just imagining such a thing left her feeling crushed. Maybe that's why, until this moment, I had pushed from my mind Takada's revelation, made so soon after first meeting Shungetsu, that he had loved a woman 'long, long ago'. Better to forget the unattainable. Human beings are creatures capable of blocking their memories like this.

But why had Takada's love for Lady Kusuko entered my consciousness now?

A contraction swept over me like a great wave: the baby was coming. And I wanted it to come. Surrounded by nurses and midwives, my body was trying its best to embrace the excruciating, maddening waves of childbirth.

Where did the maddening part come from, I wondered, as I lay there bathed in sweat. From my belated recollection of how Shungetsu felt on hearing of Takada's ancient lady love? Or from the natural, physical reaction of any woman who brings a child into this world?

*

Don't push – not yet.

The midwife restrained me. My body, however, wanted to go full steam ahead. In fact, it was screaming for the baby to be born.

I knew the baby was a boy. Would he resemble Naa-chan? Or me?

Now you can push! the midwife exclaimed. Don't close your eyes. And inhale! Breathe in, not just out. Push with everything you've got! He's crowning, so one last time. The baby's doing a great job!

It puzzled me that the midwife was speaking to me like an old friend. I had met her for the first time only the night before, when the contractions started. We'd never eaten lunch together, or studied or worked at the same desk.

And here he is! the midwife sang out. It's a healthy baby boy, Madam. Congratulations!

Her friendly manner had been suddenly replaced by a more distanced, professional tone. What a strange place, I thought. The afterbirth was quickly cleaned up, and the baby brought to my side. Wrapped in a white cloth, he looked more purple than red.

They used to call babies sprats, didn't they? My mind seemed to be wandering.

That's right. Long, long ago it was. I was there beside my mistress, wasn't I, wondering when her baby would come, worrying whether she would be all right?

Huh? Where did that memory come from?

It was not the Edo *oiran* Shungetsu's memory, nor did it belong to my present self, Riko, who had just given birth. No, it had travelled an even greater distance, from some faraway place and time.

*

'You did a fine job, Madam!' the midwife said. 'Shall we call your husband?'

I could hear Naa-chan's voice. The sound of his feet running in my direction.

'Oh, Riko,' he said. 'You were wonderful. Thank you. Thank you so much.'

His body cast a shadow over my face. The hands enfolding my cold fingertips were warm.

Time had passed since the day Naa-chan and I had agreed we wanted a child. Spring and summer had come and gone, and when I awoke to the fact that new life was growing in my body it was already autumn. Then we had welcomed a new year, a second spring had come round, and June's rainy season had begun. Now I had given birth to a baby boy on a summer day in my thirties.

Both Naa-chan and I had eagerly anticipated the birth. I prepared for it as I rearranged the house and looked after my garden. Still, it's hard to truly relax when you're waiting for something to happen. When I reached my limit, I would meet Mr Takaoka at the coffee shop near the river and we would talk over a cup of tea.

Mr Takaoka was very solicitous about my pregnancy.

'Did Lady Kusuko have any children?' I asked him once. The question came out of the blue, yet he answered without hesitation.

'She did,' he replied.

'I see. So then, were you like a son to her?'

'No. She wasn't a mother to me, nor a lover, nor a friend, just someone who I deeply cared about, as she cared about me.'

I shrugged. Mr Takaoka tended to turn sentimental when he talked about Lady Kusuko.

'So, what do you think – does carrying a baby make a woman stronger?' he asked me in return.

'What nonsense,' I answered a bit frostily. 'Having a baby isn't simply a means to strengthen yourself.'

Mr Takaoka just laughed. I laughed with him. But his question unnerved me. It felt like I'd been crammed into a new category, that of 'women who have children'. It was a fleeting feeling, but Mr Takaoka turned serious.

'I'm sorry – I spoke without thinking,' he apologized.

Unlike with Naa-chan, my conversations with Mr Takaoka never left me frustrated.

'So, when's your due date?'

'Around the time it gets really hot.'

Mr Takaoka kept eyeing my belly. My maternity clothes couldn't hide my pregnancy. 'Don't worry, little baby,' he said with a warm smile. 'You'll be fine.'

We named the baby Toji. He cried a lot, so much that I was at my wits' end from morning till night.

I had never imagined that looking after an infant could be such back-breaking work. Naa-chan and I became like the couples in the old children's stories: the husband going to the woods to gather firewood each morning, the wife with the baby on her back, dragging laundry down to the river to wash, doing all the cooking, and so on and so forth. Carrying all that firewood home must have worn the husband out in this case, since he had no energy left to hold his son.

To put it bluntly, Naa-chan wasn't all that helpful with Toji. I had no big objection to being a full-time housewife, in charge of the cooking, cleaning and looking after the baby. I had not known, though, how much work the last part entailed.

Toji cried when my breast milk was insufficient; cried when the back-up milk bottle still wasn't enough; cried when he couldn't fall asleep; cried when he needed his diaper changed; cried when he wanted to be held; cried when he was lonely; cried when an activity he liked ended; and sometimes cried for no reason at all. In other words, Toji cried for the greater part of the day.

His crying demanded a response. I had to let him nurse longer when my milk was meagre, sterilize the bottle, warm the formula to a precise temperature, change his diaper, rock him in my arms, strap him to my back to do the laundry, rock his cradle with my foot as I swept the floor, grab the moments he was sleeping to do the cooking, and strap him in the stroller to go shopping, taking care on my way to avoid the many potential dangers.

Had I three heads and six arms like an Indian Asura, it still wouldn't have been enough. I felt like shouting my frustrations from the rooftops.

I was always running on empty.

Please, Toji, I prayed each day, be a good boy, please sleep more than three hours. But he never did, just went on bawling with all his might. Day or night, he never slept more than two hours at a time. He'll sleep longer once he's three months old, they told me at his first monthly check-up.

Yeah, dream on. Toji hit the three-hour limit and stopped. He turned four months old, then five, and still his eyes would pop open after three hours, and those ear-splitting cries would echo throughout the house, summoning me. The little sleep I got came at night, when I nodded off during the intervals when he wasn't crying. What could I do? Finally, I became adept at grabbing snatches of sleep lying beside him. But it wasn't deep. Not by any means. Instead, I hovered between sleep and wakefulness, unsure of which realm I was inhabiting. A far cry from those days when my sleep was deep and uninterrupted, a happy respite from the world.

And yet it was during those difficult days that, for a second time, I returned to the dream world . . .

Let me speak now of that time, when sleep was shallow, and I found myself slipping in and out of a new and unfamiliar realm.

In that dream, I was a *nyōbō*. *Nyōbō* means wife today, but long, long ago it referred to something quite different: a woman who served a noble princess as one of her ladies-in-waiting. Why on earth had I become a *nyōbō*?

The present me was flummoxed. The term, and the position it described, was as unfamiliar to me as Yoshiwara and *oiran* had once been. Didn't this word come from an era even older than Edo? I was aware that the rank continues in today's imperial household under a slightly different name. Nevertheless, the *nyōbō* of my dream seemed to mean what it had a thousand years ago, back in the Heian period.

This new dream world was hazy at first. Yoshiwara had been a realm full of sharply defined colour from the outset – even my body had an outline that was clear and distinct. True, when I woke the dream receded into the mists, but while I was dreaming it felt like a real world that I was physically inhabiting.

This time, though, it was hard to grasp the flickering dream world that beckoned to me as I lay drowsing beside Toji. At first, I wasn't even sure who I was, or to which era I had been transported.

Still, that world gradually became clearer as my dreams of Heian piled up. It turned out that the lady I was waiting on was the eldest daughter – *ōiko*, back then – of a noble who served the emperor.

I was ten years old. My mistress was ten as well. You might think it strange a girl that young would be assigned a position of such responsibility. Yet this was long, long ago, when people's lives were much shorter, and the age of maturity far younger. Even so, ten was still below what was considered the age of adulthood. At that age most children still lived at home, looked after by their parents – only the most precocious were permitted to serve a person of such high rank.

Yes, waiting on the princess was considered work of great importance. Since my family was less exalted, it was an honour for us as well.

The princess was a demure young lady, but she had a mischievous side as well.

On the day of my arrival at her family's estate, I was so stiff and formal in her presence that I couldn't glance in her direction. It continued like that the next day and the day after that too. I was acting like a real ignoramus, sitting there like a bump on a log. Finally, on the third day, she deigned to break the silence.

'Do you like *oto*?' she asked, using the old word for cat.

In the dream, I had a memory of growing up in a house literally swarming with stray cats. I recalled that they would all start yowling on spring nights when the moon was out, much to my brothers' amusement. The cats sounded like wailing babies, and they weren't just outside our home but inside as well. My dream mother loved cats.

'Yes,' I answered, trembling.

'You're a brave one,' the princess giggled.

I didn't understand – why would she call me brave just for saying that I liked cats?

'Brave,' I said, stupidly echoing her.

'Yes. After all, Chinese cats are really scary.'

Huh? This baffled me. Were cats from China really so terrifying? The princess let the matter rest without further explanation.

For my part, I was so new in my position I didn't have the nerve to ask anything more. I had to wait a while for the princess to fill me in on the fearsome cats of China.

Finally, one day she spread an old painted scroll in front of me and let me take a look. It depicted people in unfamiliar dress, as well as a number of trees and animals I hadn't seen before.

'This is a Chinese cat,' she said, pointing to an animal in the corner.

So that's what it was – a tiger!

It was Riko who noticed this – though I may have been a ten-year-old girl, Riko was there, too, inside me. I could also tell that the surroundings depicted in the scroll were likely Chinese. The archaic style conveyed some of the affection Japanese felt for the people and landscapes of that foreign culture in Heian times.

'My father gave me this scroll,' the princess said, carefully rolling it up.

I was impressed. At the detail of the painting, first of all, but also at the princess's quick mind. The princess had known that the characters for cat could also mean tiger in Chinese, but by omitting that fact she had turned my love of cats into something else. Had she explained at the outset that 'cat' could refer to a far more terrifying beast, that information would have flashed across my mind for a brief moment and then, just as quickly, disappeared. By allowing time to elapse, she had made the visual impact far greater – having been thus surprised, I would never forget.

The princess's mind worked like that. The longer I spent with her, the more I witnessed her keen intelligence in action, and the more I came to admire her. If one were to ask her future husband if her cleverness made her easier to get along with, however, his answer would probably have been no, for it could not be said that in Heian men's estimation of women, intelligence ranked particularly high.

But I digress. The princess was not to meet her future husband for some time yet. No, at this point the story revolves around the ten-year-old princess and the ten-year-old me, and how we drew closer to each other as time passed.

The princess's father was a kind and gentle man. It warmed my heart to watch how he treated his wife, the princess's mother.

The marital system among aristocratic Japanese during the Heian period considered the groom's official residence to be his bride's home. However, that did not mean that he gave up his own home – on the contrary, he could return there whenever he pleased. This was a practice which today's anthropologists call duolocal marriage. If a man tired of his wife and wished to pursue another woman, he would return to his own home first, then begin visiting the residence of his new love. The upshot was that there were numerous married men who seldom slept at their wife's home.

My princess's father, however, lived permanently with his wife and her family, for he loved her deeply. She was the daughter of a man who had closely attended a former emperor. She was thus of very high rank – much higher, in fact, than her husband. Yet the princess's mother loved the princess's father every bit as much as he loved her.

Back then, however, being in love bore little connection to getting married. No, the overriding factor in choosing a husband for one's daughter was his family's political status. That meant it was very rare for a couple to be wed who loved each other from the outset.

The princess's parents were a striking exception to this rule. Her father's rank at court was not especially high. Nevertheless, his wife paid him the greatest respect, looking after his needs in every regard and making sure that he was always dressed in beautiful clothes, which she perfumed with the most elegant incense. For his part he always spoke to her with great affection and gratitude, and never so much as looked at another woman.

Showered with affection from two doting parents, the princess was raised as a perfect jewel – there was not a day she wanted for anything.

I wish I could say that I devoted my time to taking care of my baby and only occasionally strolled through my dream world, but I found that I was anxious to escape. In the intervals between my dreams of the Heian princess, I slaved away looking after Toji. More accurately, perhaps, I dreamed in brief spells while looking after him, even though I wanted to experience my dream world in a more leisurely fashion. It was my chosen sanctuary, for taking care of him was so draining.

To tell the truth, I was growing increasingly irritated with how little help I was getting from Naa-chan. Apart from bathing Toji on holidays and making a big deal of looking after him when my parents came upstairs to visit, he hardly ever played with or even held the baby.

'We could break our backs trying to get our men to help with housework,' Michiko-sensei laughed when I complained. 'I resigned myself long ago, but young women today don't give up so easily.'

Hoping to force Naa-chan to spend more time looking after Toji, I began fleeing to Michiko-sensei's house on occasional Sundays, ostensibly to continue my koto lessons. Perhaps I should have been more direct, but I couldn't have managed to ask Naa-chan for help otherwise. A character flaw, I suppose. I have heard that other mothers, believing it their natural right, have been able to devise ways to get their husbands to share the load, but somehow I've never figured out how to do that.

'Maybe it's because your parents raised you the old way,' Michiko-sensei said, savouring her tea. 'How about Naa-chan – does he like little kids?'

'He seems to. From a distance, that is,' I replied, whereupon she laughed again.

'Boys look after their mother when they grow up,' she said, taking a slice of the sweet *yokan* that I had brought.

For the first time in ages, I remembered her third son, the one who had been there when Michiko-sensei had spoken about a certain junior high school student called Naa-chan, whom she had just met. Of her three sons, only he had understood her feelings; then later, after she and my husband started seeing each other, he had been the one to intervene, taking care to consider my situation as the wife even as he dealt with his recalcitrant mother.

'I wonder,' I said sceptically. If Toji took after his father, he might look after me when I needed him, but he would also be tending to a bevy of other women just as eagerly. I had had enough of men so readily distracted.

'You're pretty hard on men,' Michiko-sensei said.

'Living with Naa-chan does that to you,' I answered. 'Like it or not.'

'Still, it was you who fell in love with him, right?' Michiko-sensei teased. Sure, I had been totally smitten when I was young, who could forget that? But hadn't what he had done since thrown a cold blanket over that love?

'So then, have you fallen out of love with him?' Michiko-sensei asked artlessly.

'Our relationship may have passed the point where simple words like "love" and "hate" make much sense.'

'Really?'

'Yes, I think so.'

'After all the trouble it took to get together,' Michiko-sensei said, envy in her voice. Clearly, she still had a crush on Naa-chan. Should I tie a ribbon round him and hand him to her? I was tempted, but only for a moment.

A year passed after I was elevated to serve the princess, followed by a second year. Then the princess's mother began entertaining the idea of marrying her to the gentleman she favoured. Of course, the princess herself played no role in this search. Nevertheless, unbeknownst to her, we who served her were privy to a lot of gossip, much of it quite detailed, about the ongoing negotiations. Whispered rumours suggested that she might be married to someone in the imperial line.

I had been there a full three years when those whispers reached their peak.

Finally, around the time the princess was celebrating her coming-of-age ceremony, it was formally decided whom she would marry. It was the end of winter. The nightingales were singing, not the full-throated serenade that would come later in the year but rather the chirping of young birds – I remember well because the princess took such delight in their immature voices.

'They're so cute when they sing like that,' she said.

'If nightingales are the harbingers of spring,' I laughed, 'and these can only chirp, we may be forced to wait for some time.' But the princess was serious.

'It's not necessarily a good thing when something finally arrives,' she said, shaking her head.

In my heart of hearts, I knew that she was right about this, as she was about so much.

It's not always for the best when something reaches its fruition. The princess was aware of this at thirteen; yet I, as Riko, still hadn't attained that level of understanding, though I had lived nearly three times longer. Was that because girls reached maturity earlier back then, or was it solely due to her intelligence? I couldn't tell. After all, she was the only young woman I had served.

Was it fortunate that someone so astute, so able to discern beauty in the incomplete, was destined to marry that particular gentleman? Once the princess was wed, I found myself pondering that question time and time again.

At last, Toji began sleeping through the night. A four-hour stretch became five hours, then six, until, eight months after his birth, it was no longer unusual for him to make it through to morning without waking once.

Not surprisingly, I began to recover – I was gradually able to stem my anger about Naa-chan's refusal to help with the baby (sigh) and, more generally, at Japanese men's stubborn immersion in the old patriarchal system (sigh, again).

I resumed my get-togethers with Mr Takaoka, now taking Toji with me. Obviously, quiet conversations at the coffee shop were out of the question, so on sunny afternoons I loaded Toji into the stroller and pushed it down to our old meeting place on the riverbank, where I often found Mr Takaoka waiting. He would lift Toji from the stroller like an old pro and bounce him in his arms, much to the baby's delight. When I spread a blanket on the grass and placed Toji on it, he immediately began to roll around. When he grew excited, he'd thrash his arms and legs about, trying to crawl.

'What a coordinated little kid,' Mr Takaoka laughed, watching Toji squirm. 'And strong too.'

Toji was crawling within a month – two weeks after that saw him motoring about on his hands and knees.

'He's a quick learner,' Mr Takaoka said in admiration. 'I envy him,' he continued, going to retrieve the baby, who had scrambled off the blanket. This process repeated itself until, finally, the baby tired himself out and began to fuss.

The time had come. I mixed some powdered milk with hot water from my trusty thermos and fed Toji. Sure enough, it worked like magic – within moments, he was out like a light. My oh my, how things had changed!

'It's so much easier these days,' I murmured as I spread a bath towel over the sleeping infant. 'Now, can I tell you about my dream?'

Mr Takaoka gave me an encouraging smile, whereupon I launched into a detailed account of the latest events in my dream saga.

Where was I? That's right, it was just before the time of the princess's coming-of-age ceremony that all the daughters of the aristocracy went through. After the ritual, they replaced the simple smock they had worn up to that point with a *mo*, a long pleated skirt that trailed behind them on the ground.

Back then, coming of age meant that a girl had to start preparing herself for marriage. Indeed, the ritual indicated that a prospective groom was already on the scene, which in turn meant that he and the girl would begin 'sharing a pillow' – in other words, that the girl would lie with a man for the first time.

'Not very complicated,' commented Mr Takaoka casually. 'A girl becomes a woman by changing her dress. That makes perfect sense, but it's sad somehow that it directly leads to her sleeping with a man.'

I felt the same way. The princess had been raised with great care, wrapped in soft cotton you might say, only to be given away to some man of high breeding. That was how Heian aristocratic society worked.

'I guess modern women are luckier,' I replied. 'We have the freedom to choose.'

'Freedom can be a problem in its own right,' Mr Takaoka countered.

That's certainly true. Freedom can raise all sorts of gnarly problems. I had been free to fall in love with Naa-chan, and free to marry him. If my parents had opposed my decision, if they had tried to foist another man on me, I would have married Naa-chan anyway.

Was I any happier as a result? I don't know. Happiness strikes me now as a flat, monotonous notion, nothing more. Not that I share the princess's preference for a baby nightingale's chirps over the song of the adult bird. It is impossible for me to characterize my days with Naa-chan as simply happy or unhappy – they are a mixture of happiness and unhappiness, joy and sadness, anger and inner stillness, as well as a multitude of other emotions.

'You're right,' I whispered in reply. 'Gnarly problems, for sure.'

When the princess changed her manner of dress after her coming-of-age ceremony, so too did I. This was the so-called 'investiture of the lady-in-waiting'.

I've been calling myself a lady-in-waiting to this point, but I was really just an apprentice for that role, someone expected to serve as the princess's playmate and help look after those little things she needed done. A handmaid, in other words.

A fully fledged lady-in-waiting played a more extensive role. Some were assigned the task of educating their mistress in the writing of poems and letters. When an aristocratic woman married a high-ranking man, she was supported by others more experienced in literary skills, a position filled in later years by eminent authors like Lady Murasaki and Sei Shonagon. Then there were those like me, who were to look after the intimate side of things, sharing our mistress's confidences and worries.

It was not until shortly after her coming-of-age ceremony that the princess's mother informed her of the man she was to marry. As I remember, the princess conveyed this news to me with the single word 'Finally.' She didn't specify, but there was no question what she meant – her future husband had been decided upon. I already knew, however, exactly who he was.

It's entirely possible that the last person in the residence to learn his identity was the princess herself. For everyone in the place was in a fluster with rumours about the match, from the lowliest servants to those who personally attended the princess's mother and father. The man was well known all over the capital, so it was no surprise that the entire staff became embroiled in the gossip.

The name of the man the princess was to marry was Ariwara no Narihira. The previous year, he had been Junior Sixth Rank and was now at the Imperial Archives and on track to rise through the ranks to an illustrious career.

Lord Narihira was nobly born, too. His father was the eldest son of the former emperor who had stepped down three reigns ago, while his mother was the *ogousama* – daughter – of the emperor before that. But what made Narihira exceptional was more than his lineage. His handsome face and elegant form had been lauded in the capital for quite some time. Apparently, he had stolen the hearts of a number of women who were now left pining away, waiting in vain for him to call again.

The reason why my princess's family were able to secure such an outstanding match was, surprisingly, the relationship that had developed between Narihira and the princess's father, Ki no Aritsune.

I think I've already mentioned that her father was not of terribly high rank. That was certainly the case. His station and his wealth were unremarkable – indeed, it is no exaggeration to say that, compared to most aristocrats in the capital, he was lacking in both those areas. Yet he was known as a man of great moral virtue. Not wealthy in property, perhaps, but wealthy in spirit. That's probably the best way to describe him. Although Narihira was considerably younger, they became comrades of a sort, despite the age difference. When Lord Narihira was young, Lord Aritsune had shown him much affection; now that Narihira had risen in the world, he looked out for the older man in a multitude of ways.

Narihira was already frequenting the homes of a number of ladies (as I have mentioned, men customarily visited their lovers' residences), but he had never taken an official wife, so Narihira's decision to wed the princess caused a commotion. Of course, neither the princess nor I could tell how many of these rumours of women tearing out their hair in grief were exaggerated for effect, and how much was real.

Whatever the case, preparations for the wedding moved forward, step by step.

'Do you mean *that* Narihira from *The Tales of Ise*?' Mr Takaoka asked me.

'Yes, that Narihira.'

'I remember there was an *oiran* in Yoshiwara who loved *The Tales*,' he said nostalgically.

That was Komurasaki. She had a shelf of illustrated books that she read while waiting for customers. I had been a *kamuro* at the time, and had found it hard to take my eyes off the picture of the startlingly handsome Narihira as she turned the pages.

Neither Mr Takaoka nor I dared bring up the fact that Shungetsu and Takada's flight from Yoshiwara so closely paralleled the 'Akutagawa' chapter in *The Tales*.

'So, what was your impression of the real Narihira?' Mr Takaoka asked, as if brushing away a fly.

I spent a moment collecting my thoughts about the 'real Narihira.' No, 'real' was the wrong word – the Narihira I had known existed purely in dream.

But since I have this chance, let me introduce you to what I, a modern woman named Riko, knew of that poet, lover and hero of the ninth-century collection of poetry and prose, *The Tales of Ise*.

Ariwara no Narihira: the man whose love affairs spanned his life, from youth to old age. Whose lovers included an empress-to-be and the sacred priestess of the Ise Shrine. Who shared love poems and took to bed a great many wives and daughters of the aristocracy, as well as their ladies-in-waiting. Who followed the emperor he served with unswerving loyalty, even after that emperor's abdication. A man rich in friends, whose parties involved poetry, singing, conversation and wine. A man who lived a colourful life, yet whose affection for men and women alike was deep and lasting – that was the image of Narihira projected by *The Tales of Ise*.

How, then, did that Narihira appear in my dream?

Well, if I had to choose a word to describe my initial reaction to him it would be 'shock'.

Why? Because he somehow reminded me of Naa-chan.

It's the Heian period we're talking about, so of course Narihira was shorter in stature, but like most aristocratic men of that era he was trained in the military as well as the literary arts, which made him more muscular than Naa-chan. There was also some similarity in their faces. The better I came to know Narihira, the more difference I saw in their characters. Nevertheless, at odd moments, when Narihira was before me and his voice was ringing in my ears, the two men would still overlap in my mind.

At the point in my dream when I first met Narihira I was a young girl, the same tender age, more or less, as I was when I fell in love with Naa-chan. To be that age, and to serve a man who reminded me so much of Naa-chan, gave rise to complicated feelings, to put it mildly. Narihira was younger than Naa-chan at the time of our marriage. My best guess is that he was twenty-six when he wed the princess. Just being near him brought back vivid memories of a young Naa-chan in all his beauty and charm.

Was I therefore jealous of the princess? Not really. There, in the dream world, I may have been a girl the princess's age, but here I was a woman in her thirties who had already borne a child.

Still, I was conflicted. I felt a tinge of envy that my princess would become the beloved of such a handsome, charming young man. Yet I sympathized with her too, for the similarity between the two men suggested to me that the kind of turbulence disrupting my marriage would disrupt hers as well. Finally, I was uneasy about how I would react if I were placed in close quarters with such an attractive man for a long period of time.

So many emotions swirled within me.

Yet not for a moment did I ever dream of taking the princess's place. To repeat all that I had gone through with Naa-chan? No, not for anything in the world!

*

I will never forget the morning after the first night Narihira and the princess spent together.

Narihira had already headed back to his estate, but the princess remained sequestered behind her blinds. His morning-after poem was delivered by one of his attendants, but she made no move to answer it as the rules of courtship required.

The princess's senior ladies-in-waiting were worried. They paced back and forth in front of where she was lying in bed, declaiming: 'Why won't she write to him? After all it took to bring such a shining young courtier to her side!'

A marriage was not finalized until the groom had journeyed to sleep with his bride for three nights in succession. So, although it appeared that the marriage was as good as done, all bets were off if the princess rejected him in the end.

Narihira had consulted with diviners to ensure that he had chosen an auspicious day and followed an auspicious route for his visit. All the more reason, therefore, for the princess to send him a proper missive to seal the deal. Once she had, then he would visit the next night, and the next, following which ceremonial rice cakes would be served to everyone, cementing the marriage.

'Princess,' I whispered through the blinds. She had responded to no one to that point, but I could see her shadow sit up. 'Are you all right?' I asked. She didn't answer, but she did raise the blinds just a little. I gulped.

For the princess I glimpsed through the blinds had changed. How glowing her skin! How moist her eyes! How enticingly tangled her long hair!

It had been some time since Narihira's departure, yet the after-effects of the night she had spent with him were as clear as day. Looking at her rapt expression, it felt as though, for the first time, I was witnessing with my own eyes the transformation of a woman whose heart had been captured by a man. The princess had fallen in love. In a single night.

'I want to write a poem,' she said in a quiet voice. 'Bring me paper and a brush.'

I hurried to her low desk in the corner of the room and retrieved the implements she customarily used. The princess raised the blinds and wrote her poem in a single fluid motion. It appeared that she had been mentally crafting her reply ever since Narihira's missive had arrived.

'Fix it on white paper with light-blue backing,' she said in that same quiet voice, handing me the poem, which was written in a most graceful hand.

It was mid-autumn. The white paper with blue backing, a style we called 'plumed grasses', reflected the season. To use this pairing – taken from the kimono world – for a love letter was considered the height of courtly elegance. Lord Narihira was known for selecting just the right colour combinations, evoking the season while displaying his ready wit. By layering coloured paper, he mirrored kimono's layering of coloured fabrics.

The princess knew this, without a doubt. I had thought that she was in the dark, yet how prescient she was in discovering the talents of her prospective husband! How was that possible? Had she asked someone to make enquiries? Or had she picked up her information from the gossip of the ladies who served her?

And, to my surprise, the use of overlapping colours wasn't the only skill with which the princess hoped to impress Narihira.

'I'd like to apply some of the Chamberlain's Perfume too,' she went on.

The Chamberlain's Perfume – the fragrance most associated with the subtle poignancy of autumn. I was profoundly moved by the princess's ability to combine the aesthetics of colour and smell to fit the season. Yet at the same time, I cannot deny that the precociousness of her reply worried me a little. Was it really a good idea to leap ahead, as it were, showing off her talents in their first exchange of letters?

I sound like an old woman, I admit, but that was my first reaction. It was one thing if a woman more experienced in love should craft a reply that mirrored Narihira's consummate skill. Such a woman might be seen as tasteful and refined. Yet how would Narihira respond to such a sophisticated, polished response coming from a girl barely on the cusp of adulthood?

Perhaps my concern stems from the situation in present-day Japan, where so many men prize immature girls over women. I prayed that in the Heian world, a girl who outshone others her age would be accepted and admired for the keenness of her intellect and the depth of her feelings. But I worried that the princess would encounter hardship despite her qualities. Or rather, I worried that hardship might descend on her *because* of the fineness of her heart.

That's right. The princess's very excellence made me sad. I couldn't help but feel that hidden within the fragrance of her brilliance lurked a faint, somehow threatening, scent.

Toji was now a real toddler who loved to babble. It was by common consensus the cutest age; yet what took me by surprise was that not only were my parents and I smitten, but Naa-chan was as well.

For months, Naa-chan had, somewhat fearfully, watched from a distance as our child grew from a limp newborn – a primitive form of life requiring constant care – into a little baby. Now, abruptly, he took on the role of a proper father.

I know that watching one's husband become a true father should be cause for gratitude and happiness. When Naa-chan started taking Toji to the park every Sunday, I was supposed to feel those emotions, without a shred of criticism. Yet something was gnawing at me. For a while, I couldn't put my finger on what that something was. Then, one day, it hit me. I had become a little jaundiced.

It was a strange state of mind. I wasn't envious of Toji for the love he was receiving from Naa-chan. Rather, it was the incontrovertible reality that now, right in front of me, I could see Naa-chan head over heels in love with someone who was not me.

Of course, Naa-chan had shared his love with a number of women. He was generous in that way: there were women I knew about, and those I was doubtless unaware of. Yet all the while he had loved me as well. That was what made him so endearing, but at the same time it was his greatest defect.

Fickle.

Of all the words that might be used to describe Naa-chan, this, I think, rings truest.

If he were a water bird, he would not be the sort that skims above the water single-mindedly looking for his prey and then, like an arrow, plunging deep to capture it. No, he was the type of bird that swims around beneath the surface, then pops up to follow first one set of ripples, then another. He might pledge his heart to a lover, but his feelings never ran all that deep. I think that more or less sums up Naa-chan's love affairs.

Toji, however, was an entirely different story. For Naa-chan loved him like a boy besotted with a girl for the first time. That Naa-chan was entirely new to me.

I was envious, but also a bit curious. Having watched him continually since I was two, I thought I knew all there was to know of the man, inside and out. But I was wrong. Naa-chan could devote himself to another person. Unswervingly.

Perhaps at one point that had characterized his love for the fiancée of the vice-president of his company. Could he have been as head over heels in love with her as he now was with Toji? On the other hand . . . I'm sure that the more deeply he fell in love with her, the more he bent over backwards to respond to all her needs. That may constitute the true joy of loving, I guess, but such constant self-abnegation can be awfully taxing. Wasn't Naa-chan secretly worn out that way?

Yet loving Toji required no such prudence – no such considerations were involved. For Toji returned his love unreservedly, irrespective of any faults his father might have.

Children are strange creatures. On the one hand, they have to trust in their parents' love, for the sheer fact that there is no one else to look after them; on the other, they have only those parents to love, however cruel, or unjust, or unreasonable they may prove to be.

Perhaps Naa-chan had never experienced unconditional love of that kind until Toji. That's what I thought, anyway.

In spite of my concerns, Lord Narihira and the princess continued on their path to wedlock without a hitch. Narihira came on the first night, then again on the second, until, finally, the third night arrived. If that were to pass successfully, they would officially be man and wife.

I couldn't sleep a wink that night. Happiness for the princess's good fortune and my desire that all would go well kept my eyes wide open.

The bridal chamber consisted of two rooms joined side by side. This 'chamber', however, was unlike the rooms we have today. Back then, a room did not serve one specific function. During the daylight hours, screens and curtains were set aside so that everyone could write, eat and talk to one another; in the evening, bedding was spread on a tatami mat and the screens and curtains replaced so that it could serve as a bedroom; then in the morning the room became a space where, in this case, Narihira's clothes could be laid out in preparation for his return to the palace. In short, a room was an ever-changing, protean space.

Tatami mats too were movable, not set in the floor as they are today. When not being used, they could be stacked in a corner or stored elsewhere.

A corridor called a *hisashi* encircled the room. Today, *hisashi* refers to the eaves that jut from a roof, but back in the Heian period it referred to the corridor itself.

The place I was assigned to sleep was on the floor of that broad corridor, as close as possible to where the princess lay. That way, I could hear her during the night. Often, when she woke and couldn't get back to sleep, she would raise a corner of the blinds and wake me in that quiet voice.

The first night that Narihira and the princess slept together, however, a much older lady-in-waiting took my spot. That was because it was necessary to have a woman with ample experience present were the princess to need guidance or assistance.

I felt very strange positioned further away than usual in the corridor, listening to the sounds coming from the princess's room. A muted rustling of clothing. Sighing. Stifled cries. There was something else too, that made no sound yet lay heavy in the air.

I was a Heian lady-in-waiting, a girl with no experience whatsoever; yet I knew in that moment exactly what was taking place inside that room between my princess and Narihira. It felt as though the princess had moved to some faraway place. As her handmaid, one who, like her, had barely reached her teens, I was struck by an indefinable loneliness.

The following night, too, I held my breath and tried to inter-
pret whatever sounds emanated from the bridal chamber. It
seemed to me that, somehow or other, the atmosphere between
Narihira and the princess had become easier and more relaxed.
I could feel it on the air. From time to time, the princess would
murmur something and Narihira would answer in his deep,
soothing voice.

The part of my consciousness that was Riko, of course, should
have known all about the acts that were taking place, yet the
atmosphere between the couple was reaching a level of eroticism
I had never experienced. Yes, an atmosphere at once secretive and
fierce was wafting from their room.

I couldn't tell – was this purely the result of who Narihira was,
or did it come from an intimacy between the two that had already
budded by the second night? Whichever the case, it was clear to
me that the sex taking place between Narihira and the princess
was more erotically charged than anything I had experienced as
an Edo *oiran*. This was a real revelation.

Perhaps I had underrated the physical side of Naa-chan's and
my relationship. The Riko now inhabiting the body of the young
lady-in-waiting felt that might well be the case.

That didn't mean that a night spent breathing in the atmosphere generated by Narihira and the princess made me want to go
jump in bed with Naa-chan. It did, however, set me to thinking.
Had I failed to give my body the consideration it deserved? Come
to think of it, I hadn't paid much attention to my physical self
since childhood. You could say I had left my own physical pleasure on the back burner all that time. Shutting myself up at home
with my books, pottering in my garden. Those were the things
that had absorbed me, not hanging out with friends or family, or
cavorting and sweating under the blue sky.

What joy was I finding now in Naa-chan's embrace? I tried to recall, but lying there in the corridor outside Lord Narihira and the princess's bedroom left me feeling it was all awfully long ago.

The princess's love for Narihira was making her more and more endearing in my eyes.

Lost in the clouds, mooning over her husband. Fixating on what clothes to lay out for his trip to the palace. Smiling happily while wafting incense over the outfit she had selected for him. How pure was the princess's love! She revered Lord Narihira, that's really all I can say. There were no hidden intentions, no ulterior motives.

As Riko, it was impossible not to compare the princess's marriage with marriage today – hers was so complicated, involving so many external factors, it would boggle anyone's mind.

For the princess's marriage was a form of political union, bound by the fetters of her society. All aristocrats had to participate in that system to preserve the rank and status of their house. A woman might diverge from her assigned path while young, even take lovers, but once she was officially married she was to devote her life to her husband, thinking of no other man. The idea that a woman should have a life of her own had no place among aristocratic ladies of the Heian period. Her life was her husband's – that is, unless she renounced her marriage or became a nun.

I found this way of life somehow refreshing.

A wife had to take great pains to ensure her husband got ahead at the palace – no hint of the plain or the shabby should attach itself to him. One could say that that was her job.

That's right. The princess's utter devotion to Narihira, the respect she paid and the care she took, can be seen to have its parallels in today's world – for example, in the way office workers rally behind their superiors to make their work as easy as possible. In that sense Heian women were career women, who pursued their jobs as wives with great zeal. Such simplicity and purity of purpose was what I found so appealing.

How does modern marriage compare? What is its true nature?

For one thing, a modern marriage follows no set pattern; rather, it contains a host of individual variations, depending on the environment in which one is raised and the ideas that one comes into contact with as an adult.

Of course, the modern marriage system is freer and more liberated. When you think that, not so long ago, most marital relationships were still coloured by Confucian attitudes which placed women below men, you can only marvel at the freedom today's women have to fashion their marriages as they see fit.

Yet the fact is that this new view of marriage contains its own challenges and pitfalls. Freedom forces us to exercise our discretion in so many ways: how to handle our relatives. How to deal with our neighbours. How to raise our children. How to divide the housework. How to allocate the family finances. How to decide who brings home the sushi.

Apart from these practical issues, emotional considerations also have to be taken into account. How to preserve romance within marriage, for instance. Or, conversely, how to let it slide. The unspoken rules that govern romance outside marriage. Or the decision to talk about those rules together. The realities of sex. Couples have to synchronize their positions on each one of these issues, either by discussing them or by reaching some sort of unspoken agreement, and each side has to exercise his or her own judgement.

Heian aristocrats followed a single path. Today, however, a hundred married couples will follow a hundred different paths.

Freedom is great, no doubt about it. But it brings its own complications. Perhaps we could say that people strong enough to handle those complications can exercise their freedom wisely, while the rest can't.

Was I, as Riko, properly exercising my freedom in my marriage to Naa-chan? I couldn't help but ask myself that question as I, a Heian lady-in-waiting, watched the union of Lord Narihira and my princess unfold.

What I found most interesting was the princess's ability to express her feelings freely, despite her subordinate role and strictly regulated life. A freedom born from a lack of freedom. I felt this strongly as I watched her in the days that followed.

And how did my marriage compare? Had I asserted my own likes and dislikes with Naa-chan – had I opened up even once as the princess was now doing? Such were the questions foremost in my mind during those months that I spent with the princess.

'My *omake* hasn't started,' the princess said. It was early November, the 'month of frost'.

Omake, or bonus, was what she laughingly called her period. Now that she was spending nights with her husband, the princess had doubtless been instructed about pregnancy by one of her older ladies-in-waiting. So she must have known what missing a period might signify.

'Are you nauseous – do you feel like vomiting?' I asked her.

'Not really,' she said. She seemed slightly dazed. Her long black hair framed her face beautifully, like a princess in a picture scroll.

I was torn – I was happy that she had conceived a child with her beloved Narihira so quickly, yet I also felt pity for a girl about to bear a child at the tender age of fifteen, and I guess it showed.

'It's nothing to fret about,' the princess said, studying my face. As someone who would be giving birth for the first time she must have been worried about herself, yet she was the one reassuring me, a mere lady-in-waiting.

The princess seemed far more mature now than she had been a year earlier, when her relationship with Lord Narihira had begun. Then I had been the one protecting her and looking after her needs, but now she had shot ahead, leaving me behind. I couldn't have been happier.

I prayed that the princess was indeed pregnant, and that she would bear her baby safely when the time came, even as I weighed the huge difference between childbirth then and now, in our age of modern medicine.

There were no maternity specialists, no doctors or midwives, in the Heian period. Who, then, took up that task? We, her ladies-in-waiting.

As the birth approached, we worked as a group. Those who were older and more experienced helped the mother. Others focused on reciting prayers and incantations. All of us were dressed in white, and everything in the room – screens and curtains, cushions and bedding – was white as well. In other words, it was an aristocratic version of the age-old Japanese parturition hut.

White purified the 'pollution' of childbirth. Without doctors, many women lost their lives at that time, as did many babies. Thus, while we today might regard the offering of prayers as mere consolation, it was a crucial part of the process for Heian people.

It was afternoon when the princess began to show signs of labour.

'I think it's started,' she murmured. I loved this side of the princess, her capacity to stay calm in even the most trying circumstances. Had she lived in today's society, I am sure she would have been an outstanding employee, for she had the personality to endear herself to fellow colleagues and the tact to get along with her bosses. If we had worked in the same office, it would have been she, not me, who came out on top.

The labour dragged on. It had grown dark, and there were long intervals between contractions, during which the princess nibbled on some small dumplings.

'They're delicious,' she would say one moment; then cry out in pain the next. Finally, the intervals began to grow shorter.

Two ladies-in-waiting were supporting her shoulders. The princess would give birth in a seated position.

The birth went smoothly. I thought back on my own experience. How the midwife had encouraged me as I lay there on the birthing table. How she had first instructed me not to push. Then, at the end, to push as hard as I could.

I could see no real difference between that midwife and these ladies-in-waiting. The latter's diction may have been more elegant, but their instructions were basically the same: 'Don't push yet,' 'Push now,' 'Push from your diaphragm,' all delivered at the appropriate moments.

Women have been delivering babies like this forever, I marvelled. That realization really struck home. Sitting birth, crawling birth – whatever form it might take, childbirth and the tremendous effort it required had been the province of women since humans began walking on two legs.

The baby was born without complications. The princess's ladies-in-waiting collected the placenta and the membrane that had covered the baby – the afterbirth, in other words – and placed them in a plain clay bowl set aside for that purpose. The person in charge of the prayers then took the bowl away to bury

it somewhere. In the meantime, the infant was given his first bath
and wrapped in a white cloth.

'It's a boy,' said the woman who had been holding the princess's right shoulder.

'Wonderful,' said the princess, and closed her eyes. Actually,
there was no preference for boys among the aristocracy – that
the baby was healthy was all that mattered. A boy could rise to
become a government official, while a girl might marry a man of
higher rank than her family. In both cases, the onus was on the
child to elevate the status of their family.

The princess's son was left beside her for only a few minutes. Soon
he was taken away by one of her ladies, who was to serve as wet
nurse and keep him clean. The princess lay on her side in a daze,
watching her as she bustled about. When, eventually, the wet
nurse left, the princess closed her eyes a second time.

'You must be very tired, my lady,' I said. She gave a faint nod.
Then her eyes opened again.

'He's so sweet,' she whispered. Her voice was hoarse, but her
eyes were shining. How lovely, Narihira would have thought, had
he seen her in that moment.

The princess's gaze kept wandering to the screen behind
which the wet nurse had disappeared with the baby.

The princess's spirits were a little low after the birth.

Although her health returned immediately, her face was wan
and lifeless. My concern for her made me think back, in as much
detail as I could, on my own experience with childbirth and the
days that followed. I remembered how busy I had been. And how
sleep-deprived.

Toji had cried such a lot. When he needed changing, when he

wanted to be fed, and sometimes for no apparent reason at all. I'd done it all, nurse him, change his diapers, cuddle him and much more, more in fact than was really necessary. Nor was this only a daytime matter. Like all new babies, Toji woke at regular intervals throughout the night, so I'd had to repeat the process over and over again, nursing him, changing his diapers and cuddling him . . .

I know I am repeating myself, but it was such hard work, it's impossible to stress it too much. I'd had to use the intervals during the day to do the housework, attend to my own recovery from childbirth, write a 'baby diary' to show to the doctor, talk to Naa-chan and look after our relationships with our neighbours . . . That's right. I'm sure I looked as wan and lifeless then as the princess did now. Accumulated exhaustion was the culprit.

Yet the princess's experience was quite different from mine. Her baby was being cared for by her ladies-in-waiting. They would bring him to her when he was in a good mood, but otherwise she never fed or looked after her own child. When the baby was brought to her, the princess would hold him in her arms and lovingly rub her cheek against his. Yet all too soon, one of her ladies was sure to come and sweep him away as the princess looked on sadly.

It took a full six months for the princess to fully recover that innocent, lively personality we all knew so well, but even then, on occasion, the downhearted expression she had after childbirth would return. I had an idea where that look might have come from. Might it simply have been that she was yearning to spend more time with her child?

I am perpetually amazed at the role of human desire in our lives, how intrinsic it is to our basic selves. Right after Toji's birth, when

I was overwhelmed by so many things, I would have leaped at the chance to have help, but now that my baby is a toddler I thank my lucky stars that there are no servants around.

Toji loves me more than anyone in the world. Naa-chan may be fun to play with, and my parents may ply him with gifts, but in the end I'm the one he counts on.

Sometimes I find myself musing that, actually, it's all about power. The sense of authority that helps you secure the attention of an infant. When I watch Naa-chan pour out his love on his son, I am struck by the way children love their guardians – and how overjoyed Naa-chan must be to reciprocate that trust. Nevertheless, however much Toji trusts his father, he will always place the most trust in she who spends the most time with him – in other words, yours truly.

Raising children is hard; yet in return one gains so much. Can there be any greater pleasure in the world than that which comes from monopolizing the love of a child? For Toji, I am irreplaceable. This period of his life may last only a few years, but the fulfilment I get from it is immeasurable. Perhaps it resembles a dictator's pleasure when he exercises absolute power, for I too hold absolute sway over Toji.

Observed from the vantage point of a Heian lady-in-waiting, I must confess secret misgivings about this aspect of my modern self. Watch out! I want to say. My selfless love for Toji could morph into something quite different, which could bring down misfortune on both of us.

The princess played a much more distanced role in the raising of her child. Milk was provided by the wet nurse; and the baby's playmate was the wet nurse's child. In such circumstances, it was entirely natural that the baby would feel closest to the wet nurse and the other infant sharing her breast.

I realized that the aristocratic system of raising children might have its strong points. Yet, as her lady-in-waiting, I worried about the gloom that could descend on the princess when access to her own child was so restricted. I wondered if the princess felt the same desire as I had to exercise control over her baby. To create a sweet, honeyed world for just the two of them, a place where an intense bond between caregiver and cared-for could develop.

I started out talking about the role desire plays in our lives, right? In an aristocratic society where the mothers who suffered through childbirth and their children were customarily kept separate – indeed, where most women considered this separation only natural – the princess's deep, unrestrained desire for control set her apart from the rest and made her moody. How sharp her mind was! And how I worried about that cleverness, and what fate might hold in store for her.

These years pass by so fast! Only yesterday, it seems, Toji was just beginning to walk, and now he loves running about. And he understands many words too. He doesn't know how to manipulate them yet, but judging from the way he listens to what his parents say to him, he seems to be picking up a lot (though this could be a doting mother talking).

Naa-chan saves the photos we have taken of Toji on his computer. When I look at how carefully he has arranged them, with mine in one file and his in another, I get a sense of what he must be like in the office.

As in: wow, I bet he's really good at what he does.

I don't equate computer proficiency with job performance, yet when I watch him deftly downloading to his computer the photos I've taken on my smartphone while studiously avoiding the personal information I have stored there, and when I realize how easy it is to discuss with him which photos we want to keep, I can well imagine how skilled he must be in managing human relationships.

In that context, Naa-chan is really something. He can be warm and attentive, but when the time comes to make a decision, he doesn't hesitate. I find it somewhat ironic that I can gain such a basic insight into Naa-chan's character from something as simple as watching him arrange our photos of Toji. I had once burned with love for Naa-chan, yet it is only now, when going through photographs, that I can see his finer qualities with a fresh clarity. I can even see now that these qualities are what has made him so attractive to women.

I'm beginning to compare Naa-chan and Lord Narihira more and more often.

I mentioned that there's a resemblance between the two men, and certainly there is a similarity in their facial features, and the way they comport themselves. Yet, after keeping an eye on the love between Narihira and the princess for a full two years, and serving Narihira up close, I reached the conclusion that my first impression had been mistaken, and that the two men aren't all that alike.

Narihira is a much simpler man than Naa-chan. If he finds a lady attractive, he sends her a poem, visits her house and sleeps with her. Even if he isn't especially attracted, he will still compose a poem if the lady so desires, visit her house and sleep with her.

Beyond his love affairs, however, he is known at the palace for being a hard and conscientious worker. Narihira has imperial blood running in his veins, but that has not made his rise any easier. On the contrary, his royal connections complicate his position at the palace and work against his career. Yet that does not discourage him, not in the least.

Men are known to hide their emotions from women and children, but in fact the men of Heian were quick to cry, and their feelings were often an open book. Thus, if the political environment turns against him, even Narihira will vent his displeasure openly. Overall, though, Narihira keeps his cool. Like tall grass in a meadow, he shifts with the breezes, never showing sarcasm, anger or self-pity and following the most natural course of action, whatever the circumstances.

'He strikes me as a man free of desire,' I say to Mr Takaoka.

We are sitting on the bench beside the river, eating a simple bento while Toji plays at our feet. Toji has become very attached to Mr Takaoka – more attached, perhaps, than to his own father. He is in seventh heaven when the three of us picnic together. I feel more relaxed with Mr Takaoka than with than Naa-chan, which may have something to do with it too.

'But he was a real playboy, right?' Mr Takaoka laughs. 'That doesn't sound much like a man free of desire.'

'Maybe so, but there is something terribly straightforward about him,' I reply.

Mr Takaoka looks doubtful. 'Perhaps that's because he's a man who never wanted for anything,' he said.

'You're pretty hard on Narihira, aren't you, Mr Takaoka,' I reply.

He shrugs. 'That may be so,' he answers. 'Men normally don't like to see a man so popular with women – it offends us.'

Whatever he might say, I can't help thinking now that it's Mr Takaoka and Narihira, not Naa-chan and Narihira, who are actually quite alike. True, there's no similarity in their voices or their faces, but both of them project an air of cool detachment. A lot more than Naa-chan does, that's for sure.

'If he's without desire, then why did he make love to so many women?' Mr Takaoka asks.

'Because women desired him.'

'Seriously?'

'Maybe he's like a *yorimashi*, you know, one of those dolls that shamans and spirit mediums used to summon the gods.'

'*Yorimashi*,' Mr Takaoka echoes. He sounds surprised. 'Spirit mediums, huh?' he asks.

'Yes. In his case, though, it wasn't a god that was summoned, but women's love.'

'An amazing idea. Nevertheless, I wouldn't want to be a *yorimashi* – that could turn out to be a real headache.'

What Mr Takaoka says certainly rings true. Narihira is a man beloved by many women, yet it doesn't seem to be making him particularly happy. Perhaps that helps explain why I sense something dark lurking beneath Narihira's bright, impressive surface.

Lord Narihira and the princess's son was really thriving. This New Year's he turned six, five by today's count.

Narihira and the princess had been getting along well, but recently his visits had become more irregular. No question. Before, he had graced us with his presence almost every day, seldom returning to his mansion in Ashiya.

In fact, there were only two kinds of occasions when Lord Narihira returned to his home: first, when directional taboos, imposed in the case of death or other forms of pollution, blocked his return to the princess's mansion; and second, when his long absence caused worry among his household staff. For the past month, however, Narihira had been acting strangely, his visits to Ashiya more frequent. Perhaps I could say that he had itchy feet. Or that his mind seemed to be elsewhere.

'He's been here almost all the time, so it stands to reason,' offered one of the older ladies-in-waiting, but the princess's sad face told a different story. Her sighs had become more and more frequent.

'Shall I bring your son to you?' I suggest. Her face brightened a little. Her love for her baby never falters.

It doesn't take long to discover why Lord Narihira is spending less and less time in the princess's house.

Narihira has fallen in love.

The ladies who look after the princess are gossipy sorts, so rumours quickly begin to circulate.

'It appears the woman he's seeing lives in Gojo.'

'Is she a great beauty?'

'She must be, since he goes to such lengths to see her.'

Her ladies take care to hide the gossip from the princess, but they love scandal, so it continues unabated. It appears that there is indeed a very high-ranking princess whose mansion is in the Gojo area.

'She may be a Fujiwara,' remarks one of the senior ladies-in-waiting.

I'm beside myself with worry, for I remember that Narihira's legend, handed down through the centuries and recorded in *The Tales of Ise*, included an affair with a Fujiwara princess. That woman's name was Fujiwara no Takaiko, later the consort of Emperor Seiwa, who bore him a son.

Yes, I had read about the love between Lord Narihira and Princess Takaiko in the *Tales*. Chapter five describes how Narihira had secretly visited the princess by slipping through a hole in the fence that surrounded her mansion. The following chapter, the 'Akutagawa' episode, portrays their thwarted elopement. The two ran away, with her elder brothers in hot pursuit. The brothers managed to steal her back, which is why we see Narihira in

Chapter four (the story jumps around), after her entry into court, travelling to the home she no longer occupied to lament his loss, weeping throughout the night.

How completely the Narihira of *The Tales of Ise* was captivated by this torrid affair. Here was a courtier who enjoyed exchanging witty poems with women, whose talent for romantic courtship seemed to know no bounds, suddenly transformed by love into someone too besotted to compose a single poem, whose only concern was finding ways to continue his visits.

I guess we could say that he had gone mad. The roof had collapsed on this once cool and resourceful man, now buffeted by the gales of love. Or perhaps it is more accurate to say that Narihira himself had been transformed, reshaped by this experience. That was how life-altering Narihira's love for Takaiko must have been.

What will my princess do if she discovers Lord Narihira's new and burning passion? The prospect worries me no end. For I know how different she is from other women of her era.

Women's emotional attachments to their husbands and lovers today are somewhat different from Heian times, when aristocratic men were permitted numerous lovers. Back then, women were far more pragmatic and down to earth, whereas today those feelings are couched in terms that derive from Western ideas of romantic love, which entered Japan during the late nineteenth and early twentieth centuries.

Certainly, Riko was taken aback by much of what she witnessed within her community of ladies-in-waiting. Many of the women were wild and uninhibited. Some were having multiple affairs. Some preferred one-night stands. Some were exchanging amorous missives with men not their husbands. Such ladies-in-waiting seemed to be everywhere.

While those long-serving women who made up the princess's permanent retinue were, by and large, prudent and proper, there were other women, the 'migrating birds', who came and went depending on the season, and many of these women dared to sleep with whomever they fancied.

Migrating birds weren't attached to any particular estate; rather, they moved to wherever their labour was needed, working on fixed contracts. They shared with each other details of conditions in the different aristocratic houses – which courtiers were the most handsome, who seemed most likely to ascend to the top, which houses were on the brink of penury. It was through one of these migrating birds that the rumour of Lord Narihira's visits to the Gojo princess began to circulate.

At around this point in the story, my relationship to my dream world shifts. Until now, dreams had served as a kind of retreat, a diversion from the trials of motherhood and my concerns about Toji. These days, however, it is actually a relief to leave Heian and my worries about the princess to return to being a wife and mother. Now it is my life in the present that provides me with emotional sustenance.

My concern for the princess knew no bounds. At the same time, I was being tossed in every direction by the unfathomable nature of the man, Narihira. The longer I knew him, the stronger my conviction that, contrary to my first impression, he and Naa-chan were extremely different. I was growing to like Naa-chan more and more.

'You've changed, Riko,' he said to me one day.

'Changed?'

'Yes, you're sweeter now.'

'So, I wasn't sweet before?'

'Yeah, to tell the truth, you were a little scary.'

'What do you mean, scary?' I said with a laugh. How could I be scary?

'As if your eyes were always following me,' he went on.

'Following you.'

'Yes. Your love was almost too much.'

'I still love you,' I said lightly.

'Yes, but now you have Toji too. He's the important one.'

'Who's more important, my husband or my son – is that what you're asking? I've never given that a thought. Why would I – what meaning could a question like that possibly have?'

'No meaning at all. Toji's important to me, too. Just as much as to you.'

'So then, what made me so scary?'

My love for him had been stressful, Naa-chan went on to say. Its intensity made him happy, but it also wore him down.

'You overrated me. I'm not the great man you thought I was,' he wrapped up.

Could that be true? I whispered in my heart. Maybe it was. Naa-chan was always surrounded by women, but he lacked Narihira's depth. If Narihira was the ocean, perhaps Naa-chan was a lake. Both were repositories of water, but the scale was vastly different, whether the weather was calm or stormy.

'Women always scare me a little,' he said as if reading my mind.

'Who has scared you the most?' I asked. He didn't reply. Toji had started to fuss, so he picked up the baby and began walking around the room.

I was sweeter now, Naa-chan had said. Did that mean I had stopped staring at him? Had my love for him faded? Is that why I had become more accepting of who he was?

If that were true, what were my true feelings about him back in the days when my passion was riding high? Were they best described by a word like love, or were they closer to something like hate?

These were the thoughts that ran through my mind as I sat there, vaguely watching Naa-chan dandling the baby.

'Do you think the princess is holding a grudge against Lord Narihira?' the wet nurse said to me one day. She was the newest of the women serving in our house, having arrived just before the baby's birth. She had been a lady-in-waiting at a house near Sanjo, had fallen in love with a man there and had a child with him, but his affections had cooled, so she had picked up and moved to our house as a wet nurse.

'It really hurts when a man dumps you,' she said.

'For sure, but then our princess has got to get out there and snag a new man to replace him,' burst out the youngest of the group. She had recently struck up a lively correspondence with a man from a house not far from ours. Watching the princess had taught her how to add perfume and somewhat witty poems to her missives, which was apparently delighting him no end.

'Don't be silly,' the wet nurse lectured her. 'Our princess has borne Lord Narihira a child. She's no longer in a position to find another man.'

'I wonder about that,' the girl shot back undeterred. 'A woman who's got it doesn't lose it, however many children she has.'

The wet nurse looked in my direction and sighed.

'You're young,' she said when the girl was out of earshot, 'but I can see you're quick to learn, so I can say this. It's terribly painful when you truly love a man and then you drift away from each other. Women who are happy with a man's love, however brief, who treat it like foam on the water, don't understand this. The princess feels things deeply. It's no wonder she gets so sad when Lord Narihira becomes distant.'

I took the wet nurse's words to heart. She was right. The princess's unswerving love for Narihira was that of a naive young girl. She had borne a child, yet her heart remained innocent. At the same time, though, she could discern what was going on around her like an experienced older woman. She was fully aware that Lord Narihira was seeing someone else, I had no doubt.

The wet nurse, like me, must have realized how much that pained her.

'Have you ever been jealous?' I ask Mr Takaoka as we sit there on the bench beside the river. He almost gags on his can of coffee.

'Where did that question come from?' he asks, as Toji clambers up his leg. Toji is one and a half, and full of mischief. These days he's fixated on climbing – he climbs on our sofa, on chairs meant for adults, on the kitchen table, in short on anything that happens to be around. I can't take my eyes off him for a minute. He especially loves climbing on people: if Naa-chan is sitting on the living-room floor relaxing, Toji's eagle eye is sure to spot him. Then, like a baby animal, he runs to latch on to any part of his father's body he can – his arm, his back, his side – and starts scrambling up.

'Not sure you can make it to my knee – the road is pretty steep,' Mr Takaoka says. He flips his toe and Toji loses his hold, sliding down on to the ground beside the bench. The soil is soft, though, so he doesn't hurt himself. Toji laughs merrily and begins another ascent up Mr Takaoka's leg.

'Of course, I've been jealous,' he says.

'Really?'

Why does his answer surprise me? I guess I was convinced he was a stranger to the 'lower' emotions like jealousy.

'Who was she?'

'My, oh my,' he teases. 'You're a curious one, aren't you?'

'It's just that . . .' Actually, I'm burning to know who it was, and when, and where.

'It was a hopeless love from the start,' he says offhandedly.

A hopeless love.

Might it be somehow connected to the story he had told me about the emperor's beloved Lady Kusuko, that tale from 'long, long ago'? Or was it a love that the flesh-and-blood Takaoka experienced in this present, 'real' world of ours?

'Yes, I was in love,' Mr Takaoka begins in what is clearly an account of events from his own youth.

The woman might have been his father's mistress.

His father was popular with women at a time when it was not at all strange for a man of means, married or not, to have a mistress or two on the side, so it was likely that Mr Takaoka's object of desire was indeed attached to his father. Nevertheless, to quote Mr Takaoka, 'I never knew, right to the end.'

But I'm getting ahead of myself.

Let's start when Mr Takaoka first met the lady in question. He was a schoolboy at the time. One Sunday afternoon, his father announced that he would take his son to the Ginza.

'I'd love to go to Ginza too,' his mother put in, but his father shook his head no.

'I have to meet a difficult business associate. This guy loves kids, right? He doesn't have a family of his own, though, so if I bring my wife along too, he might think I was flaunting mine in his face.'

For a moment, his mother looked as if she wanted to say something, but she didn't argue.

Ginza was lively that day. This was the third time Mr Takaoka had been. The first time was to buy a backpack for school at a shop that sold suitcases. On the way home, his father had taken him to a department store restaurant where he had eaten grilled eel (he hadn't been able to finish, so his father had eaten the rest for him). The second time was when he accompanied his mother and grandmother to see Kabuki (he fell asleep halfway through the performance and was scolded by his grandmother).

What kind of man was his father's 'business associate'? A portly gentleman with a walking stick and derby hat? Or a skinny, shrewd operator with a sly face? Or a beetle-browed fellow who resembled some movie star? Those were the sorts of characters that the excited Takaoka had pictured while waiting at the coffee shop. Instead, lo and behold, it was no business associate – not a man at all but a woman!

'This is Fujiwara-san,' his father said, showing no discomfort.

'Please call me Kusuko,' the woman said with a bewitching smile. In that instant, Mr Takaoka fell in love. Her smile was at once gorgeous and graceful, beckoning him into an unfamiliar world.

'Don't tell your mother,' his father had told him afterwards, but that was unnecessary – Mr Takaoka would never have breathed a word to his mother about 'Kusuko-san'.

Kusuko and Takaoka had vanilla ice cream. His father had jet-black coffee. Kusuko returned home before it got dark.

'So how did you like Ginza?' his father asked in a conspiratorial tone as they rode a taxi home.

'There are all kinds of women in Ginza, aren't there?'

'All kinds of women?' His father laughed.

'Yes. There were women the first time, in the restaurant where we ate grilled eel, and the next time too, at the Kabuki, and now this time with Kusuko. And they're all so different.'

'And who did you like the most?' his father asked.

Mr Takaoka didn't reply. In fact, he said nothing at all the rest of the way home. Beside him, his father sat gazing out of the taxi window.

Mr Takaoka had a hard time believing that his father and Kusuko were anything as commonplace as ordinary lovers.

After that first meeting, Kusuko often suggested that he come along on their outings. If they were really lovers, wouldn't she have preferred to be alone with his father?

'Do you and Kusuko ever meet at night?' he asked his father one day in the taxi on their way home.

'No, never,' his father replied. 'She's married, you know.'

Mr Takaoka didn't find that at all surprising. Kusuko was older than his father. Unlike his mother, who told him repeatedly never to ask how old a woman was, Kusuko spoke openly about that and other things as well. She was the one who brought up her age, and that she had lived for several years in China, where she had learned to prepare and prescribe traditional herbal medicines, and that she and her husband didn't get along.

'Do you love my father?' he asked her point-blank one day.

'Sure.'

'More than anyone in the world?'

'No, the person I love the most is myself,' she said, just as directly. Mr Takaoka was greatly relieved. For he and his father were rivals in love.

'Then who is second?'

'A great many people.'

'How many?'

'More than I can count on my fingers,' Kusuko said, flashing that inimitable smile.

The period when Mr Takaoka accompanied his father to Ginza to see Kusuko lasted less than a year. One day, the visits ceased. It hurt to imagine that his father might be seeing Kusuko secretly. Mr Takaoka was just a schoolboy, but he was aware that jealousy was behind the pain he was feeling.

Mr Takaoka's father died before he could ascertain if those secret meetings were real or a product of his imagination. A number of years passed by. His family had fallen on hard times, and he still had no inkling where Kusuko might be. Yet he thought back on their time together during breaks while he worked delivering newspapers and doing odd jobs for the small shops on the shopping arcade. His father may have been dead, but the young man's jealousy lived on.

Nor was that jealousy directed solely at his father. No, one could venture to say that it was aimed at everything and everyone. Mr Takaoka couldn't stand it that she was living in a place he had never seen. Why wasn't she there with him now? Why weren't they breathing the same air? Why wasn't she sharing her feelings that moment?

Kusuko should belong to him – he had felt that from the outset. She's mine, he thought, just as I am hers. He was barely in his teens, yet he was absolutely certain.

Apparently, Mr Takaoka and Kusuko were never to meet face to face again. No one ever spoke her name, nor did rumours of her ever reach him on the wind.

'Have you looked her up on the internet?' I asked, trying to be practical. He shrugged and gave a faint smile.

'At first I wanted to avoid doing anything that unromantic, but in the end I gave in and checked anyway.'

'You checked.'

'Yes. I didn't have a cellphone, but on one of my bike trips I stayed at an internet cafe in – where was it? Hakata, I think – so I looked her up while I was there.'

Toji sneezed. I glanced at my watch – it was late afternoon. The air had grown cold, and the tall grass was rustling in the breeze.

'Did you find her?'

'Nothing definitive. My guess is she's no longer of this world.'

'Do you mean she's dead?'

'Maybe yes, maybe no, but she's no longer here in any case.'

'What does that mean?'

Mr Takaoka didn't answer. You should be heading home, he mumbled, sweeping Toji up in his arms.

I didn't dare ask him about the possible connection between Kusuko and the story from 'long, long ago' that Takada had told me back in Edo, whose heroine had the same name. As someone whose own life involved moving back and forth between dream and reality, I knew how hard it was to explain such matters succinctly. Toji had closed his eyes and was nestled in Mr Takaoka's arms.

Several months after Lord Narihira's visits declined so markedly, we had confirmation that he was spending his time with a Fujiwara princess in her mansion at Gojo.

He had grown haggard. His cheeks were sunken, his hair had lost its lustre, and his lips were always dry. His eyes glittered in a way I found quite frightening. Although he was in good shape from years of martial arts training, so that whatever he wore became him, he looked for all the world like a ruined man, perhaps because his eyes were always turned to the ground, perhaps because his whole body was slack, as if his mind had gone blank.

The princess looked serene. I found that terrifying too.

She continued to tend to Narihira's needs as if nothing had changed. We had to accept that he was now seeing the Gojo princess. Yet it appeared that he was not being adequately looked after by the people there. Thus, he came back every few days to be taken care of by my princess. As if it were entirely natural, she made sure he was turned out properly, matching the colours of his clothes and infusing them with incense. And although she knew full well that he was seeing someone else, she saw him off in the morning as she always had, without a hint of displeasure.

So far was she from showing her disappointment, knowing he would be going directly to the palace after a night spent at Gojo, she would even pack the clothes for his official duties and entrust them to one of his attendants.

Despite her outward serenity, there was nothing at all calm about her inner feelings. Her turmoil surfaced when she failed to place the bamboo hood over the incense burner while infusing his clothing, almost setting the fabric on fire, or when her knee landed squarely on her long, glossy hair so that she almost pitched forward on her face. These uncharacteristic mistakes left me thoroughly shaken.

The princess did not look well. And yet she grew more and more beautiful with each day. Sparkling eyes, pink cheeks, lips gently parted as if about to pose a question.

What on earth was taking place within her heart?

The princess's baby, the princeling, was growing hand over fist. He had already surpassed my real-world baby, Toji, in age. He was about to turn six, though two years had not yet passed since Toji's birth.

The princess spent more time with her son now that Narihira's affections had moved elsewhere.

The day began early back in Heian. The sun was barely up when courtiers headed off to the palace. If it started early, though, it ended early too. Almost everyone was home by one in the afternoon, the only exceptions being those on night duty.

Formerly, Lord Narihira had spent his afternoons at home talking to the princess, writing and, on occasion, playing with their son. Now, however, he came home only to change his clothes before darting off like a dragonfly for Gojo.

During those brief moments when he was home, the princess would prepare a fresh set of clothes for the next day, then follow him with her eyes as he rode away. As long as he was there she would perk up like a flower placed in water, but as soon as he was out of sight she would droop, a picture of total dejection. How pitiful she looked then.

She might collapse face down on the floor, as if her beautiful clothes, which normally seemed weightless on her shoulders, were bearing down on her with many times the force of gravity, or the smile on her face might give way to an expression of sheer emptiness. The nursemaid and I would try to comfort the princess by bringing her son to her in those moments.

The princeling was an extremely bright child. By now he could recognize many characters, and write a few himself in a well-formed hand. Today Lord Narihira is celebrated as one of Japan's greatest poets, so perhaps it was only natural that his son would have inherited much of his father's skill, but in truth the boy's precocious development was spurred by the long hours his mother spent with him, reciting poems together, helping him practise the cursive syllables in which they were written and drawing pictures.

The princess was a devotee of poetry and stories, a literary connoisseur of her time. While others might choose to pass the hours chatting or nibbling on sweets, she preferred to while away her days immersed in the writings of her ancestors, reading each old poem and tale over and over. This was one of the many reasons why she and Lord Narihira had enjoyed each other's company so much, which meant that she was not just sad when their time together shrank – she was bored.

The hours she spent with her son were therefore her greatest diversion.

As I mentioned, the day started early and was close to being over by the time it grew dark. The idea of eating a meal after sundown, as we do today, was inconceivable: after all, true lamps didn't exist yet. Night-time in Edo's Yoshiwara had also been quite dark. There, though, lamps were common: they bathed the Quarter in a soft light, despite the surrounding black. But Heian's nights were darkness itself. True, lanterns were set out here and there, but the oil they used must have been inferior to that used in Yoshiwara, for the light they produced was feeble.

The people of Heian therefore placed great value on sunlight. The princess, for example, loved to play with her son on the sun-lit veranda, under the eaves. Their favourite games were shell-matching and kanji-building.

Chinese characters, or kanji, are composed of many 'radicals', pieces joined together in various combinations to form characters. In this game, a number of those radicals were written on cards, and the challenge involved calculating how many characters could be constructed from them. Radicals meaning water, hand and path, which commonly occupy the left side of a character, for example, might be paired with other radicals commonly used on the right side to form a number of characters. Once the cards were laid out, players would rush to construct as many kanji as they could.

While the princess gracefully chose her cards with sleeves elegantly rippling in the breeze, her son scampered about rapidly putting his cards together, his small hands a blur.

'You're too fast for me,' the princess said. That fed his pride and encouraged him to move with even more speed, so that he would begin roughly knocking his cards about on the floor with his hands and feet.

'No, no,' cautioned the nursemaid. 'You've got to be more careful.' But the boy ignored her. After all, his mother the princess was right there, looking on with an indulgent smile.

The princeling probably should have been disciplined at such moments, but all of us – the nursemaid, the ladies-in-waiting, myself as well – refrained from commenting on his rudeness, for we were keenly aware that the calm and happy face the princess had shown when Narihira was living with us now surfaced only when she was playing with her son. So we sat by as she lovingly watched her child run amok.

'All right, then let's play shell-matching instead,' the princess said. The boy rushed off to fetch the old bucket filled with the clam shells used for that game.

'Don't race around like that,' said the nursemaid, running after him. Our residence was a harmonious place those days, except for Narihira's absence. The other women and I all inwardly sighed, praying that such peaceful moments could last, yet fearing that they might prove fleeting.

*

'How did Narihira love his women?' Mr Takaoka asked.

'In what sense?' I replied, shocked at the directness of his question.

'I'm talking about sex, whether it was different then.'

It was certainly a topic guaranteed to pique one's curiosity. We had a good, albeit somewhat distorted, idea of sex during the Edo period, thanks to the ukiyo-e prints and stories passed down to us from that time – augmented in my case by my dream identity as an *oiran* who slept with her customers. Yet the only literary accounts of sex during Heian were vague, phrased in roundabout, euphemistic terms.

'I guess what I mean,' Mr Takaoka went on, 'is whether Narihira sexually satisfied your princess.'

I rolled my eyes. For heaven's sake, how could I answer a question like that?

'I guess so.'

'Was Narihira a particularly lusty fellow?'

'About average, I would think.'

'So then how should we look at his obsession with the Gojo woman?'

'I wonder about that myself.'

I felt like a gossip doing it, but I had told Mr Takaoka how Narihira had shifted his affections from my princess to the woman at Gojo. I knew that Heian society accepted Narihira's behaviour, but I wanted to make it clear just how much the princess wilted when he was off with the other lady, a matter that didn't seem to concern Narihira at all. Yet how could I, a mere lady-in-waiting, speak against the great lord? On top of that, I sensed that, when I was in Heian, my mental and emotional make-up was slightly different. I wanted Narihira to be totally devoted to the princess, but at the same time I wanted him to be the great lover embraced by women wherever he went. These conflicting emotions marked my days in Heian.

'It's like he's some kind of rock star,' I told Mr Takaoka, trying to explain why my Heian self admired him.

'Rock star,' he echoed.

'Yes. If not that, then the alpha male in the herd, with dozens of females at his beck and call.'

'Narihira as alpha male?'

'Elevating such a figure,' I said, 'makes a certain sort of biological sense, don't you think?'

'Is that what the world of Heian is really like?'

'Yes, I think so. There's more to it than that, though, all the same . . .'

I broke off there. I wanted to explain that, in Heian, my body and its surroundings felt like they were fused together, but I didn't have the words.

It was a powerful feeling. There I was, a lady-in-waiting, living in a world of impenetrable darkness, exposed to extremes of heat and cold and subsisting on, by modern standards, a most limited diet. It was natural, then, that I would come to see my body not merely as a vehicle to carry me through my daily tasks but rather as directly linked to my spirit. My mind and body were a single entity.

I was continually amazed at how fresh and alive everything felt: the soles of my feet on the wooden corridor, my fingers against my simple silk kimono, the voices of the insects amid the silence, the smell of a wild animal foraging for food in the kitchen, the rising sun filtered through the latticed shutters.

I often think back to when Naa-chan and I first slept together. I was still in high school. Barely had he touched me when I was overcome by an intense joy at being alive. When he became more forceful, the feeling grew stronger, and when he turned gentle again, it increased further.

Yet now I believe the ecstasy the princess experienced on her first night with Narihira was even more powerful.

I've already described the depths of the darkness of the Heian world, but it struck me that there were corresponding depths of joy and sadness, and of anger.

'Do you like your body?' I asked Mr Takaoka, searching his face, his arms, his torso with my eyes.

One would not call him handsome. Nor was he particularly well proportioned. Nevertheless, I loved how his body looked – it made me feel at home, though in a very different way from my feelings for Naa-chan.

'Sure, I like my body,' Mr Takaoka said without hesitation.

'How long have you felt that way?'

'Since I met Kusuko, I think.'

Toji was beginning to fuss. I wanted to hear more about Mr Takaoka's thoughts on spiritual and physical joy, but that would have to be another time. What would I say when that time arrived? I had no idea.

On the way home, Toji fell fast asleep in his stroller, his head at a right angle to his body. I pushed the stroller as quietly as I could, but my thoughts were on Narihira and my princess the whole way.

Lord Narihira's odour had changed.

The incense that scented his clothes was the same, yet when he returned from the palace, or at the crack of dawn from one of his visits to the Gojo princess, the aroma his body emitted was unlike anything I'd known before.

At first, I thought someone at the Gojo princess's residence was suffusing his clothes with a different incense, but that seemed unlikely. My princess took pains to perfume both his clothes and hers with the same incense. I always felt that she was doing that in order to feel his presence more strongly when he wasn't there. That was how much she loved him. If her perfume had been overlaid by another, different aroma, she and we, as her ladies-in-waiting, should have known immediately.

No, the incense was the same, but the smell was different.

The fragrance of modern perfumes varies slightly depending on who is wearing them. This was probably a similar situation. It was as if Lord Narihira's body was changing now that he was spending so much time with the Gojo princess. No longer did his odour match that of my princess: their clothes might be imbued with the same scent, but as time passed the smell of his body mixed with that familiar fragrance to produce a different result.

At first, I found Lord Narihira's new odour repulsive. At some point, though, the smell that had first repelled me began to exert a secret attraction.

I found this shift baffling. After all, the new odour was the physical and emotional residue of his sleeping with the Gojo princess. It was the tangible proof of the growing rift between him and my princess. Yet I now found it terribly enticing. When Lord Narihira and the princess had emitted the same smell, I had felt none of this pull. Instead, I had regarded him as a handsome courtier, nothing more. As I might regard a beautiful flower in the field.

Now, however, I was drawn to him, as a moth to a flame.

Lord Narihira didn't exert the simple, easy attraction of a good-looking man any more. His face was gaunt, he was more on edge, and his mind often seemed to be elsewhere. In other words, he was no longer the kind of man who most women flock to. Whereas I found him irresistible.

What on earth was going on?

It was the seventh month, the 'letter-writing month', whose seventh day marked the most romantic festival of the year, Tanabata, celebrating the annual coming together of the Weaver Star and the Cowherd Star.

For unexplained reasons, several weeks had passed since Lord Narihira's last visit to Gojo – since then he had been at home.

He had changed once more. Now he appeared more relaxed, fulfilling his duties at the palace and talking pleasantly with the princess.

Rumour quickly spread among the ladies in our residence that an unseasonable autumn wind had cooled his relationship with the Gojo princess. At their get-togethers, some ladies even shared poems remarking on the strangeness of autumn winds that blow in midsummer.

I was not so sure. Lord Narihira's odour persisted, which unnerved me. It clung to him like that of a wild animal, though his visits to Gojo had ceased.

As Tanabata drew near, Lord Narihira suggested that we might hold a *kikkōten* on the day of the festival. A *kikkōten* was a party that joined poetry and song, wind and string instruments, to celebrate the meeting of the Weaver and Cowherd stars on that auspicious night. This caused great excitement in our residence. It was highly unusual that Lord Narihira would hold a party of such consequence at the princess's home.

Lord Narihira had many courtier friends. In the Heian world, this set him apart. While men serving at the palace were colleagues, competition to get ahead could turn them against each other. Much of their time together was spent at court events, but bosses and subordinates alike considered such affairs to be 'just part of the job'. When work ended, the courtiers dispersed: some returned home, while others went to visit the woman they were seeing at the moment. Almost never did they make an unscheduled detour along the way, or go out with colleagues to enjoy a bit of inconsequential fun. In short, their private and work lives were kept almost entirely separate, which meant there were few opportunities to socialize. The courtiers who gathered around Lord Narihira, however, spent a lot of time together outside the palace.

Modern men often meet after work, for a game of indoor soccer, perhaps, or Japanese chess, the main point of those activities being the drinking that follows. They also participate in male-only recreations, such as mountain climbing and camping – indeed, they have almost limitless choices, few of which involve women. For whatever reason, modern men love hanging out together. Heian men, by contrast, almost never engaged in male-only pursuits. Another way of putting it is that they seldom sought to distance themselves from women, either in their public or their private life.

As Riko, I found this surprising. In a sense, Heian men and women were on equal footing. Certainly, aristocratic men had precedence in the public sphere – they were the officials who ran the country. There were restrictions on women's private lives, too. Women did not play the ball-kicking game known as *kemari*, nor did they join the archery contests, where men on horseback shot arrows at straw targets. In such areas, roles were clearly divided by gender. Nevertheless, as I came to see, there was another side to that world, where male and female roles were valued equally. Men did the jobs that took physical strength, while women looked after any work that required manual dexterity. Both were of critical importance. All aristocrats recognized this in their daily lives. Women walked proud – their rank was recognized in the palace, and they had licence to love as they saw fit.

How could it be that, in a society where men were permitted multiple lovers, the power imbalance between men and women was less pervasive than it is in the present day?

'Maybe it's because dealing with nature, not other people, posed the greater challenge,' Mr Takaoka said on one occasion. 'Though I doubt it can be explained away so easily.'

But I'm digressing again. My point was that Lord Narihira, unlike most other men of his times, was, for whatever reason, always surrounded by a cluster of male comrades. They travelled together, shared their worries and complaints, and then drove those cares away with music, poetry and wine.

My princess was in high spirits. How long had it been since Lord Narihira had hosted an event at her family home? When the day finally came, there was a great hustle and bustle from early morning on. An altar was set up in the south-facing garden, which was bounded by a roofed mud wall: on it were placed melons and peaches, black-eyed peas and steamed abalone, while a five-colour cloth was hung on a screen as a backdrop. Mulberry branches were carted down from the mountain and arranged in a corner. Biwas, kotos and other musical instruments were offered to those able to play: we could hear snatches of music from the crack of dawn, with bursts of ensemble playing when the musicians felt inspired. Around midday, small groups of guests began arriving in ox-drawn carts, and our residence, normally so quiet, turned into a hub of activity.

Narihira's chief concern was the ice he had arranged to have brought down from the icehouse. His idea was to help his guests forget the heat by serving them white sake in ice cups together with chilled rice porridge. Though, of course, more than cold wine and porridge was served.

The norm for such parties was to provide each guest with a single tray holding several smaller dishes. In this case, however, guests received two rimmed cedar platters of delicacies placed atop a one-legged tray and accompanied by earthenware cups for liquor, hors d'oeuvres and an assortment of sweets.

Our entire household was in a fluster, though we attempted to appear as calm as possible. Was everything in place? Would our plans proceed without a hitch? Were the guests all being properly escorted on to the grounds?

Most guests showed up with faces wreathed in smiles. Some smacked their lips at the food, others were enchanted by what the musicians were playing, while a few began surreptitiously trying to charm the ladies-in-waiting, now so close at hand. Still others practised reciting whichever poem they would perform later (written on a mulberry leaf, as was the custom at Tanabata), changing a word here or there, then reciting it again.

The princeling was a ball of energy. At first he tried to sit quietly beside his father, but before long he was up to his usual mischief, plaguing the ladies until, finally, the nursemaid had to scold him. When the food was served, he had a taste of the white sake and grew even more boisterous, joining the biwa players with an impromptu song of his own. Then he ran to the princess, seated demurely next to Narihira, and threw himself on her lap.

'Try some octopus,' she said, placing a morsel on his tongue with her chopsticks.

'I don't want any,' he laughed, turning away. The princess raised her eyebrows. Then she swept him up and pressed him to her chest.

Narihira looked at the two of them as if regarding something very unusual.

The festivities were now in full swing. The musical instruments had reached a crescendo, and a lively and charming 'children's dance' was being performed by those yet to undergo their coming-of-age ceremony. Watching them, the princeling was transfixed. He jiggled his body and moved his hands in time with the music – all the guests had to smile at how cute he was.

The princess watched him with eyes full of love. At first, Narihira too seemed intently interested in his son's reaction, but after a while his gaze shifted to the dancing children.

Truth be told, Narihira didn't seem all that focused on the dance either. While we from the residence were on tenterhooks hoping the party would come off without a hitch, he alone seemed entirely detached, an island of repose within a sea of activity. What on earth could he be thinking?

I was serving sake to the guests, but I kept peeking in his direction. His face showed no emotion. Yet it was such a beautiful face that, even then, it seemed to carry some meaning. Was the party a blessing for the lord, or a curse?

The sun had passed its summit, and the shadows in the garden were beginning to lengthen. In the Heian world, everything had to be done in accordance with the rising and setting of the sun. People arose when the sun came up and went to bed when it went down, and if audible rustles and sighs came from lovers consorting beneath the moon and stars, well, that was a private world, and none of anyone's business.

It was after three in the afternoon, by modern count. The sun was still high enough in the sky, yet the party was winding down and a poignant sense of a precious moment slipping away was in the air.

*

Naa-chan had moved up a notch or two in the world. Until recently, it looked as though his company had put him out to pasture, but the faction he belonged to seemed to have made a comeback, and he had been given a promotion.

'So, are you a section chief or something like that?' I asked him.

'We don't use terms like section chief and department chief any more,' he laughed. Apparently, all the positions had been given English names.

'Sounds like a TV drama,' I said.

'You're really a child of Showa, Riko,' he laughed again, referring to the long period that ended in 1989.

Come to think of it, what would Narihira's rank be today? He was working for the government, so a high-ranking bureaucrat or politician, perhaps? Whichever it was, it would have to carry elite status. After all, his grandfather was an emperor!

'Do you want to get ahead, Naa-chan?' I asked.

'Yes, I'd like that,' he replied. 'That way I can do more for the company.'

'So you want to do more for them – is that it?'

'I do love my company, believe it or not,' he said.

That answer surprised me a little. Given how depressed he had been when he was shunted aside at work, I had assumed he had accepted defeat and retired to sulk in his tent. But he didn't care so much about winning or losing: rather, he wanted to devote himself to a cause – in his case, the company he worked for. That had been his goal from the outset. I just stared at him.

'Don't give me that look,' he said. 'OK, loving one's company may be a bit much.'

'No, it's not that,' I said, shaking my head.

I didn't mind Naa-chan expressing such an old-fashioned sentiment, not at all. On the contrary, I had always loved that naive side of him. Naa-chan may have looked like a man of the world, surrounded by women as he was, but at his core he was surprisingly strait-laced. How did that fit with his willing response to the women he attracted? Apparently, he felt no conflict.

Of course, everyone is a mass of contradictions, and I have no desire to single out Naa-chan for his. Case in point – if I were asked today whom I preferred, Naa-chan or Mr Takaoka, I would have a hard time answering.

Yes, you heard me right. I am coming to like Mr Takaoka more and more. But as I have said, that doesn't mean I want to jump into bed with him. No, I just want him near me all the time.

My heart calls out: where did you come from, Mr Takaoka? Why are you so close to me now? Where will you go next? When did Mr Takaoka become so important, I wonder?

As my affection for Mr Takaoka grows, I think back more often on the things he has said to me.

What weighs on me most are the 'two Kusukos'.

When my nights were spent living as Shungetsu, I had thrown myself into the study of the Yoshiwara pleasure quarters and related topics, yet travelling back and forth between Heian and the present was fostering no desire to read up on that period.

There were two reasons. One was because looking after Toji left me too busy to read. The other was that the Heian world was so much more natural to me than I had expected – indeed, I wondered if perhaps I had been born and raised there, in which case it was the modern world that was the dream.

If I had started to regard the present as a dream world, it may have been because I was growing tired of life with Naa-chan.

Humans, after all, are a species able to transform what they see to fit their hopes.

But let me return to the story of the two Kusukos.

It didn't take me all that long to discover the basis of the connection between Lady Kusuko and the modern woman Kusuko. It wasn't books that taught me, though, but my own eyes and ears.

The person who enlightened me was one of the guests at Narihira's Tanabata celebration. His name was Shinnyo, and he was Narihira's uncle.

Shinnyo quietly arrived when the party had passed its peak and the sun was beginning to sink in the sky. He came alone, and not by ox cart but on foot.

I was on the veranda looking after the princeling, who was throwing a tantrum triggered by a lack of sleep. Normally, it was the nursemaid who tended to him at such times, but she had her hands full helping out with the party.

The princess gazed at the two of us wistfully when we slipped away from the throng to retire to the veranda. The festivities had been going on since the morning, and she appeared a little tired herself. She and the lord looked like a pair of beautiful dolls sitting there beside each other, but I doubted they were really sharing the moment, perhaps because Narihira's detachment created a distance between them. No doubt that only added to her fatigue.

I found it hard to wrench myself away, but I knew that she couldn't leave – the party was being held in her home, after all – so I had taken her son to the veranda, where it was cooler. Although the sun was on its downward path, the heat and humidity were still oppressive.

'Hello,' I heard someone call. The voice struck me as familiar.

It was a Buddhist monk. He removed his sandals and briskly strode down the corridor to the princeling and me. It appeared that no servant had welcomed him on his arrival, for he was entirely alone.

'Who are you?' I asked, shielding the child with my robe.

'My name is Shinnyo, and I am Lord Narihira's uncle,' he replied.

Lord Narihira's uncle?

Ah, now I remembered. That's right. The man standing before me had to be Narihira's father's younger brother. The monk Shinnyo. His name before entering the priesthood had been Takaoka Shinnō.

I had first heard the name Takaoka Shinnō not long after my princess and Narihira were married. Sure, I was slightly taken aback, for it was the name of the young prince in Takada's story of 'long, long ago'. Nevertheless, I felt something fateful in the way the various names fitted together: Takaoka Shinnō in Takada's story, Takaoka the young prince (now Shinnyo the monk), and Mr Takaoka, to whom I, as Riko, was drawing ever closer.

Might there be some kind of connection between them? Could there be a link between the forbidden desire that Takaoka Shinnō felt for Lady Kusuko, as related in Takada's story, and the love Mr Takaoka had felt for the woman Kusuko? These were the thoughts now swirling in my head.

The monk Shinnyo sounded exactly like Mr Takaoka – their voices were one and the same. I shuddered. Then I took a long, hard look at the monk Shinnyo's face.

He looked back at me. Then he smiled.

'So, we could meet after all,' he said. The words, their cadence, were modern, not at all the way people in Heian Japan spoke. And while his face bore only a faint resemblance to that of Mr Takaoka, weren't their smiles identical?

'Ah, yes, we really could,' I answered.

*

Following this exchange, Shinnyo went straight to see Lord Narihira. According to the ladies-in-waiting who gathered after the party ended, the two of them hadn't met for something like ten years.

I was able to pick up a pretty detailed account of Shinnyo's life from those chatterboxes. He was a disciple of the great Buddhist sage and teacher Kūkai, with whom he had been extremely close. When Kūkai died – or passed into Nirvana, as his followers said – Shinnyo had attended the funeral.

After the funeral, Shinnyo went to holy Mt Kōya and practised austerities for some time, but five years ago, when an earthquake had decapitated the huge statue of the Buddha at Tōdaiji Temple, he had been summoned to lead the restoration, testimony to the high regard in which he was held. He truly was a revered monk, the ladies-in-waiting marvelled.

I had to cover my smile when I heard the phrase 'revered monk'. Mr Takaoka, a revered monk? Give me a break! And yet Mr Takaoka had himself undergone rigorous training on Mt Kōya, and his laid-back nonchalance could certainly qualify him for revered monk status.

It appeared that Shinnyo's sole reason for accepting the invitation to the party was that he was about to depart on a long journey. His austerities would normally have prevented him from participating in the 'mundane world', but he wanted to see his beloved nephew's face one more time before sailing away to foreign shores.

'I'm off to Tang China,' he is reported to have told Narihira.

'That's an awfully hard journey,' Narihira replied.

'Not really. In fact, I'm itching to get started,' Shinnyo said before his words were drowned out by the surging biwas. How I wished to know what they talked about after that!

'What's wrong?' the princeling asked.

'What?'

'Does something hurt?'

'Why do you ask?'

'You look like you're in pain,' he said, giving my hand a squeeze. Then he started patting it.

I certainly wasn't in any physical pain. Emotionally, though, I was tied in knots. To think that Mr Takaoka and I had been able to meet, here in Heian! I was happy. And excited. Yet I was shaking inside – it felt like my heart was being put through a wringer. An indefinable loneliness had found its way there too.

'Thank you,' I said to the boy. 'You're sweet.'

I seem to have worried him, for he kept on patting my hand.

The next time I met Mr Takaoka it was the end of summer, just as it was in the Heian of my dreams.

It was most unusual for the seasons of Heian and the modern world of Mr Takaoka, Naa-chan and me to dovetail like that. The present chases dream, and dream chases the present. Although it seems inevitable that the two will catch up with each other, that never comes to pass. For me, dream time and present time run along entirely separate tracks.

Still, it was the end of summer in both places: the cicadas of late summer were shrilling, and when darkness fell a host of other insects raised their voices in chorus.

Earlier that day, I had given in and phoned Mr Takaoka for the first time. It was a weekday afternoon. Until now we had met by chance, but I had asked for his contact details some time before and had jotted them down. This was the first time, though, that I had put them to use.

Feeling a bit like a housewife arranging a tryst with a man not her husband, I dialled the number. Though there had never been anything physical between us, I had never mentioned my meetings with Mr Takaoka to Naa-chan.

It had been a fortnight since I met the monk Shinnyo in my dream. I had wanted to contact him afterwards, more than once, in fact. But I shrank from mentioning how we had met and spoken in Heian. Perhaps my memory of that meeting was faulty. Had I misheard the line, 'So, we could meet after all'? Was my assumption mistaken, that Mr Takaoka was there inside Shinnyo, some misconception on my part? These doubts held me back.

Of course, Mr Takaoka and I had met when I was the *oiran* Shungetsu, but that hadn't unsettled me like this. Later, when we looked back on that meeting, Mr Takaoka had said, 'We overlap, but Takada is not a hundred per cent me.'

I knew exactly what he meant. Although Riko's consciousness had mixed with that of the Edo *oiran* Shungetsu, Shungetsu and I were always two separate individuals. It was never, 'Shungetsu, in other words, Riko.'

I was quite sure that Mr Takaoka was no different. For sure, the man Takada had strongly resembled Mr Takaoka, and Takada had spoken of his 'long ago' love for Lady Kusuko, yet not once had I felt that the two men were one and the same person. Both Mr Takaoka and I had been taken aback when the relationship between Takada and Shungetsu turned out to be so passionate. Could our present-day, flesh-and-blood selves fall in love like that? No, that love was exclusively theirs, not ours.

I am discovering, though, that my feelings as the Heian princess's handmaid do not fade so readily. Her secret attraction to

Narihira, her admiration for the princess, her deep affection for the princeling, the inner quivering that accompanied her meeting with the monk Shinnyo – all weigh heavily on Riko's heart.

No, this is not a matter of vaguely observing the handmaid's emotions from the outside, then making occasional forays to try and reach her deeper feelings. There is nothing furtive about this. In fact, I can no longer draw a hard line between the emotions of Riko and those of the handmaid. Although I can't know everything about her – I can't be with her all the time, however often I take her place in dreams – there is always a point at which she is me, and I her.

Almost half a month has passed since Shinnyo's visit to the princess's residence, in Heian time as in the present. As her hand-maid, my nerves have been in tatters all that while. My mind is too full of Shinnyo.

What will become of me? If it goes on like this, will I be drawn to Mr Takaoka in this world, just as my Heian self is being continually pulled in Shinnyo's direction?

Anxiety and ecstasy swirl within me. I wobble to the river, feeling so shaky that the ground beneath my feet seems turned to cloud.

Mr Takaoka is waiting for me on the bench, looking as relaxed as ever. Toji throws his upper body forward in his stroller and calls to him.

'Well, well, little Toji. What do you want?' Mr Takaoka laughs, poking the toddler's cheek. Toji squeals in excitement, like he does when tossed in the air.

'Ta!' he calls again.

'That's my name, isn't it?' Mr Takaoka asks.

'Ta!' Toji repeats. Yes, that's Mr Takaoka's name, no doubt

about it. Although he has never addressed me that way, nor his father. He's not shown much interest in words like Mama or Dada.

'He must really like you,' I remark. The tension filling my body has made my tone unintentionally harsh.

'That's great,' Mr Takaoka says, as laid-back as ever. What a horrid man, I think. When I'm floundering like this.

The instant I think him 'horrid', my level of anxiety shoots up even further. Could I be wrong in assuming that Mr Takaoka and the monk Shinnyo are somehow connected?

I am badly shaken, but what Mr Takaoka says next puts my worries to rest.

'I almost said "It's been a while" when I greeted you, but in fact we met just the other day, didn't we?'

My jaw drops and I freeze. Toji can't resist trying to stick his tiny fist inside my mouth.

'Stop that!' I choke. Yet, thanks to him, I snap out of my momentary paralysis.

'We did see each other, didn't we?' Takaoka continues. 'At your princess's residence.'

'That's true,' I reply, nodding as a child might.

'I live as Prince Takaoka. I love what Tatsuhiko Shibusawa did with my story.'

'Tatsuhiko Shibusawa,' I parrot his words, again like a child. 'Who is that?'

'I guess the simple answer is that he was an author.'

'I've never heard of him.'

'That's because you're young.'

'I'm not that young any more.'

'I guess you're right – it was over a thousand years ago. You and I go way back.'

We go way back? For a second time, I am at a loss for words. There are so many questions I want to ask Mr Takaoka:

Were you living in Heian until I met you there as a lady-in-waiting?

How did you feel when you saw me?

Are you and the monk Shinnyo one and the same person, or are you a part of Shinnyo, in the same way you were part of Takada back in Edo?

Were you really smitten by a forbidden love, as Takada described, before taking a monk's tonsure and changing your name to Shinnyo?

Does that history bear a relationship to your feelings for Kusuko?

How do you feel about me now?

'Is something wrong?' Mr Takaoka asks, peering into my face. 'You know, you seem different here than you do in Heian. I like this you better.'

I almost burst into tears. I'm overjoyed that he finds the present me more attractive; yet it hurts that I failed to impress him as the princess's handmaid.

It takes me a moment to pull myself together. 'So, are you the monk Shinnyo?' I ask when I am able to speak again.

'It appears so.'

'Since when?'

'Well, he's a Buddhist ascetic, that Shinnyo fellow,' he says, as if referring to someone else.

'That fellow?'

'Yes, there's a lot more of me in Shinnyo than there was in Takada, but then Shinnyo is so superior to Takada that I find it hard to call myself by his name. It feels like I'm putting on airs.'

But you're a superior man, too, I am tempted to say, but stop when I realize I don't actually know him that well. I encountered him as a small child and I've spent hours conversing with him on a bench by the river, but now that I think about it, our conversations have seldom touched on his personal life. He has always been there for me, listening to me talk, soothing me, helping me regain my mental equilibrium, but what have I given him in return?

'I think I became able to enter Shinnyo once he joined the monastic life,' Mr Takaoka explains. 'But I can't say for sure when he and I became one – time gets wonky when you're meditating.'

'But you *are* superior,' I insist, finally daring to say it.

'Heaven save us from superior people, right, Toji?'

Toji has clambered on to his lap and made himself at home, jiggling about as he watches the river.

'Say, who was it that Shinnyo fell in love with when he was still Prince Takaoka?' I throw the question out as dispassionately as I can.

'Yes, Takada had that one right. It was Lady Kusuko,' Mr Takaoka replies, sounding equally at ease.

'So then, are she and the Kusuko you talk about one and the same person?'

'They're the same, and different too,' Mr Takaoka says, and goes quiet.

My mind jumps back to my time in elementary school. The uninviting classrooms. Whole days spent without talking to a single classmate. Time that dragged at a snail's pace. And in the basement, the janitor's room, where Mr Takaoka and I would talk, just the two of us.

Come to think of it, he had taken our photo there on his last day as janitor. I decide to pull it out when I get home and take a look. To see the two of us as we were long ago.

*

The monk Shinnyo left in the afternoon before the party ended, but he returned to the residence several times after that to converse privately with Lord Narihira. Word quickly spread throughout the residence that Shinnyo was planning to travel to Tang China and, beyond that, to Hindustan.

'Hindustan?' the princess's son asked, wide-eyed.

'Hindustan?' the princess echoed. 'I wonder what kind of place that is?' The mention of Hindustan seemed to have a trance-like effect.

Copying and reading Buddhist texts were activities usually reserved for men, but I often witnessed my princess at her desk engaged copying sutras or reading books – some in Chinese characters from her father's collection, others in hiragana, the script used primarily by women – or else writing in her diary. Rare for a woman in those days, the princess could read Chinese, which was why she could play 'kanji-building' with her son. In fact, I often wondered if her knowledge might rival that of the great women writers – especially Lady Murasaki, author of *The Tale of Genji*, and Sei Shōnagon, who wrote *The Pillow Book* – who lived a century or so later.

Hindustan, India today, was the birthplace of Buddhism. The leading Japanese Buddhist teachers of the time were Kūkai and Saichō, who had journeyed to China to study the religion and founded the monastery enclaves on Mt Kōya and Mt Hiei on their return. No Japanese monk, however, had made it all the way to the Indian subcontinent.

The princess's knowledge of Buddhism and its history went way beyond that of most people. She knew the religion's roots were not Japanese, that it had been brought to Japan from China. And that, furthermore, it had traversed many lands to reach China from India. This is why mention of Hindustan set off such a powerful yearning in the princess. She had a faraway look in her eyes, as though gazing at a distant dreamscape.

'Do you really think that Shinnyo can make it all the way to Hindustan?' she asked me.

'It's a long, long way away,' I said. She nodded.

'Is it really so far?' the princeling asked.

'Oh yes, it's really, really far. No one has been there yet,' the princess said brightly.

After the *kikkōten* party marking Tanabata, Narihira resumed his frequent visits to the Gojo princess's residence. This had cast a cloud over the princess, but now I was cheered to see her vigour had returned at last.

'Wouldn't it be marvellous to speak to Shinnyo in person?' I said to her. Her face lit up, and she clasped her palms before her chest as if in prayer.

'I must speak to Lord Narihira about that,' she replied. 'And you should be there too, to hear what Shinnyo has to say. There aren't many opportunities to listen to so eminent a monk.'

Her words set my heart pounding. I would be able to hear Shinnyo's voice again. See his face up close. I flushed at the thought, and my hands began to tremble.

'Yes,' I said, struggling to hide my excitement. I didn't want the princess and her son to glimpse my inner turmoil.

Shinnyo agreed to appear at our residence to talk to the princess and her ladies.

Lord Narihira had originally conceived of the event as another big party, with guests invited from outside the residence. But the prospect of such a formal gathering made Shinnyo uncomfortable, so Narihira reluctantly abandoned the idea. In response, he came up with a new plan. Instead of a party, Shinnyo would lecture, not on the grounds, but within the residence's inner quarters. Of course, this greatly surprised the princess. These were the rooms where she and her ladies lived, and no man besides her husband was permitted to enter. The princeling was allowed there, of course, as was, on rare occasions, his 'breast brother', the little son of the nursemaid. But a grown man? When even the princess's male kin were excluded?

'That's true, but then Shinnyo is a monk, which makes him different from other men,' Lord Narihira said nonchalantly.

'But all the same . . .' the princess timidly remonstrated.

I could sense what was going on. Narihira was being uncharacteristically petty. He had taken pains to offer Shinnyo the chance to talk about Buddhism to a large group of people in a public setting and had been turned down. Meanwhile, not just the princess but everyone at the residence was thrilled that Shinnyo might be coming, and were counting on him to arrange it.

Generally speaking, Narihira was used to being the star of the show wherever he went, beloved by men and women alike, so he wasn't accustomed to having another man grab the attention. At court, of course, he had to take a back seat, since the Fujiwara clan, which enjoyed the support and trust of the present emperor, was politically dominant. Away from the palace, however, he lived surrounded by those drawn to his charm, who flitted merrily about him like insects around a flame.

To have his wife and her women dazzled by another man was a new experience for him. It wasn't hard to understand, then, why Narihira was showing a bit of spite.

'Shinnyo has taken the most rigorous path to enlightenment,' he said. 'Being surrounded by women isn't going to distract him.'

The princess had no ready answer for that – all she could do was nod. I thought that Narihira was being a little childish, but shrugged it off. What really excited me was seeing how Shinnyo would surmount the hurdle that Narihira had placed before him.

'So, choose an auspicious day and get on with it,' Narihira ordered the princess.

It has been a long time since I looked at the photograph of my elementary school self and Mr Takaoka standing side by side, so it triggers a number of emotions.

Back then, he reminded me a little of an 'Indian prince'. Big eyes. Thick lips. A nose unusually pronounced for a Japanese. Still, his face was a bit of a mishmash, and to be honest I never would have called him handsome.

When, as an adult, I met Mr Takaoka a second time, it never crossed my mind to think about how his face and body were put together. He was always there beside me, fully himself, able to soothe my worried mind. But that was it. Whether he was attractive to women or not didn't matter. Now, however, as I study Mr Takaoka's face in that photo taken nearly thirty years ago, I can see how manly he looks.

He's not the type all women would find captivating. His features are slightly out of whack: his large, bright eyes, aquiline nose and sensual mouth, taken together, come across as somehow excessive. Yet that very imbalance, combined with his overall bearing, makes Mr Takaoka the kind of person you'd like to hang out with. That's for sure.

I remember Naa-chan's comment: 'He's the sort of person I'd like to be a disciple of.' Now it strikes me that, from the time I was in elementary school, I was the one fated to be Mr Takaoka's disciple. He may not have been a conjuror yet – that took longer, it seems – but aren't both he and I now living in a magical world?

Perhaps Mr Takaoka and I, sensei and disciple, have been training in the art of magic for the past twenty years.

Now the results of all that training would be tested in the inner quarters of a princess's residence in the Heian period.

The ladies of the residence were quietly excited. It wasn't the sort of excitement that can be openly displayed, but it was keen and deeply felt.

Did I mention before that Heian women's work was valued more than you might think? Yes, compared to Japanese women today, their work was appreciated and unencumbered. Women today leave their homes to join the working world, true enough, but barriers of various kinds await them there, while the women of Heian could sit back and enjoy things a lot more. This shouldn't be taken to mean, though, that Heian women were liberated. They were not. But the fact that they worked apart from men made their lives easier and more relaxed.

While Heian men did the jobs that involved the public, like politics and scholarship, Heian women worked out of sight in the palace and the residences, where many of them, including the ladies-in-waiting, had ample opportunity to showcase their talents. To have a man come striding into their inner sanctum, where men were banned under any circumstances, was therefore bound to stir up the women. This might be a stretch, but it reminded me of the Japanese response when Admiral Perry's black ships forced their country open in the 1850s: a mixture of excitement and fear, resistance and expectation.

The day was bright and sunny. Narihira had not visited Gojo for several days, and the princess seemed quietly appreciative of the attention he was giving her.

My own view of of Narihira's decision to avoid Gojo was

somewhat jaundiced. Could he be regretting, at this late stage of the game, the trick he was playing on Shinnyo? Thanks to his perverse plan, the women's quarters were abuzz with Shinnyo's visit. Narihira's decision to remain at home struck me as an attempt to best Shinnyo in the eyes of those in the residence – to prove, in other words, that he was the more attractive man.

I don't mean to imply, of course, that he was consciously competing with Shinnyo. I doubt that the princess in her wisdom would have been drawn to him if he were so petty. And yet, Narihira's unconscious drive to compete fascinated me. For I found this flustered, disconcerted side of him more human, and thus more endearing, than when he was coolly monopolizing the attention of those around him – at those times he was so self-possessed he could seem almost hollow.

Shinnyo's visit was planned for October, the 'godless month', when Japan's countless gods were said to be off visiting the Izumo Shrine.

Although there would be no formal banquet, there was still to be a meal shared with the invited guest. It would feature dried persimmons, *kuzuko* delicacies and a generous assortment of seaweed and nuts, including chestnuts. In fact, Narihira was much fonder of abalone, crabs and small birds, but Shinnyo never touched meat, fish or fowl, and the princess had given orders that everyone at the residence should follow his diet for the day – no creatures of ocean or mountain were to be served.

Narihira did not seem pleased with this menu. But the princess was unfazed, and her orders were followed.

'Well, I guess matters regarding the ladies' quarters should be determined by those who live there,' he said in a resigned voice to the women nearby. That he should speak directly to them only drove their excitement to an even higher pitch.

I observed what was taking place between Narihira and the ladies. Narihira was exerting his charm now, captivating everyone in the residence. The princess calmly watched from the side. The women revelled in their lord's attentions, even as they carefully avoided provoking the princess's ire.

The scene reminded me of a herd of animals in the wild.

I took a second, closer look. Even if one dispensed with the 'herd of animals' comparison, there clearly was a herd mentality at work in Heian society. A strong and dominant male had the right to conquer whichever female pleased him. Authority was power. Status was power. Good looks constituted power. Combined, they exerted a spellbinding effect on women.

Do you see such an era as barbaric? Looked at from Riko's perspective, the answer is a definite yes: Heian ways of thinking were very primitive. Yet at the same time, speaking from the standpoint of one of those ladies-in-waiting, they were the most natural thing in the world. If a woman was strongly attracted to a dominant male, she felt the urge to couple with him. This attraction did not involve her mind, but rather her heart and body – her desire was simple and straightforward.

It's difficult to describe the emotional trajectory of Heian male–female relationships in a way that makes sense. Even to my modern self, Riko. So let me look back for a moment on myself as Riko, and the steps that made me who I am now.

It started when I was very young, with my burning love for Naa-chan, my desperate longing to be with him every spare moment. The joy when we were finally together. The ecstasy the moment our bodies joined. I can recall all this as if it happened yesterday. I wonder, though, if it can be explained in terms of simple physical desire.

'You're leaving out the mental part,' I can hear Mr Takaoka say.

Having reached this point, I have to agree – the greater part of my feelings for Naa-chan were probably connected to my thought processes at the time.

Back then, I couldn't see it that way. I was convinced my desire stemmed solely from my visceral, physical self – that it was far removed from the values of my society. Now that I have experienced how male–female relationships worked in Heian, however, I can see that my attraction to the 'best man' in my vicinity had a practical origin, which fitted the social and aesthetic standards of my culture.

Naa-chan was handsome. His future prospects were excellent. He was nice. He was unmarried. And he made me feel that he liked me. I think I put all these qualities in a kind of checklist, either right away or in stages. Social acceptability? Check. Human warmth? Check. Compatibility? Check. Makes me feel good in ways words cannot describe? Check.

I think my younger self put hours and hours into mentally adjusting this secret checklist. Of course, I never put that checklist into words. Half of it existed in my unconscious, where I was reviewing all sorts of points and making adjustments accordingly.

Aren't human beings amazingly gifted? I mean, there I was, a young woman of below average ability, dealing with problems so complex they would stump today's artificial intelligence apps, a woman who from a very early age was making judgements on the basis of pure intuition. Women today make these kinds of calculations all the time, probably with no better results than mine. We have to, I think, in order to survive. We need socially shared values, and the checklists they create, to get along in a modern environment.

The drive to survive, however, took a specific form in the Heian period. True, it was important for ladies-in-waiting like myself to form a special bond with a good man. Our feelers were always out to locate one of these, just like women today. Those feelers, however, moved in a very different way. For one thing, the element of play was a big factor. Perhaps it could be said that the feelers were left to dangle, rather than stiffly pointing out.

In today's monogamous world, choosing the wrong companion is synonymous with misfortune. If one strays temporarily from one's relationship, even if only to find someone to relax with, it leads to that dark stigma of infidelity. Turning away from an unsatisfactory partner is a deviation from the proper path, causing him or her heartbreak and bequeathing a host of problems to any children you might share.

Men in Heian aristocratic society were able to have multiple lovers, as were women. Meanwhile, every woman worked. There were ladies-in-waiting and handmaids like myself, nursemaids, property owners like the princess (for looking after the residence was real work), and others who presided over things like housecleaning and the care of musical instruments. The structure of the family was also unlike what we see now. A high-ranking woman's children were raised by nursemaids, while even those of middling rank weren't expected to look after their children by themselves, the result being that far fewer kids bore the emotional burden of their parents' break-up than is the case today.

It was desire that drove Heian women to seek out attractive men. The more attractive the man, the more women flocked to him, few of whom cared whether he had other women in his life or not. There *was* jealousy. How much fluctuated according to the woman's rank. An official wife was free to vent her jealousy when her husband spent his time visiting other women. If a high-ranking woman took a lover, that lover could also be the target of her ire, a response appropriate to the pride her high status conferred. On the other hand, if a woman of low rank was involved with a high-ranking man, she would see it as a stroke of good luck, and thus be unlikely to broach any dissatisfactions about his other relationships. Seen from this perspective, Heian aristocratic society was a claustrophobic, unjust world where people's innermost feelings had to be constantly edited and arranged according to their rank.

Unjust it certainly was. Claustrophobic, however, is another matter.

Jealousy today is a bit different from jealousy in a society where extramarital affairs were standard, not tabooed. On the one hand, this makes a functional difference; on the other, it is unadulterated and pure.

To separate from one's companion in Heian times was an emotional blow, but not a major material loss. Well, I guess there were times when financial consequences did figure, but they were minor compared to today's monogamous world, where even a superficial glance reveals not just emotional but economic loss on a drastic scale. When a man or woman becomes estranged from their spouse their family is torn apart, their assets are divided, and both have to rebuild their lives. That's right. Today, if a husband or wife runs off to be with someone else, they leave behind not just an ocean of pain but also a mountain of financial distress.

In that sense, the men and women of Heian were able to enjoy the parry and thrust of love affairs in a much freer spirit.

I want a good-looking man.

I want an attractive woman.

Relationships formed on such a basis may not survive for long, but they are certainly fun while they last.

These mutual sentiments, played out against a backdrop of

Heian social norms, led to a lively and colourful culture of love. Love direct and free, like that of creatures in their natural habitat.

'You're always happiest when you're waiting for something to arrive,' the princess sighed, then fell quiet.

'What do you mean?' I asked. The princess just smiled to herself.

'When is Shinnyo coming?' her son asked.

'He said it would be right around the boar festival,' she replied. Although she was beaming, I sensed a shadow of loneliness hovering behind her smile.

'Pounding rice cakes is so much fun!' the princeling crowed. He was remembering the *omochi* cakes we all had made on the 'day of the boar' in October, the godless month, to guard against illness. 'And there were lots of toad lilies too!'

'What a good memory,' I exclaimed. 'You even remember the flowers!'

His cheeks flushed the colour of peaches. His bashful side was showing – he was no longer the baby he had once been.

You're always happiest before something actually arrives.

I ponder the princess's words. What in particular was she referring to? The question occupies my mind even after I wake from my dream.

Before something arrives. Did that point to the time before one actually falls in love? Or before a secret stratagem is put into action? Or maybe it meant something much smaller, like waiting for Naa-chan to come home the evening I cooked an elaborate meal for our anniversary, or diving into that night's dessert, something new that we had never tried before.

What is the 'something' about to happen to me?

I have a premonition. It involves not just my modern self, Riko. Nor just the dream me, living as a handmaid in Heian times. Instead it concerns both of us, Riko and handmaid, perfectly joined together.

That premonition is filling me to the brim, drop by drop. A sense that something is about to happen to me. No, that's not exactly right. It's not so much that something is going to happen – rather, I am going to cause something to happen. That's right. I will be the catalyst. My hope is that whatever I cause to happen will bear fruit in the end.

Does the princess have any idea what is in my heart?

What should I do? I still don't know.

The day of Shinnyo's visit to our inner sanctum is drawing closer and closer. August, the 'leafing month', has come and gone and the 'long month', the silent approach of autumn, is well under way. The cicadas' shrilling has died away, replaced by the chirping of autumnal insects.

It was not quite dark, and I was drowsing in a corner of the veranda.

In Heian we went to bed when the sun went down and got up when it rose again. Our evening meal took place shortly after mid-afternoon, and our preparations for sleep were usually complete before nightfall.

The evening cleaning was over and done with, the screens and mats rearranged and the princess's bed prepared. It wasn't her normal bedtime yet. My custom was to remain by her side for a while longer, in case she needed anything. Today, however, she was feeling poorly, so shortly after midday a Buddhist priest had come with his rosary, and now prayers were being chanted on her behalf.

Though already autumn, the heat of midsummer had returned. For the past ten days or so, autumn breezes had been cooling things off, but now those breezes had turned sultry, a complete turnaround. We were led to wonder if a bad storm might be on the way.

The princess was not the only one under the weather. A number of her women were unwell – some were having their period, while others were so on edge they would fly into a rage over the most trivial thing.

For some reason, the women around the princess, myself included, all had our periods at the same time. Newcomers varied at first, but after they lived with us for a few months their menstrual cycle would come to match the princess's. When the princess was feeling poorly, we too would become heavy and sluggish.

Lord Narihira and the princess presided over our residence. We who worked within seldom ventured outside, so that our entire existence centred around the noble couple – watching them, picking up on their moods. In that sense, our service to the lord and princess involved not only our hearts and minds but our bodies as well. Perhaps the best way to put it is that, while each of us was a separate individual when we began our service, our roots gradually intermingled. Like Yoshino cherry trees that bloom at the same time, or a stand of amaryllis that blossoms and withers together, we who worked in the inner rooms flowered and fell as a group.

Narihira had returned to the residence that afternoon. He had not been at work at the palace, though: instead he had stayed at his family estate in Settsu overnight. The lord had visited both his mother and his younger brother, so he looked happier than we had seen him in some time. As soon as he heard that the princess was ill, however, he hurried to her side.

'How do you feel?' he spoke through her blind from his seat on the veranda, his voice filled with worry.

'Not nearly so tired,' she replied in a muffled voice. Even after his visits to the Gojo princess had begun, Narihira was as attentive to her as he always had been. True, the times he came home had declined in number, and he often seemed quite preoccupied, but he was never cold to her.

'How was Settsu?' she asked from where she lay.

'Everyone is well.'

'I'm glad to hear that.'

It was a simple exchange, but the warmth of their feelings was apparent.

I had been dozing off when their conversation started, but now I was fully awake. The intimacy of their exchange – their obvious closeness as a married couple – had brought me close to tears. Why did Narihira feel the need to visit other ladies when his home life was so harmonious?

All of a sudden I was pained, and angry too.

'I think it's best if you stay in bed today,' Narihira said.

'Yes, you're right,' the princess responded.

Her voice was quiet. But I could tell that the princess was sad. Narihira would not be sharing her bed that night. He would be in Gojo instead, that was clear.

Why? My modern self called out to my Heian counterpart. How could our lord happily trot off to see the Gojo princess with his wife so sick? Even as I did this, though, my other self on the Heian side rebutted me. Men are creatures made to unite with women, she countered. Women are creatures who yearn to unite with men. Anyone who wants to step outside this cycle should take Buddhist vows.

Lord Narihira's clothes, scented with a cool fragrance, rustled

as he stood to leave. He would walk the length of the veranda and
out of the door at the end.

'Ahhh,' a loud sigh escaped me.

Lord Narihira stopped and turned. Who had sighed, he wondered, peering through the gathering gloom in my direction.

I sighed again, this time under my breath.

'Heian food is tasty, isn't it?' Mr Takaoka said to me.

'You didn't eat much fish or meat, though, did you?' I asked.

Mr Takaoka and I were alone on the bench beside the river.
My father and mother had taken Toji to the department store.

Toji was growing fast. What he couldn't reach yesterday he
was sure to grab today; what was too far to walk last month could
now be covered in a trice. As his height shot up, his clothes grew
too small.

'Kids wore hand-me-downs back in the old days,' Mr Takaoka
said nostalgically.

'You too?' I asked.

'Everything I wore was new until my father lost his money,'
he said. 'After that we bought second-hand – my school uniform,
everyday clothes, the works.'

'How about your shoes?'

'I think those were new,' Mr Takaoka said. They were canvas
shoes that he kept wearing even after his toes poked through the
front.

'I'm a rich man now, compared to back then.'

'Rich?'

'You bet. I have no worries about finding food for today –
that's rich enough for me.'

Buddhist monks like Shinnyo had no possessions or money.
Unless they were fasting in the mountains, they would go

out with a begging bowl each morning to gather that day's sustenance. Shinnyo subsisted on a diet of thin gruel and a few pickles.

'A monk's diet must have been awfully restricted – was it really so good?' I asked.

'Sure, it was. Things taste better on an empty stomach you know. And I can remember some wonderful banquets too, at least when Emperor Heizei was still on the throne.'

That's right, Shinnyo was Heizei's son.

What was served, I wondered aloud, at those banquets?

'My favourite was abalone.'

'Lord Narihira is the same!' I cried. 'Maybe that's a family trait.' As uncle and nephew, they would have shared DNA.

'I liked the *so* cheese too,' Mr Takaoka said.

'I haven't had a chance to try that yet,' I said.

So was made by boiling down cow's milk over many hours. Only a very few could afford such a delicacy.

'Lots of cattle were raised in Narihira's family home, Settsu, so I bet he ate buckets of *so* as a boy,' Takaoka said.

'You're right,' I said. 'When he visited Settsu, he sometimes brought it back for the princess.'

Come to think of it, the other day he had taken some to her when she was sick. She was too ill to taste it, though. I bet he had carried it off to give to the Gojo princess. That had stuck in my gut. In fact, it bothered me even now.

'Why the angry face?' Mr Takaoka said.

'Huh?'

'Have a look,' he said. He took my hand, raised me from the bench and led me to the river.

'See down there?' he said, leaning over the water. 'That's your scary face looking back at you.'

'I can't see. The water's too murky,' I laughed. Mr Takaoka laughed with me.

'You know, you're kind of sexy when you get angry,' he said.

'Give it a break,' I replied, flustered. In that fleeting moment, my attraction to Mr Takaoka sparked again. That feeling was immediately replaced by jealousy, though, which mounted as I imagined Lord Narihira carrying the delicacy to the Gojo princess.

Jealousy, however, is a loaded term. What is it, exactly? I mean, it fits naturally when I'm describing the princess's feelings as Lord Narihira rode off to Gojo, but why would I feel jealous in *this* situation?

'My oh my, your scary face is still hanging around!' joked Mr Takada, easy-going as always. That brought me back to myself, at least for the moment.

The river was gurgling. Birds were singing in the distance. The wind had died down at some point, and the air weighed heavily on our shoulders.

'I wonder why,' Mr Takaoka said out of nowhere, 'humans become so attached to others instead of looking into themselves.'

'Attached?'

I repeated the word under my breath. I certainly didn't want any of my sticky attachments laid out in front of him.

'Yes,' Mr Takaoka went on. 'Attachments can give us strength. But they can also make us very vulnerable.' I felt he was shining a spotlight into my soul.

The autumn was deepening, and preparations for Shinnyo's party were steadily progressing. Although the invitations were in Lord Narihira's name, it was the princess and her family who were running the show.

In personality, the princess's father, Lord Aritsune, was the polar opposite of Lord Narihira – a reclusive man, he preferred to return home to his family and his books when he finished his day at the palace. Although Narihira had been barely ten years old when they first met, he was already peeping at the pretty ladies at court whenever he had a chance, while Aritsune was buried deep in his books. When it came to promotion, though, Aritsune's impressive learning could not overcome his deficiencies, namely his shy and retiring personality and his modest family fortune. As a result, although Narihira was a decade younger, strangely, he behaved as an older brother might.

Remarkably, despite the difference in their ages, the friendship had continued to flourish. Even when he was paying visits to his various conquests, Narihira would always find time to pop in to chat with his old friend. When Aritsune was posted to outlying districts like Shimotsuke and Shinano, too, Narihira would ride all the way there to keep his friend company.

Rumours persisted that Narihira and Aritsuna's friendship lay behind Narihira's marriage. And that Narihira was ready to come to the rescue whenever necessary by backing up the deficiencies in Aritsune's finances. This added to the difficulty in preparing for the monk Shinnyo's visit, since not only was Aritsune financially pinched, the relatives he might have turned to for assistance had already passed away.

Nevertheless, the princess spared no effort in gathering all the things she thought Shinnyo was likely to enjoy.

'Well, at least we don't have to worry about crab and pheasant,' she said. 'He wouldn't eat those.'

Freshwater crab and pheasant were the delicacies most often chosen to headline feasts, but they required property near a lake where crab could be caught and hilly land for the pheasants;

moreover, each required skilled hunters and fishermen. Aritsune's domains had none of those things. To replace the crab and pheasant, the princess sent for a supply of pine nuts, dried dates and pomegranates brought from the districts where Aritsune had formerly been posted, and made arrangements for a variety of Chinese sweets to be prepared by highly skilled artisans in the capital. These were especially popular among Heian aristocrats, Chinese-style dumplings made from stone-ground wheat, salt, sesame and a bit of sugar and then lightly fried in sesame oil. The makers of these sweets were judged by how well they selected and mixed the ingredients and the shapes they created, from confections that looked like ropes or *magatama* beads to elaborate depictions of turtles, cranes and other auspicious creatures.

The princess consulted with a number of confectioners before making her choice and placing her order. Her ladies especially looked forward to the delivery, since they would sample the sweets when they arrived.

The sweets came in a box with a pearl-inlay lid. When they removed the lid and peered inside, they saw the sweets lined up on platters of unglazed clay.

'Oh, this is delicious!' the first lady to sample sang out.

'This one may be heavy to digest.'

'This one's too hard.'

'Here's my favourite, this one here.'

The ladies dug in but the princess did not join them. The princeling, however, leaped at the chance.

'They're beautiful, aren't they?' he said, taking one moulded in the shape of a plum blossom between his fingers and holding it up to the light. 'Yes, it would be a terrible waste to eat the whole thing,' he said, popping it in his mouth. The ladies all laughed merrily.

'You said it was too beautiful to eat, yet you swallowed it in one gulp!'

'Yes, but it was delicious, so I don't care,' the boy said. The women laughed again.

'What's this uproar?' came a man's voice. We fell quiet immediately.

Lord Narihira was back from his day of work at the palace. We had lost track of time, but sure enough the shadows were lengthening – how could the day have passed so quickly?

'Since when is my house home to so many ill-bred women?' Narihira's voice rang out. He strode through the open veranda door and down the corridor to where we were sitting. If we were going to ignore the dictates of propriety, it seemed, so would he.

The princess was looking down. She swept her son beneath her long sleeves to remove him from his father's sight. As the prized heir, it wasn't appropriate for him to be seen in the company of so many of her ladies, especially when they were behaving in such an indecorous manner.

All of us were excited to have Lord Narihira so close at hand, without the normal distance. Usually, we dressed properly only when a special guest came to visit; at times like these, when we were together as a group, we wore only a layer or two of under-garments or else *hakama* pleated trousers. Lord Narihira's sudden return, however, caught us unprepared – there was no time to change. Were it today, it would be the equivalent of standing before your boss in a negligee.

Ladies' maids, however, can be a tough lot. I see one of us over there right now, trying to attract Narihira's attention by provoca-tively raising and lowering her knee beneath her *hakama*.

The formal way men and women sat was different in Heian times than it is now. Women raised one knee, while men either crossed their legs or raised a knee like the women. Thus, while the *hakama* and the copious outer garments made it look like they were sitting properly with their feet tucked under them, in fact all had one knee elevated. Since they wore nothing under those garments, well, if a camera had been placed near the floor, it would have revealed the female form at its most carnal. Nothing of the sort existed, of course, so it made sense for Heian women to sit as they did. Actually, it was the most comfortable position: your legs didn't fall asleep, and you could shift your posture without attracting attention.

No one would describe the layers of clothes that the princess and other noble ladies had to wear as comfortable, though – far from it. Their cumulative weight was considerable. First, the princess put a *haribakama* next to her skin, then a *hitoe*, then five layers of *uchiki* and then *uchiginu*, *omote-ki* and *karaginu*, and then, finally, the trailing *mo*, a total of twenty to thirty kilograms of fabric! This was a heavy burden to bear for women who had so little exercise; there were no gyms yet, of course, nor any chances to go hiking in the hills. High-born women therefore tended to laze around most of the day, since carrying so much weight left their bodies fragile and weak.

Should their life be considered easy or hard? If you were to order my modern self to wear all that bulky clothing, I'd tell you to forget it. Yet put that same question to my Heian self and I would call it the most natural and elegant way to dress.

The kimonos that the *oiran* of Edo wore when they promenaded down the streets of Yoshiwara were heavy too, but the Quarter was not large, so distances were short, and their work required that they take those clothes off once they were entertaining guests. And compared to Heian women, the *oiran*'s physical exercise necessarily peaked once she was in bed.

We may see the *oiran*'s life as hard, and it was, but how then should we view the life of someone like the princess? Was there 'princess's work' in the same way that there was *oiran*'s work? I for one think the princess's job was every bit as difficult and demanding. Physically, there was all that heavy clothing. As for the psychological side of things, Heian women were forced to deal with, even approve of, their men's numerous affairs.

Maidservants like me had much freer lives than princesses. Right over there you'll see one of my colleagues, emboldened by the sight of someone else flashing him, giving Narihira the eye. Nothing further was likely to happen when the princess was around, but all the same, it would be hard to exaggerate the amorousness of the ladies of our residence.

Narihira barely glanced at the covert come-ons being directed his way. His first words were to the princess:

'I'm home, dear,' he said quietly. 'I plan to stay here for three days. Please see to my meals.'

The princess nodded in response. As if waking from a dream, her ladies immediately leaped into action, each returning to her designated task. The only exception was the young princeling, who went back to savouring the sweets with a big smile and a sesame seed wedged between his teeth.

I often found myself comparing Toji with the princeling, wondering how my son would fare if he were growing up in Heian times.

I think the reason may have been that I was spending so much time thinking about Narihira. I still couldn't help comparing him to Naa-chan, but in many ways the two men had nothing in common. Narihira was just so much more manly. On the other hand, were I to try to compare Mr Takaoka and Narihira, or my own father and Narihira, I would find even fewer points of similarity.

Narihira could never exist in today's world. Why? Because he was so totally a creature of that most rare and special society, the aristocracy of Heian Japan. Not many men today would be forgiven for his lifestyle, consorting with a string of women and engaging in elegant pursuits with his friends.

Nevertheless, Naa-chan and Narihira did share some features, most notably their popularity among members of the opposite sex. Like Narihira, Naa-chan let his relationships run on without breaking them off. The girl from Kyushu. Michiko-sensei. The fiancée of the vice-president of his company. And those are just the ones that I know of, three down and still counting. I never snooped into Naa-chan's life by checking his cellphone or calendar, or anything else of that sort. Not because it felt morally wrong, but rather because my love for him had been whittled away to nothing.

My head reels when I reflect on how innocently I loved Naa-chan in the beginning. I was so open, so loving, so willing to trust him, body and soul. And I did trust him. Not to the extent that I thought he'd never fall for another woman, but because I saw my love for him as being on a higher level, the most precious part of my life.

Loving someone, if you think about it, is dangerous. I mean, how well can we know anyone? How well can we know even ourselves? When I first loved Naa-chan, I did so with unshakable confidence. As an expression of my own unimpeded free will. But can love ever be conducted in such a clear and direct way? After our marriage was decided, I never wavered in my love, even when I learned of the other women. In fact, the thought of leaving him never entered my mind.

Then I was faced with Naa-chan's 'platonic' love, Michiko-sensei, which shook my self-confidence, though only a little.

Then I was hit by Naa-chan's affair with his boss's fiancée, which left me wandering in a dense fog for days.

Then my heart flew off to Edo, where I came to know what sleeping with men other than Naa-chan was like.

Then, in Heian Japan, I met an extraordinary man – Narihira – whom I have come to both love and hate.

Finally, at this very moment, I am distinctly aware of my faint yet deep-seated attraction to Mr Takaoka.

Where in the world have all these feelings come from, only to bedevil a woman like me? And if I can understand my own love no better than this, then why should I be surprised if I fail to understand its object of desire, Naa-chan? It's only natural.

Naa-chan's and my love is a fragile thing, built on a shaky foundation of fantasy and mistaken assumptions. Is it any wonder that this realization leads me to worry about Toji, our son?

A child of the Heian aristocracy was raised by an entire household. Today, however, only those few enmeshed in the 'loving' ties that bind a family, amorphous though those ties may be, are responsible for the child. A shaky edifice housing an even shakier activity. That is how we look after children in modern times.

Toji was happily running about with his building blocks. 'Toji,' I blurted out. 'What shall we do? You came to me as my son, yet I lead such a dubious existence.'

'Mama!' Toji answered. He smiled the world's most innocent smile, an expression of complete and utter trust in me.

It was an inky night at the residence, and passions between the men and women who lived there were piling up like snow.

Nights at the residence were like this, pitch-black and writhing with hidden desire. Maidservants who were having affairs with valets were now waiting for them at their places of assignation. Those seeing lower-ranking men were less self-controlled – they would slip into the men's quarters and send their lover a signal to draw him outside. There were several ways to signal. You could imitate a birdsong, or wear a distinctive perfume to broadcast your presence, or even, as one lover did, release fireflies into the room on a summer's night.

Men and women alike were faithful to those desires. If the upper crust had its elegant court poetry, so we who served them had our own varied ways of communicating love. Even those without a partner seldom hesitated when the chance for love came along. If a maidservant caught the eye of a gentleman visitor to the residence, and received from him a missive, usually a poem, she would immediately reply with a poem of her own if she was up to the task. If not, she might ask a more experienced lady to help her compose it.

The gentlemen came secretly, under cover of darkness. The women helped one another, escorting the gentlemen to their meeting places. There were cases, too, of gentlemen who slept, not just with the object of their tryst, but also with the woman acting as their guide. Women showed no jealousy in those situations. Just being noticed by men above their station was satisfaction enough.

Of course, a woman had the right to refuse a suitor, however high his rank. It would be unseemly to make that refusal public, though, so she had to find an indirect way to discourage him: she could fail to tell him the way to her quarters, for example, or compose a decidedly inelegant poem in response, or even leave her empty nightclothes on top of her bedding while she went somewhere else to sleep. In all cases, the man was expected to accept these veiled rejections. In fact, aristocratic men were so easy-going they treated rejections from lowly women like us as just part of the game.

Marriage was fairly flexible throughout the Heian period. If a husband and wife had not been with each other for three years, for example, that marriage was considered to be over.

During my time in Heian I've already had two lovers.

The first was a man who had worked as a valet at the residence for many years. Our affair began shortly after the princess became the wife of Lord Narihira. He was much older but well liked by everyone at the residence for his gentle ways. His wife had passed away several years earlier, and he had been celibate ever since. Watching me grow from a girl young enough to be his daughter into womanhood, however, had awakened his passion, until one day he passed me a clumsy poem he had written himself.

I was better educated than the other maidservants thanks to my daily contact with the princess and her bookish ways, so I could tell right off the bat that his poem lacked sophistication. Yet that made his true feelings stand out all the more, so I gave myself to him without hesitation.

Our relationship lasted a year. When it began, he was still mourning his wife, which had physically diminished him, but he was revived by sleeping with me – his complexion became ruddier and he was physically more vigorous, as if the clock had been turned back and he was a generation younger. Yet that was only temporary, and six months later he was exhausted again.

A rumour was circulating in the residence that I had sucked the energy from his body. Of course, no one ever told me this directly, but somehow I knew. And I had to acknowledge that our affair was overtaxing him, for he was just too attached to me. Every night he came to make passionate love – or it might be more accurate to say he came to devour me. It was an era when the food supply was limited and standards of hygiene were low. Perhaps it was unavoidable, then, that the lives of some older men were whittled away by their unbridled desire for younger women.

And so it was that, one year after our affair began, my valet left the residence and returned to his home in Kazusa. I stood alone at the gate to bid farewell to this man who, because of me, had aged so much. We whispered our farewells, and though he looked drained I could tell from his smile how satisfied he was with the time we had spent together. Surely, no one would call him unfortunate, for we had been true and constant lovers.

My second lover was an official of the sixth rank who had attended the Tanabata festival at our residence.

This gentleman lived on the fringes of the capital, and was the polar opposite of my first lover: capricious and mean, but very sexy too. There was always a buzz among the princess's ladies-in-waiting when this official came to call. Maybe 'buzz' is the wrong word. You see, the presence of a man of rank constricted their behaviour – they couldn't whisper among themselves or flirt, at least openly. Yet though they were quiet and reserved, it was easy to tell from their admiring glances in his direction how excited they were by this sexy noble of the sixth rank. Perhaps he might bestow a courtly poem on one of them!

The official had no interest in any of his admirers, however, for the one he secretly loved was none other than the princess herself.

I had a good idea of his hidden love. I doubt a run-of-the-mill Heian handmaid would have been so discerning, but I had the advantage of looking at the world through Riko's eyes from time to time and so was able to easily detect the telltale signs.

How liberated were passions back then!

The people of Heian totally lacked that strangely excessive concern for others' opinions shared by modern Japanese. As might be expected, the presence of Lord Narihira meant that the official had no chance to pass a poem to the princess, or even speak directly with her, yet I could see his restless gaze constantly seeking her out.

Like Narihira, the official was a very attractive man. Unlike Narihira, however, he was beloved by women alone, not by men. He seems to have accepted the fact that he could not approach an honest, incorruptible woman like my princess directly. He therefore took an oblique approach, forming a relationship with the one who was closest to her – yours truly – and then trying to use that as a bridge to achieve his ends.

The result was that I began sleeping with the official.

Did he really believe he could reach the princess through me when I was the one being depended on to protect her? In fact, by giving my body to the man, I thought I was able to stand between him and the princess, arms crossed and legs braced. The official was far more cunning, however, than I gave him credit for. He could tell that my purpose was to protect the princess. He seduced me fully conscious of that fact, so that each of us was left seeking to uncover the hidden motives of the other.

'I love the perfume you're wearing,' he might say to me. Or, 'Your hair is so soft today.' Or, 'You write with such a beautiful hand.' Or, 'I wish I could come to see you every day.' And so on and so forth. The man was a great charmer. He praised me to the skies, though I was so far beneath him. As if I were some great princess myself.

I knew he was after my princess, but he acted in ways I hadn't foreseen. I had thought that, once he had me in hand, he would waste no time making a play for her. But he made no move in that direction. Instead he continued visiting me, with all the flattery that entailed.

These clandestine visits went on for several months. He couldn't come every night, of course. As a Heian nobleman he had other women to see, and people would frown if he spent all his time with women anyway. His job at the palace meant he couldn't go overboard enjoying wine, women and song; he had his estates to look after, and his own family and relatives, who could not be totally ignored. There were also occasions when directional taboos forced him to restrict his movements; such taboos could lock down the entire capital, leaving him to twiddle his thumbs at home.

I think I've mentioned how pitch-black the Heian nights were. It wasn't just the depth of the darkness: the colour was of a richer hue. Those jet-black nights were filled with emanations we seldom encounter in modern times. There were traces of what I suspected to be supernatural beings, or the ghosts of dead warriors, or the living spirits of beleaguered aristocrats, many of whom lived their lives in dire though well-concealed poverty (especially when compared to the wealth people enjoy today) and whose suffering therefore went unnoticed.

I always felt that it may well have been to prevent such presences from curtailing their lives that the men and women of Heian placed such stress on lovemaking, and the nights they spent together. This may help explain why I too came to physically long for those visits from the official of the sixth rank, though I felt little affection for him.

The official never so much as enquired about the princess. His admiring gaze was clearly directed at her, yet he made no move, in either word or deed, to approach her. As a result I gradually relaxed my guard, thinking that, really, it must be me that he loved. How rash, how thoughtless, could I have been? Finally, after almost a year of visiting me, I believe, he extended his tentacles in the princess's direction.

I have already mentioned the great love the princess had for old Chinese books. Well, one day the official came to our residence bearing an elegant box with a mother-of-pearl lid containing a sizeable number of scrolls he said had just arrived from China.

'Could you look after these for me?' he asked. I assumed he meant to show the scrolls to Lord Narihira. Or, if not him, then to the princess's father, Lord Aritsune, who had introduced her to the world of Chinese letters.

'Are you sure?' I asked. 'These are awfully valuable.'

'What an intelligent young woman you are to recognize their value,' he replied.

I swelled with pride at that moment. Certainly, it was rare to find a handmaid like myself who could appreciate such a collection.

'I feel confident entrusting them to you,' he went on. The next morning, after the official had left, I showed the box to the princess, knowing how much she liked reading Chinese texts. Looking back, though, I can see it was vanity that induced me to set it before her: the temptation to share something I knew would give her joy overwhelmed me. What a fool I was!

The princess immediately threw herself into the collection.

'Do you think he would mind if I handled them?' she asked, picking up one of the scrolls and carefully opening it.

'Isn't the ink gorgeous?' was her first reaction. Then, after reading a bit, 'And the calligraphy is wonderful too.'

She sat there, entranced by the robust brush strokes. Hours

passed and still she remained sunk in the scrolls, letting out only the occasional sigh, until the time came for the evening meal.

For the next two days, the princess remained sequestered behind her curtains, the mother-of-pearl box beside her, reading from morning till night. Every so often she would move to her desk to scribble something down, like a modern student taking notes.

The official of the sixth rank reduced his visits after that. They had never been very frequent anyway, usually no more than once or twice a month, so when he disappeared for a few weeks I didn't think anything of it. I was much more concerned about the princess, so fixated on the scrolls that she had virtually stopped eating: she was losing weight and her face was gaunt.

The nursemaid couldn't stand stand idly by. 'No one should obsess over things like that,' she remonstrated. Yet the princess continued reading from dawn till dusk, as if spellbound.

Things reached the point where I began to hate that wretched box of scrolls.

Although the official of the sixth rank was my lover, I didn't care for him that much; yet, as the princess grew thinner and thinner, I began to anxiously await his visit as the owner of the scrolls that had stolen her heart. I planned to beg him to take them away.

The official finally visited our residence roughly a month and a half after he had brought that box with the mother-of-pearl-encrusted lid. It was late at night, and I had gone to bed assuming that he wouldn't come, when he slipped under my covers.

Back in the early days of our affair, there were occasions when he had come without sending a note, catching me off guard when I was already asleep. Not recently, though, for I had been adamant that he put an end to such impromptu appearances, as I normally slept close by the princess.

On nights when the official was supposed to visit, it was arranged that I would sleep not beside the princess but in the west wing on the opposite side of the residence. It would be unforgivable were we to make love beside where she was sleeping – and knowing that the official had his eye on her would make it that much worse. Nevertheless, a number of the maidservants were willing to bring him to me when he came, and there were times when he was able to slip in beside me when I was sleeping near the princess. Possibly, those maidservents too were his lovers. Not that I cared one way or the other.

That night, his appearance was especially sudden. I was fast asleep, and the princess too was likely dead to the world within her grand curtains. Narihira was visiting Gojo that night, and the residence was hushed.

I was woken by someone groping my breasts. I wasn't fully awake, so I lay there in a daze as that hand slowly slipped down my side until it reached the swell of my lower abdomen. Thanks to the small light burning at the end of the corridor, I was able to make out that the man pressing down on me was the official of the sixth rank.

'Please, not here,' I whispered to him.

I tried to tell him to stop, but he covered my lips with his, forcing my words back down my throat. His hands, his fingers, were everywhere, running over my skin. Wherever he touched grew warm as if exposed to a flame, then hot – I was melting in his hands. I tried to get out from under him, but my body wouldn't respond.

He had me pinned, and resistance was futile. I thought that at least I could keep our lovemaking a secret: I clamped my lips together to stifle my cries and stiffened my body. That didn't stop him, though: before long he had spread me out on the bedding, rocking me back and forth until I had lost all control and was tossing about like a leaf on the waves.

I could hear someone else breathing close by. We had finished, and I was lying in his arms. It had to be the princess. Her eyes would be wide open in the dark, her ears pricked. I guessed her body was burning for the absent Lord Narihira.

The official who had been seething with passion just a few moments earlier had been satisfied; his breathing was slow and steady and he was beginning to snore. For me lying beside him and for the princess behind the curtains, though, little sleep was to be had that night.

It didn't take long for the official to creep from my bed to where the princess was lying.

I doubt he would have been able to get his hands on her so easily had he not given her the box of Chinese scrolls with the mother-of-pearl lid.

The official continued visiting the princess using the one who slept beside her, yours truly, as a pretext. The women who guided him through the residence to where we were doubtless believed he was visiting me. But once he had gained access to the princess's bed, he never entered mine again.

The official was a very careful and considerate lover. It may strike you as strange, given how he had accosted me in my sleep, but I was actually relieved when I overheard, through her many-layered curtains, how tenderly he was treating her. Not that he had treated my body roughly while he and I were lovers. In fact, he could be overly gentle and meticulous, as if I were a flowering tree and he had vowed to ensure that I dropped not a single petal.

He may have won the princess's body, but he had no chance of winning her heart. For that was firmly set on Lord Narihira. Nevertheless, physically she found in the official a reliable lover who could relieve her boredom and provide her comfort.

Indeed, the official could be quite self-effacing before the princess. Part of the reason, of course, was that she was so high-born, but also he had the greatest respect for her learning. He had not been showing off when he gave her the box with its collection of Buddhist scrolls. Nor was it an act of caprice. Rather, in his heart of hearts, I think that he was hoping that he and she might talk about the texts together.

There were opportunities, of course, for him to discuss Chinese texts with his aristocratic colleagues, but lately those conversations had become somewhat tricky. One problem was his contemporaries' varied levels of education. Only a few of them could talk about the contents of the scrolls in any depth.

But there was another, different problem. Until recently, envoys had been sent to Tang China to learn what they could of Chinese culture and to remind the Chinese of Japan's existence, but as conditions in China gradually deteriorated and social unrest spread, the attitudes of the Japanese who lived in the capital were changing.

Tang rule had once seemed rock-solid, but now armed rebellions were flaring up in various regions. Clouds portending the end of the Tang loomed over that country, and now those clouds were crossing the water to Japan.

A new faction at the Japanese court was calling for cultural independence from Tang China and the promotion of native traditions. More generally, the opinion was growing that, rather than being measured exclusively by one's familiarity with Chinese topics, a full education should include the study of Japan's traditions as well. It was therefore becoming more difficult for Japanese to engage in pleasant intellectual conversations about Chinese texts, as such attempts could meet with accusations of 'Chinese bias'. Japanese aristocrats hid their political opinions about China while feeling out each other's views, then came up with the most inoffensive positions they could think of. In short, they behaved exactly like workers in a modern Japanese company.

With the princess, however, the official of the sixth rank had nothing to be worried about. In the palace he had to keep a constant eye on those jealous of his rank and education, but with her he could set those concerns aside and talk freely.

I'm sure the princess, too, found her talks with the sixth official liberating. As I have mentioned, Lord Narihira did not find the princess's mind to be her most attractive feature. And he was not alone: during the Heian period, men tended to avoid women deemed overly intelligent.

There may be a parallel here with modern Japan, where men have often preferred a wife who can be controlled over one who is clearly smarter. This opinion was once rampant – no, that's not quite right, it still exists today beneath the surface. Despite their silence, no one can deny that, even now, men prefer to see themselves as superior to women, while some women's response is to take advantage of this prejudice by stowing their ability safely out of sight.

Had anyone known about it, the relationship between the official of the sixth rank and the princess would have been labelled indecent, and since I had aided the princess in her duplicity, a shadow would have been cast over me as well. The saving grace was that the official and the princess shared so much in common. Of course, theirs was an adult relationship. As I said, the official's ministrations helped relieve the princess of her sexual frustration, but even more important, he freed her mind, helping her break loose from an intellectually stultifying environment. It was hard enough for a man, but almost impossible for a Heian woman, to find someone to talk to about intellectual matters freely, without rank or ceremony getting in the way.

It struck me that, had all of this taken place today, the official of the sixth rank and the princess would have made a much better husband and wife than the princess and Lord Narihira. That was my take on it anyway. Perhaps it helped ease my conscience a little.

The official and the princess's secret affair stayed secret for a long time; indeed, no word of it passed anyone's lips to the very end.

I think my lack of resentment that the princess had somehow 'stolen' my man was what made this possible. Had I possessed even a drop of jealousy, it could have swelled into an invisible wave that might have swamped the entire residence.

I could see the official's visits were having a calming effect on the princess. Certainly, she seemed more at peace now, much more so than when she had eyes only for Lord Narihira.

The lord's visits to Gojo continued. The Gojo princess's brothers, however, had apparently found out about the affair and were trying to chase him away. It is the nature of love that, the harder people try to separate a couple, the stronger their bond is likely to become.

I sometimes conjecture that, had no one intervened, Lord Narihira's love for the Gojo princess might have gone the way of his other affairs and petered out. In this case, though, rumour had it that the girl's brothers and father were scheming to make her an empress, which must have only whetted Lord Narihira's desire.

An affair doomed from the start. I think it was that element of tragedy that drove the lord's passion for the Gojo princess.

Throughout this period, Lord Narihira continued to treat my princess well. Nevertheless, his longing for the Gojo princess was causing him to grow thinner day by day. This was the state of affairs when the monk Shinnyo came to talk to us.

There are still times when I long for Naa-chan.

My love was all-encompassing in the beginning. Later, when I found out about his other women, I despaired. And some time after that, I began to appreciate him as the father of my child, and so on and so forth – yet through all that time there have been moments when my body craves him.

I love Mr Takaoka too. And that love never wavers. That's because, while we may be connected in a mental and emotional way, there are aspects of ourselves we choose to leave off the table. Simply put, I have shown Mr Takaoka only my good side, and I'm sure the same is true of him. However detached he may seem from mundane emotions, I imagine he has his full share of shallow feelings and ugly thoughts. Neither of us lets the other see that side of ourselves. I don't think that's necessarily a bad thing, either. It can be exhausting when someone reveals the chaos that lies beneath their neat and tidy surface.

There is far less distance separating me and Naa-chan than me and Mr Takaoka; while my husband and I may try to hide our chaos, the other is sure to detect it at some point. Just as I envy the women who have slept with Naa-chan, and resent the energy he drew from them, so Naa-chan resents my exasperation with him and my closeness to Mr Takaoka, at least on a subconscious level.

Every so often, I am startled to realize that Naa-chan and I are still somehow able to live together as a functioning couple. That realization always leaves me feeling more loving towards him.

He is too much for me, yet I love him. That may summarize my feelings towards Naa-chan.

Returning to the present after experiencing the simple, direct eros of Heian makes my head spin. Where is the desire that grabs me when I am in the arms of the official of the sixth rank? Does such passion even exist in this modern world? I, at any rate, have yet to encounter it. I can't recall ever feeling the rich eroticism of Heian with Naa-chan, even when we were first in love and sleeping with him still gave me such joy.

Here's how I see it. A twisted sort of eros can be found in a partner one loves yet finds utterly impossible.

I make breakfast for Naa-chan in the mornings. Then Toji and I say our goodbyes at the door and watch him head off for the office in the business suit I laid out for him. He returns in the evening wearing the fatigue of his day at work. If Toji is still awake they take a bath together; if not, he sits in front of the television and absent-mindedly picks at the dinner I have prepared or, if he comes home even later, rolls into bed without even bothering to shower.

On my side, I clean the house, look after Toji, occasionally meet Mr Takaoka, spend time with my parents, maintain contact with a few of our neighbours, and generally strive to keep our family on an even keel.

In short, Naa-chan and I pursue parallel lives in separate spaces.

Sharing a life in that fashion can be confounding. At intervals I love him, hate him, or don't give a damn. There is that thing he did. But then there's that other thing too. Or that time, come to mention it. What is she to him these days? How should I handle it? I feel tenderness. Bafflement. Hatred. Happiness. Fatigue. Sadness. On the verge of exploding. Emotionally flat. Emptied out. Our feelings are transformed minute by minute, yet our faces show nothing when we're together. If something erotic is going to emerge from this complicated relationship, won't it have to come out of this interplay of confused and constantly changing emotion?

My desire for Naa-chan flares at the most unexpected moments. When I am on my way to shopping with Toji, pushing him around in his stroller, for example. Or when Naa-chan steps out of the door in the morning. Or when I am in the kitchen, dissolving miso in boiling water for soup. The intensely erotic aura rooted in those pitch-black Heian nights seems to have broken up and scattered under modern lighting.

The eros of the present day is fragmentary, abrupt, diffuse, disjointed – and surprisingly stubborn. I have no control over when and where my desire for Naa-chan may strike. Although I ignore its existence with a studied nonchalance, in fact I half look forward to those moments when it suddenly erupts.

From the beginning, we haven't expressed our desire for each other in words. I have never asked him to make love to me. Nor has he ever said, 'I want you now.' The problem isn't just language – there are physical hurdles to be overcome as well. Toji's moods. My physical condition. Naa-chan's libido. How things are going at his work. The lingering aftermath of the spat we had the day before yesterday. Memories of my conversation with his mother at their home several months ago. All these things stand in our way. We find ourselves unable to simply act on our feelings.

Without the elaborate conventions surrounding eros in Heian society, what role can it play in modern married life?

*

My dreams of Heian, so hazy and vague at the beginning, are now vivid and textured. The more colourful life there becomes, the more slowly time passes.

On the home front with Naa-chan and Toji, time seems to fly past. It feels like only yesterday that Toji finally learned how to crawl, and now he's toddling about. Tomorrow he'll be walking, and the day after that he'll be running.

I am keeping a 'Toji diary'. So I know that, in fact, more than a month passed between crawling and toddling, and that moving from toddling to walking will require even more time. My days with Toji constantly shift before my eyes, like clouds in the sky. He is already forming sentences.

'Mommy, no burako, yucky,' is how he rejects steamed broccoli, for example, while 'Daddy, ba wii Toji' is how he asks Naa-chan to bathe with him.

If my modern life is flashing by so fast, then why is time on the Heian side dragging along? Are the shadows that darken my handmaid's heart holding it back?

Those accumulating shadows are not mine alone. My princess's feelings, too, seem to be growing more complicated as her relationship with the official of the sixth rank deepens. On days when she knows he's coming, for example, she intentionally ignores her hair and dress. This despite the fact that, at all other times, not to mention when Lord Narihira is expected, she is scrupulous when it comes to keeping herself and her surroundings pristine and beautiful. I'm confused.

Finally, though, I figure it out. By refusing to show herself to the sixth official at her best, the princess is remaining true to her husband, Lord Narihira. When I look more closely, I realize that the messages she sends through me to the sixth official are written with far less care. And the paper she uses is inferior in quality and of a single hue, not blended with another colour and delicately folded as with her missives to her husband.

Their conversations follow this pattern as well. When with Lord Narihira, the princess always looks down or to the side, never directly at him, and speaks in a deferential tone; in contrast, she and the official of the sixth rank are frank and direct with each other – their eyes meet, and they talk as equals. To my modern eyes, the princess's conversations with the official of the sixth rank are the kind you would expect when someone loves their partner, the kind that lift your spirits; yet Heian convention holds that addressing a man as an equal is at the very least rude.

Social conventions are such strange things.

Women's work was valued during Heian, but that didn't mean that women were seen as equals in all ways. They were to work joyfully, but only in their own company. In male company they were expected to always play second fiddle. This premise was never challenged.

In my role as handmaiden, I often muse that women and men are completely different creatures. Although aristocratic men and women lived under the same roof, their lives were kept separate. First of all, they occupied different spaces. Women spent virtually all their time sequestered within the residence, while men went off to work at the palace.

They ate separately as well. Apart from the occasional banquet, the princess and Lord Narihira never shared a meal. Indeed, the concept of gathering round a table to eat was foreign to the men and women of the period, as everyone was served their own private tray of food. And almost always, men and women worshipped the gods and buddhas separately.

The things they talked about were generally separate as well. What, then, did they do together, and when? In my recollection, most of their time together was spent in bed. Only then were they free to get to know each other. I'm not just talking about the physical side of things, either. No, their topics of conversation went deeper, from loving vows shared on the pillow, to whispered conversations about one trivial thing or other, to the poems they had exchanged before lying down. Only while in bed, therefore, did these two different creatures come together, shyly at first, perhaps, but cheerfully, and always with mutual tenderness and respect. When I describe their relationships in this way, I can't help but be moved.

Yet, in the end, different creatures was what they were presumed to be. And although they came together in a circumscribed way, they remained different creatures to the end, never plumbing the true depths of the other. I think this may be why most Heian women were able to countenance their husband or lover seeing another woman without getting all worked up.

But perhaps that only applies to those women who shut their eyes and accepted without question that men were completely different. I can't help feeling that a woman as bright as my princess was fully aware that she as a woman and Lord Narihira as a man belonged to the same species.

These days, I feel a compelling urge to go out and find a job. It's not because I'm bored being stuck at home, not at all. The plain truth is that I want to make money.

Naa-chan's salary isn't all that great. The benefits are good: he can apply for a lengthy leave every ten years; the company's in-house savings plan is fully funded; and, best of all, it's easy to get parental leave. Still, I'm becoming increasingly aware of the number of women working in Naa-chan's company, each carrying her own weight.

My goodness, how out of touch with the real world have I been? When I fell in love with Naa-chan, my sole intention was for the two of us to live together – I didn't doubt that our marriage would bring happiness. Now, finally, I have to accept that the knight on the white charger is just a human being, and that I am not the princess who lives happily ever after. My own ignorance appalls me – I have been living in a fog of my own making!

It strikes me that earning money doing physical labour might be fulfilling. Maybe that's because, in both Edo and in Heian, I found myself in situations where that was the type of work I was expected to do. I know such work can be harsh and demanding. Yet I am coming to think that the dignity that comes with shouldering hard work is of a wholly different order from the dignity I feel raising Toji, for example.

Yet what work is there for me in this modern world?

'Did you ever work?' I ask my mother.

'Yes, for about two years before I got married.'

Her place of work, it turns out, was a big shipbuilding conglomerate. Though it was customary for women to quit when they got married, she said she had wanted to stay on.

'I didn't know any of that,' I say.

'You never asked,' she laughs, wrinkles crinkling the corners of her eyes. I try to picture her as a young, single woman working in an office.

'Perhaps you and I are naturally inclined towards housework,' she goes on.

'Well,' I reply, 'I can go out and find work if I want to.'

'So you say, but what sort of work?'

I consider her question for a moment.

In Edo I had mastered the art of pleasing men – was that the way to go? Or should I place myself in an all-female environment, where I could comport myself using some of the skills I had learned in the Heian period?

'It could be there's nothing out there for me,' I say, hanging my head.

Just then, Toji begins to cry. 'Now what's the problem?' My mother coos: 'Are you hungry? Do you want your diaper changed? It's about time you started toilet training. I think your Mommy should forget working and look after the home front, don't you?'

She chatters away happily in this vein. As if trying to sweep away everything I said about finding a job.

Perhaps my thirst to go out and make money is connected to my premonition that, someday, Naa-chan and I will separate.

Watching my princess and the official of the sixth rank communicate with each other as absolute equals is like looking at the sun – I have to close my eyes.

My princess lived in an era when the lives of aristocratic women were so limited, yet she had an independent mind and was capable of standing on her own two feet.

Handmaids like me were of lower rank – and thus had far fewer restrictions – than princesses; yet when I see the princess talking so freely and openly with a man, I can feel the satisfaction I have taken in my easy life dwindle.

I want to stand on my own, unaided. That is how I have come to think.

Finally, the day of Shinnyo's visit arrived. The gentlewomen of our residence were buzzing with excitement, but, quite remarkably, they all settled down as soon as he started talking. What he said deeply affected everyone there.

His lecture wasn't very long, about an hour by the modern

count. Shinnyo used simple language to make a few very basic points. In fact, I could summarize what he said in a single sentence: 'To be born into this world is a wondrous thing.'

Life is a miracle, he said. Not only that, everyone had the opportunity to encounter Buddhism and the Buddha, thereby experiencing things well beyond the ordinary.

At first, I wrinkled my nose at this. There was just too much of that sort of language rattling around the modern era. I must have heard the phrase 'the miracle of life' a zillion times.

That was the extent of my appreciation of Shinnyo's lecture. Surprisingly, though, the women listening reacted strongly, peppering him with questions.

'Being born is a wondrous thing?'

'Is that true for everyone?'

'Maybe that works for lords and ladies, but what about ordinary people?'

'It's hard to see birth as a miracle when you're stuck having one baby after another!'

The women surrounded Shinnyo, chirping like a flock of baby swallows – there seemed no end to their comments.

'Nothing wondrous ever happened to me.'

'So many of us are fated just to suffer and die.'

One lady spoke, then another chimed in, and then another. Shinnyo responded to each and every one, though his words were often few. The miracle was the fact of life itself, he reiterated. Even suffering was a miracle. Both joy and pain could lead to the Buddha. Thus, living one's life fully was the most wondrous thing of all. These were the points he stressed, over and over again.

Lord Narihira sat to the side, quietly listening to the exchange. I was dying to know what he was thinking, but there was no way to tell. The princess, too, was quiet. Yet if Lord Narihira appeared to be only half paying attention, my impression was that, despite her silence, she was profoundly affected by Shinnyo's words.

When all the questions had been anwerered, the women interrogating Shinnyo fell quiet. All were in high spirits now, as if an enormous secret had just been imparted to them. And that was indeed the case – for Shinnyo had taught all of us the world's greatest truth: the incalculable value of life. Such language may be time-worn, even trite, today. Nevertheless, at the time the gentle-women were peppering Shinnyo with questions, opportunities to openly celebrate and praise life were few and far between – far more common were those teachings that bemoaned life's diffi-culties, lamented its brevity or viewed it through an ironic lens.

That's right. In those moments with Shinnyo, the gentle-women and the princess were encouraged for the first time to find joy in the lives they were living. Certainly, this floating world was filled with hardship, with much that had to be endured; yet it was still possible to celebrate our existence. Shinnyo's listeners could not physically absorb this idea in its entirety, of course. Rather, it came to them as something utterly new, a shaft of light piercing a dark forest.

Shinnyo sat there quietly, his face serious. He was seated formally before the women, buttocks on heels, a posture still un-common at that time. His straight back made him tower above the women gathered around him, while Lord Narihira watched dolefully from the sidelines.

A month passed. The 'month of running teachers' (December) was upon us. The day before it arrived, the first snow fell.

'The snows have begun early this year,' said the princess.

After remaining at home for some time, the lord was off in Gojo once again. We had not seen him for several days.

'Remember when we made a snow mountain?'

'Yes, I remember it well.'

Snow was welcomed, for it was believed to chase away harmful insects and thus increase the bounty of the harvest to come. If we had a big snowfall, we would pile it up in the courtyard and then vie to see who could predict when the last of it would disappear.

As the princess's handmaid, I remembered the biggest snowfall as occurring the year the princess married Lord Narihira. Normally, snow lasted only a week or so before melting, but that year it fell so heavily that the pile we had made together with Lord Narihira lasted until a sunny, sparkling day in spring. A bumper crop was harvested that year. The marriage seemed to have been blessed: we ate one feast after another, accompanied by great merrymaking.

'I feel I've aged a lot since then,' the princess murmured.

'No, you haven't,' I replied. 'It wasn't all that long ago.'

Nevertheless, she was right – she did seem to have aged, though only in her mid-twenties. In today's world that would be the pinnacle of youth, but in the Heian period one was a mature adult by then, who had already tasted the sweet and the bitter of life. The princess's skin was still firm and glowing, but I could see how her face clouded with fatigue when she thought of Lord Narihira. It worried me.

The snow continued without pause. It was dry and powdery.

'I guess the lord is happy,' the princess let fall all of a sudden.

'Shinnyo taught us that we are fortunate just to have been born,' I answered, 'so I guess all of us are.'

The princess gave a forlorn smile. Life may be a 'miracle'; nevertheless, its joys are so easily trampled on by the relations between men and women. I could accept this as a handmaid, but not as Riko. The sadness in the princess's face was all it took to

convince me. Was a wife supposed to accept her husband running
off to see another woman without showing anger, or even sadness?
What the hell? All that frustration with no way to express it – I
felt dizzy for a moment.

That's when it happened.

Ah! I gasped involuntarily.

Some powerful force was pulling at my body. In that split-
second, I felt myself torn from my moorings and flung into two
dimensions – Heian and modern – simultaneously.

I am with Naa-chan. Not the Naa-chan of today, the father of
Toji, but the Naa-chan of some time before that, a less distant
'long ago' if you like.

I am curled up snugly in his arms.

But where are we?

I glance down at my body.

It's not mine.

Shock and nausea hit at the same time. I feel like I'm carsick.

I'm occupying the body of someone else. It's a woman, for
sure, but her waist is narrower, her legs longer, her face far more
beautiful. Her breath emerges through softer lips, her eyes are
bigger, her nose is longer and more delicately shaped.

'It's easier to breathe now,' I mutter.

'What?' Naa-chan looks at me quizzically. We are sitting in a
darkened bar. A mirror hangs on the wall in front of me, allowing
me to see my reflection. I do look pretty, I must admit. But the
face in the mirror isn't mine. No way.

It's clear from the body I am inhabiting, though, that Naa-
chan and I have just made love. That familiar, fluttering feeling.
My lower body languid and relaxed, my head tingling.

'What's that about your breathing?'

'It's nothing,' I stammer, disconcerted. I take a long look at Naa-chan. He gazes back at me.

I can tell right away that I am inside the body of the young woman he once loved so much. Yes, I am the one promised to the vice-president of Naa-chan's company. After she and Naa-chan were torn apart, she went on to marry a totally different man; they now have two children.

'I love you,' Naa-chan whispers. 'I wish we could run away somewhere.' My back stiffens. As if I were watching the scariest horror movie imaginable.

I am snuggling against Naa-chan while he professes love for a woman not myself, even vows he wants to run away with her – the absurdity of it all plunges me into despair for a second time. Just at that moment, though, another powerful tug dislodges me, and away I go.

This time I find myself stretched out on my back in the dark. An unfamiliar fragrance hangs in the air. Although I could breathe more freely a moment ago, now my nose is as flat as a pancake. There in the dark, instinctively, I raise a hand to my face.

Something granular sticks to my palm.

It has to be *oshiroi*, the white foundation make-up women have traditionally used. I can see why my princess doesn't use much make-up, although she does apply a bit of *oshiroi* when Lord Narihira spends the night. This feels somehow primitive, even savage, with little grains that stick to my skin. I lie there stroking my face in the dark.

My eyebrows have been neatly shaved. My nose is flat, my eyes narrow and encircled by eyelashes. In contrast to my flat face, my hair is full and heavy – its long tresses lie across my body. The unfamiliar perfume is coming from that hair.

A man and I are lying in bed together. It is Lord Narihira – I

can tell that right away. The perfume is a blend that my princess herself concocted for the lord. If he's wearing this particular
perfume, it is certainly spring. And this must be the mansion
of the Gojo princess. The lord's visits have just begun – he's not
spending all his time there yet. I can be this specific because I
had watched the princess burning incense into Lord Narihira's
clothing every day, making minute changes in the blend depending
on the season and the lord's schedule. She had become even more
meticulous once the lord started his visits to Gojo. Her distinctive
perfumes could be found nowhere else in the capital. When the
lord was spending his time with my princess, she chose incense
with a graceful fragrance. But when he was heading off to Gojo,
she devised a blend somewhat more provocative. No one knew
except a very few of her gentlewomen and the princess herself.

I have no idea if Lord Narihira was conscious of this, but as
time passed it became harder for the princess to play even this
limited role, for he was spending more and more time at Gojo,
where she could not reach him.

What kind of lover is Narihira?

That was the first thing that came to my mind.

I am freer to imagine such a thing now than I had been a
moment earlier, when the body I inhabited was that of Naa-chan's
secret lover. Now I am propelled by naked curiosity.

I discover that Lord Narihira was far from the gentlest of
lovers. I recalled the Heian men I had slept with. First the older
man who worked at the residence. He was an honest, simple sort.
In the way he made love – and the way he treated me overall –
he reminded me of a wildflower in the field. And then the sixth
official who became the princess's lover. He may have been adept
at reading Chinese books, but he was no slouch when it came
to reading women either. He was someone I could count on, I

remember, but apart from our last night, he seldom did anything surprising in bed.

Contrary to my expectations, Lord Narihira is more physically forceful than either of them. Yet his aggressive style of making love betrays no lack of consideration for women – although his actions may appear violent, in fact they are natural expressions of his abiding passion for the opposite sex. Indeed, women physically reacted to his lovemaking in unanticipated ways. A woman might be swept off without warning, or be left in the lurch at what appeared to be the moment of truth. Once he is done, however, Lord Narihira becomes utterly quiet, as if the thing that had possessed him has dropped away.

'My Lord,' I say. He smiles and put his arm round me, but then the arm falls away and I can see he is gazing at the moonlight shining through the blind.

I have no idea what Lord Narihira and this princess whose body I was borrowing talked about in bed, so I hesitate to break the silence. What can I do?

'My Lord,' I repeat. That is all I can safely say.

Lord Narihira remains silent. He is looking past my reclining figure at something in the distance.

The silence lasts for a time. I have been looking forward to the delicate words the great lover Narihira might murmur after sex, so I am feeling disappointed and somehow cheated by how uncommunicative he is when, finally, he speaks.

'I wish I could take you away,' he says.

I almost cry out in surprise. But I hold on. Could this be the moment when Lord Narihira makes up his mind to elope with the Gojo princess? It seems like a divine revelation.

Good grief, what is going on? I had been present at the moment the *oiran* Shungetsu and Takada had decided to elope together, a decision that closely resembled the 'Akutagawa' episode describing the elopement of Narihira and the Gojo princess in *The Tales of Ise*. Now I have also witnessed Lord Narihira making that fateful decision, and have heard Naa-chan speak of his desire to elope as well.

Narihira's eyes glow in the shadowy room. Finally, I could understand why Lord Narihira talked so little. He was so hopelessly in love with this woman he couldn't stitch two words together.

I woke up, my neck soaked with sweat. Reflexively, I looked over at Toji's bed – he was lying on his back with his arms and legs flung out in all directions, snoring steadily.

'Are you awake?' said a deep voice.

'Yes,' I replied quietly, turning my head towards Naa-chan.

'I've been up for a while. I had a bad dream . . .'

'Bad dream?'

Might that dream have been of his whispered vow to elope with the vice-president's fiancée, made there in that dark bar, right after their lovemaking?

That's the question I posed to Naa-chan, in my heart.

'Yes, it was really nasty.'

'A nasty dream.'

Was Naa-chan trying to suppress his feelings for the young woman, relegate their affair to the dusk of memory? On the one hand, I felt vindicated; on the other, it felt somehow unfair to the young woman herself.

'Was there a woman?'

'Yes,' Naa-chan replied with surprising directness.

'Did she have a straight nose?'

'What?'

I regarded Naa-chan's blank expression with a mixture of love and hatred. He may have guessed how I was feeling, for he closed his eyes for a few moments. Then he reached out and roughly pulled me to his side.

We made love that night, rolling and bucking on the surf, stifling our cries so as not to wake the little boy sleeping beside us.

These days, I'm splitting my dream time more or less equally between serving as the princess's handmaid and inhabiting the body of the Gojo princess, the young woman Narihira is visiting. In the process, my feelings about Lord Narihira have undergone a sea change. Gone is the grudge I bore him for having turned from my princess. Gone too is the attraction I once felt towards resplendent, high-ranking men. Both have been completely swept away.

I would never have guessed that Narihira would be so passionate towards the Gojo princess. As I expected, their relationship is marked by exchanges of witty, elegant letters and poems, but it is not so much words as the energy pouring from his body, his ability to convey his feelings to a woman physically, that makes Narihira who he is.

I think back to the time of the princess's marriage. I thought then that she was so innocent she would burst into tears when touched by a man, but now I realize that the moment she saw Lord Narihira she was powerfully drawn to him. I wrote it off then as her meek acceptance of the customs dictating whom aristocratic men and women should marry. Now I doubt anything could have been further from the truth. After all, the princess is a stubborn young woman with a clear sense of herself. How could I have imagined that she would become so quickly infatuated with any man chosen for her?

Lord Narihira is a dangerous man. Being drawn to him is like being drawn to falling cherry petals. The moment he sets his heart on a woman she becomes his captive, for she senses two opposing forces coming from him: the power of his love but also a kind of despair, a clear-eyed sense of its conclusion.

Lord Narihira loves the Gojo princess so passionately, yet he has never abandoned his love for my princess. I think this is because he knows that all love ultimately comes to an end.

As my princess's handmaid, I blame Lord Narihira in my heart for rejecting her to embrace the Gojo princess; yet, if I look at the same situation through the Gojo princess's eyes, it was crystal-clear that he still loved his wife.

Lord Narihira's love is like a flawless globe. Faced with such perfection, a woman feels inevitably drawn to it. Yet when she tries to take it in her hands she finds she cannot, for it is too smooth, with no place for her to latch on to – in fact, no one can, though many try. It is the very perfection of the globe that makes it impossible to grasp, however strong one's fingers. Lord Narihira dwells at the centre of that orb. Filled with a love of women, and his own grief.

What a disaster! A man all women should steer clear of!

The New Year festivities came and went, and a new spring was at our doorstep. Lord Narihira informed my princess that Shinnyo had already set off for India.

'He's gone,' my princess said to me.

'I'll miss him,' I replied. The princess stared at me for a moment.

'You'll miss him?'

'Yes. There aren't many monks like him, and I'll miss his teaching.'

I sounded nonchalant, but I was shaken. I couldn't help thinking how bereft I would be if Mr Takaoka, like Shinnyo, left on a long journey.

'India is a great distance away, isn't it?'

'Yes, it is. I pray that he reaches there safely.'

The princess couldn't have known, but Buddhism no longer flourished in India – it was much more popular in far-flung places like Heian Japan, where it intermingled with local histories and beliefs about life and death to generate a vibrant new culture. Nor could she have known that Shinnyo would die partway through his journey.

'Nothing ever remains the same, does it?' the princess sighed.

'That's true,' was all I said.

The day was fast approaching when Lord Narihira and the Gojo princess would elope, hand in hand. Logically, there was no way my princess could have had an inkling of this; yet there were moments when I felt she did.

'Sometimes it's a good thing that nothing ever stays the same, don't you think?' the princess said quietly, smiling a soft smile.

'I think Shinnyo taught us that the principle of eternal change actually provides an escape from the circle of pain that is this world,' I said. The princess stared at me for a moment.

'You know a great deal about Buddhism, don't you,' she said.

'Not really,' I replied.

But what was Buddhism at that point in time? As Riko I had read up a bit and found its philosophy terribly difficult to understand. I know very little about Christianity and Islam, too, and was virtually ignorant of Shinto, the way of the gods. Nevertheless, compared to those religions, it struck me that Buddhism was singularly hard to grasp.

'This is how we must act,' other religions tell us. 'If we have faith we shall be saved.' Yet neither of these strictures exists in Buddhism. Instead, we are told we will reach salvation if we *don't* act, if we *don't* hope. This connection between inaction and salvation is what makes Buddhism so special. To hope, to act – these present their own challenges, yet they seem doable. On the other hand, not acting, not hoping – that sounds extremely difficult, as well as painful. If we fail to see beyond that pain, however, we can never approach salvation.

Crazy, right? That, at least, was Riko's first reaction. Yet gradually I came to accept the sense of resignation embraced by all Heian women, including my princess: in a world that treated them so unjustly they aspired to 'surrender to suffering', as it were, to rid themselves of suffering, a perspective I was beginning to appreciate.

'Sometimes I feel I should cut my hair and become a nun,' said the princess in a quiet voice. 'I'd like to be like Shinnyo and follow the one true path. That way life's sadness and transience wouldn't bother me any more.'

My head drooped. My feelings were so different from hers. When I was inhabiting the Gojo princess I was obsessed by Narihira, body and spirit. It was the polar opposite of what my princess was striving for – a quiet life far removed from all passions. Yet wasn't a life spent dealing with blood and violence also a way of being human? Inside me, I could feel the Gojo princess and the *oiran* Shungetsu both making that argument.

'I fear Shinnyo may die on the road,' the princess said. My head jerked up. She had voiced exactly what I had been thinking – could she have overheard me? 'But I imagine he's satisfied with how things are turning out. I doubt he has ever given a thought to returning alive,' she concluded.

*

As time passed, Lord Narihira's obsession grew more intense. Finally, the moment came for him to elope hand in hand with the Gojo princess.

The sky was overcast that day, and threatening rain. When the night was still young, Narihira and the Gojo princess sat outside her blinds looking at the cloud-filled sky. Presently, rain began to fall and lightning flashed.

'It's strange,' Narihira said, 'for there to be lightning when it's so cold.'

'Should we put it off?' she asked. Her words were cautious, yet she sounded exhilarated – clearly, she was hell-bent on fleeing with him.

'No,' Narihira said, pulling her closer.

Lord Narihira had arranged for an ox-drawn carriage. The carriage and its young driver were waiting outside the residence's gates. Lightning flashed, then flashed again as it raced across the sky. Rain poured down even more heavily. Narihira said very little, his lips clamped tight.

Call off the elopement! – Riko's heart cried from inside the Gojo princess.

You've got to be joking! – the Gojo princess rebuffed Riko.

Was this a dispute between two women with opposing passions, or was it one woman struggling to resolve her conflicted feelings? I was no longer able to tell.

By the time the rain slowed it was already the middle of the night. The Gojo princess donned a leather cloak and walked through the rain and dark to the waiting carriage. How cold were Narihira's hands as he helped her step in! The carriage was not the well-appointed white *biroge* he normally used, but rather a simple *itoge* that sported coloured tassels on its flanks, but few furnishings within. The wheels creaked loudly as they went. Slowly but surely, the carriage bore the lord and the princess through the muddy ruts and away. Where were they going?

'Aren't you cold?' Lord Narihira asked the Gojo princess.

'No,' she replied.

After some time, the young driver called to them from outside. The oxen were getting tired, and he wanted to let them rest for a few moments.

'How is the weather? Is it still raining?' the princess asked. Narihira raised the carriage blinds. A moonlit, barren landscape stretched before them as far as the eye could see. The rain had momentarily lifted, and what looked like a lake was visible in the distance.

'What on earth is that?' asked the Gojo princess, pointing to the dew on the grass.

Oh, I thought. Oh, thought the Gojo princess. I could hear Shungetsu echo us from far away.

Who spoke those words? Could it have been the Gojo princess? Could it have been me, the only one who knew in detail what was bound to happen? Or could it have been neither the princess nor I, but rather Shungetsu's lingering memories, which confirmed, with no trace of bitterness, what fate had in store for them.

'They look like jewels,' the Gojo princess went on. There was no turning back by this point. The question of who spoke this line – the princess, or Shungetsu, or Riko – had to remain un-answered. The lyrical *michiyuki*, the lovers' last journey so central to the old narratives, was already under way. The tale determined that the princess's brothers would come to steal her back, and that Narihira would suffer unbearable heartbreak when the sun came up. The story was preordained.

The story.

I silently spit out the word, like a kind of curse.

Far in the distance, thunder rumbled. When it drew closer, rain would pour down again.

Then Lord Narihira would hide the princess in the nearby storehouse and stand guard outside the door for the rest of the night.

When the storm was directly overhead, and thunder and lightning were crashing everywhere, the demons would come to steal the Gojo princess away.

Narihira would maintain his watch until the morning light, not knowing that the princess had been taken.

When the storm had finally passed and dawn had broken, Narihira would look inside the storehouse, only to find it empty.

He would shout to the young carriage driver to search for the princess, and then he would spend the rest of the day running madly through the fields, calling her name. Do I have the tale right so far?

When night fell, an exhausted Narihira would return to the capital, not to the Gojo princess's home but rather to his family home in Settsu.

For the next month the lord would hole up there, in seclusion.

Only when he heard the rumour circulating in the capital that the Gojo princess had been abducted by her brothers would Narihira return to my princess.

She for her part would welcome him as though nothing had happened.

The following spring, Narihira would go back to the storehouse and sit there alone the whole day, immersed in thoughts of love and loss.

Then, on another spring day more than a millennium later, a woman named Riko would react to Narihira's love for the Gojo princess with hatred, or love, or pity.

A preordained story.

What a hard and inflexible concept that is.

'Tell me more about Shinnyo's trip to India,' I ask Mr Takaoka on the phone.

'India?'

'Yes, about *your* travels there long, long ago.'

'I've forgotten almost all of it,' he says. Yet he promises to meet me for the first time in what seems like ages.

I whip together a bento lunch, grab Toji and head for the bench next to the river. Toji is very excited. Our only recent excursions have been to the small amusement park, the zoo and the botanical gardens, or with Naa-chan to the mall. Toji enjoys all of these, of course, but for some reason nothing seems to excite him as much as our trips to the riverside to see Mr Takaoka.

'He's become a real little man!' Mr Takaoka remarks on seeing Toji. 'Before long he'll be the same age as you were when we first met.'

'Not for a while, though.'

'Don't forget. Five, even ten years can pass in a flash.'

'You're right, even a thousand years!'

Mr Takaoka looks hard at my face. 'Did something happen?' he asks.

'No, nothing new.'

'Are you enjoying your life in Heian?'

'It seems I can't go there so often these days.'

That is true. I want to be closer to my princess, but something stands in my way. My sleep has been very deep recently. In fact, I'm not dreaming much at all. When I do dream on occasion they are Riko's dreams, random and confused. Normal dreams, in other words, that have nothing at all to do with my princess.

'I never made it to India, you know,' Mr Takaoka says.

'Yes, I know.'

'But the journey was fun, nonetheless.'

'Did you think of Lady Kusuko at all on your way?'

'Yes, I thought of her a great deal.'

'Is that all right? I mean, your Buddhist austerities had brought you so close to enlightenment, should you really have been thinking of a past love?'

'Not a problem,' Mr Takaoka says cheerfully.

'But doesn't that mean that all your fasting and meditation was useless?'

'Not at all. If your memories don't disturb you, you can dwell on them all you want.'

What was it like to think of the one you loved without pain? It's hard to imagine in my present state. For me, love has always been painful. It is invariably filled with bitterness, whether the me is Riko with Naa-chan, or the Edo *oiran* Shungetsu with Takada, or the Heian handmaid, so close to her princess that they suffered together or, following that, the Gojo princess, who had thrown herself into her affair with Narihira.

What is this bitterness that plagues me? I had asked Mr Takaoka to meet me to try and better understand that.

'Tell me what your trip to India was like,' I say.

'Ah yes, India,' Mr Takaoka says Then, quietly, he begins his story.

'I never made it to India. As you already know.'

Mr Takaoka looks into my eyes as he says this. His expression is playful, even slightly mischievous.

'Yes,' I reply. By this point, I had read Tatsuhiko Shibusawa's *Takaoka's Travels*.

'Leaving China aside, Buddhism was already in decline in India at that time. I knew that, so why did I presume to tag along in Shinnyo's body? I've been mulling that one over ever since I got back to this modern age.'

'Could it be you've been chasing the vision of Lady Kusuko I read about in *Takaoka's Travels*?'

'I went on such a dangerous journey just for that?'

'Yes, just for that. To brave that danger. You knew you would die on the road, so it may have propelled you to new heights.'

'Your hypothesis hits close to home.' Mr Takaoka smiles as he says this. 'I was so young when I first met Lady Kusuko. Once I had mastered how to travel back to ancient times I met her again, this time through the person of Prince Takaoka. To this day, I can't figure out if the two Kusukos were one and the same or if they were completely different beings, though they looked identical.

'Maybe it makes no difference,' he goes on. 'After all, the Kusuko I love and the Lady Kusuko I long for both reside in my heart. Isn't it a marvel? That love means they are still alive within me, though I will never meet either of them again.'

'Did your feelings for Kusuko change during your travels?'

'I feel they did, yet at the same time I feel they didn't.'

'What do you mean by that?'

'I was eaten by a tiger, you know. That's how I died.' All of a sudden, Mr Takaoka's voice changes. Prince Takaoka, the monk Shinnyo, had been killed by a tiger. I know that part of the legend.

'Did the tiger really eat you?'

'Yes, she really did.'

'Oh, my!'

'Death by tigress is an episode in Gautama Siddhartha's life, you know.'

'The life of the Buddha?'

'Yes. It's said that in a former life he willingly gave his body to a starving tigress and her cub so that they could live.'

'The Buddha was eaten by tigers in a former life?'

'Some believe those tigers were reborn as his disciples.'

'Then Shinnyo was re-enacting scenes from Siddhartha's prior lives?'

'I guess you could say that.'

'So then perhaps Shinnyo was reborn as someone on the verge of sainthood.'

'I like the sound of that!'

'And that someone is you.'

Mr Takaoka doesn't hesitate a moment.

'No, not me. I'm a long way from enlightenment. I've fallen for you a bit, you know. I love Kusuko with all my heart, so I shouldn't desire anyone else, but here I am unscrupulously attracted to you.'

I've fallen for you a bit.

My chest tightens when I hear him say those words. For I have fallen for Mr Takaoka myself.

Not a lot though, just a little. It is a gentle love, yet at the same time heartrending.

It was a riveting tale, thrilling and suspenseful, even minus the love story with Lady Kusuko: the adventure of how, having reached not India but the middle of the Malay Peninsula, the priest Shinnyo was set upon and devoured by a tiger.

There were occasions so difficult and painful that Shinnyo wanted to abandon his faith and give up the quest. When things went smoothly, he might come across places so idyllic he never wanted to leave.

But Shinnyo persevered in his quest for true enlightenment. The whistling wind, the towering mountains, the dusty paths, the steaming jungles – all beckoned him. Another week down the road and the skin colour and language of the people he encountered would be different. The next week the customs of the area would have changed yet again, and he might be welcomed in ways impossible to imagine.

The birdcalls. Tiny creatures scurrying underfoot. The menace of larger animals. The trees' dark shadows overhead. The ferns, moss and other plant life. The buzzing insects. On and on Shinnyo had pushed forward, until in the end a tigress made a meal of him.

'Did it hurt?' I ask.

Mr Takaoka winces. 'It was torture, so painful I thought I'd never want to go back to "long ago" again.'

'How about now? Do you still feel the same way?'

Mr Takaoka doesn't answer. I can see his lips curl slightly as he sits there watching the river slide by, whether in a smile or a grimace I can't tell. His brown eyes are gleaming darkly.

Yes, Mr Takaoka wants to return.

I guess that neither of us will ever be able to revisit long, long ago, or even long ago. That is why we yearn to go back. Though that might be impossible, we would never, ever forget. The many people we came to know. The sights we saw. The colour of the sky. The smell of the wind.

Neither Mr Takaoka nor I ever actually met all those people from long ago, let alone long, long ago – it was just a dream. Nevertheless, we *lived* there, lived for so long, crying, laughing and rejoicing.

'I'm not going back,' Mr Takaoka replies.

A Tale of Today

Last week, we finally got Toji enrolled in a nursery school. I started my job three months ago.

My mother was dead set against me going out to work.

'Toji's still too little,' was her first line of attack. Then she went on to point out why I was incapable of holding a job: I was bad with computers; I lacked stamina; I couldn't work well with others; and on and on, an unending stream of criticism.

'Am I really so hopeless?' I exclaimed.

'Yes, you're hopeless!' she shot back.

'That's unfair.'

'Marrying Naruya was the best thing you ever did.'

'You're just being mean!'

I didn't stop trying to win her over, though. I had to – there was no way that I could hold a job without her cooperation. The nursery school would not accept Toji unless I could prove I was continuously employed, so for the first few months I needed my mother to take over while I settled into my job.

'Leaning on me like this just shows how spoilt you are,' she said, maintaining her opposition to the end.

To my surprise, it was Michiko-sensei who came to my rescue. She dropped by to see Toji on a day when my mother and I were at each other's throats.

'Sensei, please listen to this,' my mother got in the first word. 'Riko's fed up with looking after a child so she wants to get out of the house.'

'My goodness,' was Michiko-sensei's first response. 'Are you fed up with Toji?' she asked me.

'No, not at all.'

'Then why do you need to leave?'

'It's not to enjoy myself, believe me.'

'Then whatever for?' my mother broke in.

'To learn to stand on my own two feet.'

My mother scowled. 'So you think raising a child means you're not independent? That it's so easy?'

'No, I'm not saying that.'

'Yes, you are. You're looking down your nose at the work housewives do.'

In this way, right there in front of Michiko-sensei, my mother and I began rehashing all the points of our argument. It was an ugly exchange, and I was growing increasingly distressed. After Michiko-sensei had been so kind as to come all this way to see us!

Yet Michiko-sensei was the one who helped us out of our predicament.

'I know you don't belittle what housewives do,' she said, looking back and forth at both of us. 'Riko wants to work because she's frustrated by her own worthlessness.'

My mother gasped, surprise written on her face. That Michiko-sensei would say something so negative about me apparently shocked her.

'Riko hasn't been able to set a clear course for her life the way you did,' Michiko-sensei said to my mother. 'She lacks confidence in her marriage, so if she wants to get out of the hole she's dug for herself, I think she needs to work, not just for her sake but for Naruya's and Toji's as well.'

It appeared Michiko-sensei was clued in to the bumpy road that Naa-chan and I had travelled in the past few years.

'Y-yes,' I stammered, overwhelmed.

'So, you needn't worry,' Michiko-sensei said to my mother.

'It's all very well for you to say that,' my mother said, still not entirely convinced.

'Times have changed since you and I raised our children,' Michiko-sensei broadened the discussion. 'Riko's generation lacks the solid foundation you and I had – the ground beneath their feet is full of cracks.'

'Full of cracks,' my mother echoed blankly.

'That's right. They have no solid place to stand.'

'Is that true?'

'Yes. And when they look into those cracks, they see a great many things.'

'A great many things,' my mother parroted.

A great many things. I rolled the words around in my mind. Michiko-sensei was right. There were cracks beneath where I stood. It was by peering through them that I had been able to perceive so much: things from long ago, from long, long ago, Naa-chan's various relationships, and more. What I had experienced had shaken and confused me, leaving me unsure of where to turn.

My mother wasn't fully convinced, but Michiko-sensei's words did seem to soften her heart a little.

Not long after that, I was hired as an assistant to the university professor I had studied under during my student years.

My job was mostly clerical work. Universities were not nearly as well off as they once had been, and getting government funding for research was very difficult, but luckily my old professor – he had supervised my graduation thesis – was a great fundraiser, which was why he could hire a secretary.

I don't have many friends, but one of them, Miss Sugawara, had held this job for nearly twenty years, since her graduation. Her mother had taken ill recently and needed someone to care for her, so she was looking for a person to whom she could hand over her job.

'It would be great if you could do it, Riko,' she said.

I hesitated. I had no confidence at all that I could do the work. Yet I knew I should confront my fears head on. I needed to challenge myself with something new, after a life spent studiously avoiding such challenges.

When I returned home after my first day of work, I was ready to keel over. I had been tense all day, besides which I was hopeless using the spreadsheet software, despite the workshop I had attended. Moreover, it was clear the professor was dissatisfied with how long it took to complete the tasks he had assigned me, which meant I would likely get the sack after my month-long probation ended. Until then, my job was considered temporary.

My mother looked just as exhausted when I got home to pick up Toji.

'I may be too old to do this any more,' were the first words out of her mouth.

'I'm really sorry. It's just until I can find a nursery school,' I said, but she was still grumpy.

'Even with a full-time job, those nursery places can be very hard to find,' she grumbled. 'So what are the odds for a temporary hire like you?'

I was about to argue – how could a mother be so intent on

throwing cold water on her daughter's plans? – when I heard Toji's laughter.

'Mama!' he called, happily running to hug me. As I embraced his warm, slightly damp body, my grudge against Mother melted away.

'Anyway, I really do appreciate it,' I told her with a brief bow, then lugged my son up the stairs to the second floor.

No sooner had I shut our living-room door and plopped down with Toji on our little couch than I could feel fatigue oozing through my body.

'Are you hungry?' I asked him.

'No, Mommy. Gramma gave cookies,' he said, smiling.

I could feel my irritation returning. I had given my mother clear instructions not to feed him between meals, but I gave my head a shake and told myself to cut it out. I had leaned on her for so long. How could something this trivial irritate me so much?

'Work is hard!' I said, as much to myself as to Toji. 'Your daddy works hard for us every day too. So, who wants to take a bath?' I sang out.

'Toji. Bath!' he happily chimed in.

Our dinner that night was fried chicken I had picked up at the store, chopped cabbage and miso soup with cubes of *fu*, wheat gluten. As I fell into bed, the thought hit me: I guess I won't have much time to look after the flower bed for a while!

I had been working full-time for a few weeks when a question began to plague me: why was work performed 'outside' valued much more highly than work done in the home? When I had devoted myself solely to housework I was, clearly, a professional; yet once I was hired by the university and began working at a computer or running errands for the professor or managing the budget, I felt like a rank amateur at home.

'Amateur!' my friend Miss Sugawara laughed, throwing the word back at me. She had stopped by my (formerly her) office – she had an errand nearby, she said – and now we were eating one of the lunch specials in the university cafeteria.

'Aren't housewives all amateurs, really?' she went on. 'Cooking for a family is easy compared to what professional cooks do, same for vacuuming and laundry.'

'I see,' I said, nodding.

'Yet,' she went on, 'even if we can't match the pros, none of them could master all the skills that go into housework. No such professional exists. In the past you could hire live-in maids to cover for you, but they still needed to be directed by the woman of the house. In my opinion, nowhere is that sort of amateur professionalism needed more than in the home.'

'I see,' I said again. Miss Sugawara had rather overwhelmed me – all I could do was nod. Then I remembered that she had just taken up the most taxing sort of 'amateur' housework, as caregiver to her ailing mother.

'How are they different, office work and housework?' I asked.

'The hardest thing about office work,' she replied, 'is that your course of action is set by other people. The hardest part of housework is that you have to set that course yourself.'

The greatest stress working in an office, she went on, comes from having to deal with decisions made by others, while it's the constant need to come up with major decisions all on your own that makes looking after a home so stressful. She continued in this vein – all I could do was nod in agreement. In her view, so many Japanese women (and a few men) lived a divided existence, a subordinate employee on the one hand, the independent manager of a household on the other. In return, they received the stresses and the pleasures of each.

'We're being torn in half, aren't we?' I offered.

'That's about the size of it,' she replied, her head nodding in agreement. I could hear the pickles crunch as she ate.

It suddenly hit me – I wanted to see Mr Takaoka.

I think I had been working for about six months by that time.

Leaving the other office staff gathered in the conference room to eat their bento lunches, I went and brushed my teeth, then returned to the office. After making sure no one was there, I pulled out my phone and entered his number. His familiar voice came on the line after the second ring.

'Hi,' he said. I could hear wind blowing in the background.

'How have you been?' I asked, suddenly stuck for words.

'I'm fine. How about you?'

'I'm fine too.'

'Let me guess – you're not calling from home, are you?' he asked.

'How did you know?'

'Cause your voice isn't muffled.'

I could feel my love being rekindled – slowly and silently, I was opening like a paper flower placed in water.

'Where are you now?' I asked.

'Near the Inland Sea.'

'You're so far away.'

'No, it's not that far.'

'You're right, it's a lot closer than India.'

'I'd love to see you,' he said in a low voice. I felt as though I was sinking in the sea.

'I want to see you too.'

'When will we be able to meet, I wonder?'

'I don't know. But we will see each other again, I'm sure of that.'

'Yeah.'

We fell quiet after that exchange and just listened to each other breathing. On his end, the wind was blowing in the background; on mine was the sound of people's footsteps and doors being opened and closed.

I felt a tap on my shoulder. Could it really be past three already? I'd finished my phone call some time ago, slipped my phone in my bag and returned to my desk. I was supposed to be working on the task the professor had set for me, producing a spreadsheet laying out how our finances were being managed. At some point, however, I seem to have left my body to hover a short distance away from the Riko sitting on the chair.

'Are you tired? Would you like some tea?' Mrs Nakata, the secretary from the office next door, asked me, lightly massaging my shoulders.

Jolted from my reverie, I jumped up. 'Thank you. Wouldn't you like some too?' I asked. 'Black tea or Japanese? Or how about some coffee?'

I had been with Mr Takaoka until only a minute earlier, of that much I was sure. He might be near the Inland Sea in reality, but he was also standing right outside the professor's office with a smile on his face. Though it was a daydream, there was nothing stopping me from trotting out of the door to talk with him.

We had ended the phone call, but that didn't mean our conversation had ended. I can't recall what we talked about. But Mr Takaoka was definitely here.

'You look like you've been bewitched by a fox!' Mrs Nakata said, laughing.

'You may be right.'

'Sounds dangerous.'

'Thanks. I promise to be careful.'

I'll be careful. I silently repeated the words. But I knew I was all right. Sure, Mr Takaoka had been with me until a moment ago, but I was aware he wasn't physically present.

Mrs Nakata placed a small bag of butter cookies that she had purchased on her weekend trip to Izu in my palm and grinned. I tore the bag open and popped a cookie in my mouth.

'These are good.'

'Izu was fantastic,' Mrs Nakata enthused.

'I went there with my husband a few years ago.' I could still remember the hot springs inn where we stayed.

'What a happy couple!' Mrs Nakata teased.

'Yes, we get along pretty well,' I replied without embarrassment. I wasn't lying, either. For Naa-chan and I are now truly happy.

I often reflect on how Naa-chan has changed. In the past, we set off an electric charge when we came together: sometimes it gave off a beautiful light, at other times, it jolted us painfully apart. At this point in our marriage, though, we have stored enough electricity to make recharging unnecessary: our magnetic field has quieted, and a weak but steady flow of energy runs through the resulting calm. This could be called the mellowing of a marriage, I suppose. Or the onset of marital doldrums.

'How long have you been married?' I asked Mrs Nakata. Of the admin assistants who lunched together, she and I alone had husbands.

'Let's see. Is it ten years?' she said, cocking her head. 'No, it's twelve. Check that, make it thirteen.'

'It's easy to forget, isn't it?'

'It sure is these days. In the beginning, it wasn't only our anniversary we celebrated, but the day we met, as well as the anniversaries of our parents' and grandparents' deaths.'

'Death anniversaries?' I laughed. She laughed too. Then she slipped back to her office.

Death anniversaries? Mrs Nakata's words make me think. A death date merely notes that so-and-so passed away on a certain day, yet although we celebrate our wedding anniversary to mark the happiness of our coming together, the meaning of that date is bound to mutate as time passes, until in the end it too becomes a day of mourning. I haven't made a point of commemorating Naa-chan's and my first meeting, but had I been following Mrs Nakata's example, it would have initially been a very happy event. By now, though, it would be a day for me to reflect on how my feelings have been transformed over the course of our marriage, a chance to ponder what has been lost.

The same holds true for wedding anniversaries. A newly married couple treat the day as a joyful celebration of their mutual love. But how will they see it after three years, or five, or ten? Certainly, the significance of that day will change – as the years pass, their feelings will go beyond the point where 'joy' can encompass them, becoming tinged with ambivalence and irreparable regret. In twenty or thirty years, their joy and sadness, laughter and fury will spread out and overlap – in a way hard for me to imagine – to become layers of an undifferentiated strata of memory.

'Marriage is so peculiar,' I said out loud.

The professor was out of the office, so I was alone. My voice sounded odd, bouncing off the walls.

'Do I still love Naa-chan?' I tried again. 'I love him, I love him not,' I repeated over and over, as if plucking daisy petals.

Yet I knew those simple words could never express what existed between the two of us. What words could?

I gave my head a shake and sat up in my chair, facing the computer.

A few days after my daydream of Mr Takaoka, I got a phone call from him.

'I'm in Moji,' he said without any preamble. 'I want to see you.'

I replayed those words in my mind. Yes, I wanted to see him as well. But I didn't say that.

'OK, but how long will it take you to bicycle from Moji to Tokyo?' I asked instead.

'It's only a day and a half by ferry,' he replied.

'Oh, the ferry. So then, you could be here Friday evening.'

'Yeah. Let's make it then.'

'Naa-chan won't be back till late that night, and maybe I can get my mother to look after Toji. I'll ask her.'

'Great. I'll phone again day after tomorrow.'

We sounded like two old lovers setting up another meeting, I thought.

So it was decided. I would be seeing Mr Takaoka that coming Friday. What would we talk about? What would be left unsaid?

Friday arrived in no time. It rained all day, and Mother was less than thrilled that I was leaving her with Toji, just back from nursery school.

'Why must you go out in this awful weather?' she complained.

'Toji's staying here with you, so there's no problem.'

'And what is a married woman doing anyway, stepping out on a night like this?'

I was used to this sort of talk from my mother. I knew there was no hope of overturning the 'woman in the home, backing up her man' ideology in which she'd been raised. In fact, recently I had come to see her as a modern day Hieda-no-Are, the person (probably a woman) who, back in the eighth century, recited Japan's sacred myths from memory, which were then transcribed as the foundational myths of Japan, the *Kojiki*. In my mother's case, though, it was the decrees of a crumbling Imperial Japan that were being recited, over and over.

'I'm really, truly grateful,' I offered.

'That's easy for you to say,' she shot back, but I could tell she was somewhat mollified.

I'm sure my father cherishes this simple, unquestioning side of my mother. Might Naa-chan cherish me in the same way? Or perhaps I am the one now who cherishes him. He may not have been nearly so innocent as my mother, but at the inn in Izu when he had confessed his affair with the vice-president's fiancée, for example, or earlier, when he was hemmed in by the shadows of so many women, he had opened himself up to me as an innocent child might. As though he had no inkling of how he would be judged.

How can I help but love him?

Perhaps this realization had been cultivated during my sojourns in the worlds of Edo and Heian.

'And what might you be smiling about?' snapped my mother.

'Huh?'

'Go on. Someone is waiting for you, right?'

'Thank you, Mother,' I replied meekly.

'And don't come home too late.'

I ran out of the door before she could change her mind. Toji waved bye-bye as I left. He was more active and independent now that he was attending nursery school. In fact, he looked happier with kids and other grown-ups than with his own mother.

*

To my surprise, Mr Takaoka showed up very nicely dressed.

'What's with the fancy clothes?' The question just popped out.

'I dress up sometimes too. This is a date after all.'

'Is that what this is?'

'It isn't?'

When I say nicely dressed, I don't mean that he was wearing a suit or jacket, or anything of that sort. Just an ordinary shirt and ordinary pants. Yet compared to his usual outfit – old fuzzy sweaters and comfortably wrinkled shirts and pants that looked like someone's cast-offs – he appeared the height of fashion. Or at least someone whose cool outfits would draw others to him.

'You look really nice today,' I said frankly.

'Only today?' he said widening his eyes. I laughed.

'Yes, only today.'

'So I don't look nice at other times?'

'Then you look nice in other ways.'

'I could say the same about you.'

There we were, standing just outside the station exit, praising each other's appearance as people heading home after work streamed past. Would Naa-chan be working overtime in his office, or entertaining business associates at some restaurant, I wondered for a second. But only for a second.

'Let me take you to one of my favourite places to eat,' Mr Takaoka said.

'What sort of place is it?'

'What, and spoil the surprise?'

We walked shoulder to shoulder down the shopping arcade that led from the station. A five-storey apartment building with a brick exterior stood where the arcade came to an end, an older structure of the sort built in the 1950s or 1960s. Most windows had their curtains drawn and the balconies showed no signs of life, no laundry left hanging, no potted plants.

We walked straight through the entranceway to the elevator. When we got in, Mr Takaoka pushed the button for the third floor. There was a clatter as the conveyance crept up.

'Is there really a restaurant up here?' I asked.

'Yes, a secret restaurant,' he said when we got out of the elevator. There was no restaurant sign that I could see, just a long, featureless corridor. Mr Takaoka stopped in front of one of the doors and casually pulled out his keys.

There was a ka-chunk, and the door opened on to a perfectly ordinary sort of apartment. Beside the small entranceway was the closed door of what must have been the toilet and bath. Ahead was a dining and kitchen area about ten tatami mats in size, and on the far wall was a low window that looked out on the balcony.

'Let's hang out here tonight,' Mr Takaoka said. He pulled me to him, burying my head in his chest.

I could hear the faint rumbling of a train outside, and the occasional cawing of crows.

His heart was beating slowly and steadily, with no hint of excitement.

'Are we going to make love?' I asked, my head still buried in his chest

'There's no necessity for that, is there?'

No necessity? I smiled at the awkward formality of these words.

'You're right,' I answered. 'No need at all.'

I looked up into his eyes. He returned my gaze.

Quietly, our lips joined. It was a loving kiss, soft and full of light.

When our lips grew unsure of where the kiss was headed,

they broke apart without going any further. Whose lips withdrew first? Mine? His? Both at the same time, perhaps?

'Shall we eat, then?' Mr Takaoka said. He stepped lightly away like a leaf parting from a branch and moved into the kitchen. A pot was sitting on the stove. He turned the stove on with a snap.

The pot contained beef stew.

'I simmered it quite a while.' Mr Takaoka acted as though he had just thrown it together, yet each dish in the feast he served me had been elaborately prepared.

The appetizer was a mushroom mousse. The fish was sauteed anglerfish, accompanied by a salad filled with all sorts of herbs, most of which I'd never seen before. The pièce de résistance, of course, was the beef stew.

The meat in the brown stew was creamy soft, while the vegetables cooked with it were mashed. Together, the flavours formed a perfect whole, the beef melting on my tongue.

'Did you really make this?' I asked. He nodded.

'I like cooking,' he replied with a smile. 'Most of the time I don't have a proper kitchen, so I roast something over a fire and add a dash of salt.'

'So you sleep and cook outside when you're on the road?'

'Not a lot these days. You need a stack of permits just to build a fire.'

'Do you hunt?'

'No, I don't. It pains me to kill anything.'

'But eating dead animals is all right?'

'That's about the size of it, I guess.'

We talked about anything and everything as we ate. Mr Takaoka spoke of the things he had encountered on his journeys – the people, the animals, the sights. I did the same, talking

about Toji, my job at the university, and so on as it came to me.
This was not a mere exchange of information. Our words hung
in the room only for a moment, deepening our intimacy, then the
next moment they dissolved in the air, just a series of ephemeral
sounds with a pleasing cadence.

We ate ravenously. When we finished, nothing was left, not a
shred of lettuce, a crust of bread or a drop of stew.

'That was so delicious,' I sighed. Mr Takaoka gave a big smile.

'You were the girl who wouldn't eat the school meals, and look
at you now. A real glutton!'

He was right. I had hated lunchtime at school. The unbearable
length of the break. Set against that, the comfort of the janitor's
room, where Mr Takaoka holed up.

'It has been a long journey, hasn't it?' I whispered.

'That's true. Sometimes together, sometimes apart, but always,
always we kept moving.'

Mr Takaoka was so important to me. My irreplaceable
companion.

I felt this strongly as we drained the wine remaining in our
glasses.

Yet I have to add what linked us was not romantic love.

'Do you remember?' Mr Takaoka said quietly. 'Back then,
kanashii didn't mean sad, it meant "dear".'

Kanashii – the word brought back memories. My princess and
her gentlewomen, myself included, often used it when talking
about someone we cared for. My princess referred to her son
that way – 'my *kanashii* baby,' she would say, holding him in her
arms.

This was love, but with a different implication. Today, love
suggests an exclusive desire for a specific person, something at

once deep and narrow. Back in Heian, however, it was expansive, with permeable borders: people gravitated back and forth and from side to side, now drawing nearer, now drifting apart. To direct one's love at only one person, as Narihira did with the Gojo princess, was dangerous in Heian. It was too sharp, and too powerful.

Instead, men and women's love was gentler and more relaxed. They shared in their sorrows and their joys without ever venturing too close.

'Perhaps, *kanashii* describes the way I love you,' I said to Mr Takaoka.

'I love you like that too, I guess,' he replied. 'I think I always will.'

We looked at each other for a long moment without speaking. As if committing the other's features to memory.

We kissed one last time; then I walked out of the door alone. I doubted we would ever meet again. Mr Takaoka would continue his travels to distant places that I had never seen, much as Prince Takaoka had set off for India as the monk Shinnyo. That much I knew for sure.

I won't say *sayonara*, I called to him in my mind.

The road to the station was chilly, and the neon lights sparkled more brightly than usual. So beautiful, I thought. Only then did I realize I was crying.

The days pass.

Toji enters primary school next month. Naa-chan is terribly busy with work, having apparently been resurrected as a member of his company's inner circle. I signed a three-year extension on my contract at the university. I'm happy to continue working while Toji is in school.

I sometimes wonder if Naa-chan will ever fall in love again. He's still a very handsome man, the kind that women turn to look at when we're out together.

Not long ago, I asked him directly: 'Is there really no one else?'

'No, no one,' he answered succinctly.

He obviously feels that the path of work is broader and more fruitful for him than the path of love.

'How about you, Riko?' he asked.

His question made me sit up straight. To hear such a question from Naa-chan, who had never shown a shred of interest in my love life!

'I'm all done with romance,' I replied. Naa-chan fixed his eyes on me as if thinking about something.

'I'm glad to hear that,' he said after a long pause.

Everyone in my family is in good health, so no shadows cloud my life now. I plan to spend the rest of my days being happy.

Perhaps you think I'm too young to talk about 'the rest of my days'? But the person I treasure most in this world is gone for good, so that's where I'm at. Don't think that I'm giving up, though. No, I will fill my life with many things precisely because it is my life.

There are things that I can do.

Finding someone to love, for one thing. Not Naa-chan, not Toji, not Mr Takaoka. Just someone.

That someone might not be a man. It could very well be someone much older or younger. Then again, it doesn't have to be a human being at all. Or even a living creature, as far as I'm concerned.

I can't shake off this need to love something with all my being.

I have lived through layers of time, been close to many people, experienced one emotion after another, yet that need persists.

My new love should be neither too narrow, nor too broad – if possible, it should be like the misty light of spring. It's not even necessary for that light to fall on me, as long as it lights up that which I love. Then I can gaze upon it with a gentle compassion. Yes, soft and gentle, nothing more. For the rest of my days.

That will be the third love of my life, after passionately loving Naa-chan, after feeling *kanashii* with Mr Takaoka. I sense it quietly starting.

About the Author

HIROMI KAWAKAMI is an award-winning Japanese writer, whose fiction includes *Strange Weather in Tokyo*, *The Nakano Thrift Shop*, *The Ten Loves of Mr Nishino* and *People From My Neighbourhood*.

About the Translator

TED GOOSSEN is Professor Emeritus of Japanese Literature at York University in Toronto and has translated many writers including Haruki Murakami.